Endorsements

"With all the characteristics required of a first-rate novel, *Down to the Potter's House* delivers a gripping narrative of true love, deceptive betrayal, intense suspense, prevailing hope, malicious scheming, and bitter disappointment. Author Annette Valentine has an absolutely exceptional gift of word-craft, allowing the reader to visualize thoroughly the scenes as she paints the picture in remarkable detail. The story is set in rural Kentucky, covering a time from the late 1920s to the early 1940s as experienced by young Gracie Maxwell. She teases the reader by intimations of a terrible evil that unfolds as Gracie gradually comes to understand the horrifying effects of the evil Francine Delaney. It is an excellent novel, the second in a trilogy based on her own family that compels the reader's attention from first to last."

DAVID LAWRENCE, Ph.D.
Retired professor of European history
Lipscomb University, Nashville, Tennessee

"Annette Valentine has written a fast-moving novel of romance and redemption, intrigue and revenge with a finely-tuned protagonist who grows from naive schoolgirl to committed missionary to loving wife and mother. Written in an exquisite style, *Down to the Potter's House* is an astute study of the contrast between good and evil inside an extended family."

PATRICIA A. PINGRY
Best-selling Children's book author

"This is an entertaining and compelling novel set in Western Kentucky during the early 1900s. Annette Valentine's characters have real-life and captivating personalities that keep the novel's flow appropriate and attention-keeping. She creates a sharp contrast in the main characters' personas—one who is manipulative and controlling versus another who seeks good and positivity. Also, the reader's interest is captured as scenes flow with everything from Kentucky racehorses to Model T's to locomotives. The story is intriguing and introduces at least two unexpected surprises that captivate the reader and keep one's interest peaked. Very enjoyable!"

MORRIS HADDEN
Senior Litigation Partner
Hunter, Smith & Davis, LLP
Kingsport, Tennessee

"In the compelling sequel to her first book, Annette Valentine allows us to further delve into her father's indomitable spirit and character through the eyes of Gracie Maxwell. I was moved by Gracie's ability to rise above her stepmother's venom and her father's disloyalty, always striving to help those less fortunate. Her deep-rooted faith, strength of family, and profound love for Simon complete this remarkable story of two souls destined to become one. I eagerly await the third story in the trilogy."

NANCY DANIELS
President, Voice Dynamic
Somerdale, New Jersey
www.voicedynamic.com

"*Down to the Potter's House* is a powerfully moving continuation in the saga based on the author's family roots. She deftly captured the spirit of growing up in the South and managed to tap my emotion of happiness, sadness, reality, and hope. I regretted that the book came to an end and can't wait for Annette Valentine's next story in this series."

CHARLOTTE WOOD
Corporate Marketing/Communications Director
Amerigroup Healthcare Corporation, Retired

"I was completely mesmerized by Annette Valentine's *Down to the Potter's House*. The intriguing narrative of Gracie Maxwell, a story capturing the reader's attention from its onset, portrays lives shaped by Todd County, Kentucky. Mrs. Valentine's imagery, characterization, and her skillful use of language add to the unfolding drama of individuals who are clearly molded by God."

CAROLYN WELLS
Author of *T Is for Todd County*
Retired English teacher,
Todd County Central High School, Elkton, Kentucky

"Courage and defense of freedom mark the American World War II experience. So do devotion to family and unbridled fear about the fate of loved ones facing the enemy, half a world away. Annette Valentine's engrossing new work captures the anguish and hope of those waiting at home, digesting headlines and longing for peace.

GORDON H. "NICK" MUELLER, Ph.D
President and CEO Emeritus
The National WWII Museum

Down to the Potter's House

Down to the Potter's House

a novel

Annette Valentine

NEW YORK

LONDON • NASHVILLE • MELBOURNE • VANCOUVER

Down to the Potter's House

A Novel

© 2021 Annette Valentine

Published in New York, New York, by Morgan James Publishing. Morgan James is a trademark of Morgan James, LLC. www.MorganJamesPublishing.com

ISBN 9781631950797 paperback
ISBN 9781631950803 eBook
Library of Congress Control Number: 2020933961

Cover Design by:
Eve DeGrie and Royce DeGrie

Cover Layout by:
Rachel Lopez
www.r2cdesign.com

Interior Design by:
Christopher Kirk
www.GFSstudio.com

Disclaimer: This is a work of fiction. All incidents and dialogue, and all characters with the exception of some public figures, are the product of the author's imagination or are used fictitiously and are not to be construed as real. Any resemblance to actual persons, whether living or dead, or actual events is purely coincidental. Accounts of incidents and their locale are not intended to portray anything beyond an entirely fictional setting.

Morgan James is a proud partner of Habitat for Humanity Peninsula and Greater Williamsburg. Partners in building since 2006.

Get involved today! Visit
MorganJamesPublishing.com/giving-back

For my daughter, Jenifer Hofmann
For my son, Ken Valentine
And my grandchildren: Sarah, John, Mark, Andrew,
and Georgia Valentine, and Anna Hofmann

Acknowledgments

I wish to thank many friends whose dogged support was a pillar of strength in times when I needed it most. A good word, an encouraging word, and the kindnesses that kept me pushing never went unnoticed. Thank you for the generosity of sincere interest and constructive input that impacted me on a daily basis.

I am especially grateful for Treva Horne who willingly researched details and whose listening ear provided a valuable sounding board, for Sharilyn Grayson who kept me focused on my goals, for Karen Anderson whose graciousness revitalized me, for my brother Hal Hadden and his wife Linda who were a beacon of light—a bright reminder of the significance of a mission accomplished, for my brother Joe Hadden who breathed life into my confidence, my brother Morris Hadden who held me to a high standard, and for my husband Walt who never flagged in his affirmation or gentleness.

Thank you to Maxine Bivins, Janet Keith, Gayle Ward, Jenny Gremillion, Marsha Whittlesey, Mary Armistead, Cherie Feinberg, Brent Dickson, Michael Neal, Kathy Zimmerman, Karen Jones, Mica Copeland, and Jerolyn Smith without whose advocacy I would have been far less equipped for the writing journey.

The Characters

Gracie Maxwell–fourteen-year-old girl quickly growing into womanhood

Henry Maxwell–Gracie's older brother

Simon Hagan–young man who returns to Todd County to sweep Gracie off her feet

Senator Robert Maxwell–gentleman farmer, Gracie's father, and owner of Hillbound

Annabelle Maxwell–wife of Robert and is Gracie's mother

Felix and Francine Delaney–neighbors on the farm adjoining Hillbound

Moe Lee and Odelia–Negro couple who work at Hillbound

Children of Moe Lee and Odelia–Celia, Enoch, Bessie, Bertha

Amos–Moe Lee's brother

Clarice–Amos' common law wife and main help with Annabelle

Clancy–Felix and Francine Delaney's hired hand

Samuel Delaney–owner of Cloverdale Stock Farm and is Felix's older brother

Luke–the jockey and trainer

Bertie–Luke's wife

Millicent Carver–Gracie's older sister and wife of James Carver (grocery and hardware store owner)

Emma Rivers–Gracie's oldest sister (Emma's husband is Elmer)

Marcus Willoughby–Francine Delaney's nephew and frequent visitor to her Todd County farm

Rebecca Willoughby–Marcus' wife

Chester Willoughby–Francine Delaney's brother from Madison County, Kentucky

Lucy Willoughby–Chester's new wife

Geoffrey Hagan and Hannah Peterson Hagan–Simon's father and step-mother

Jean Morgan–friend of Gracie's during her early school years

Chapter 1

With the drought in every part of Todd County, Kentucky, and surrounding counties, survival had become more intensified. Foreclosures were threatening even the ardently industrious farmers, but for those who were exceptionally hardheaded and efficient—such as former Senator Robert Rutherford Maxwell—procedures at Hillbound in 1930 continued uninterrupted.

Harvest time had signaled the end of yet another growing season at Hillbound, and the routines of tobacco farming were not unlike the ones I had watched from my youth. Negro folks still toiled in the fields—their brows covered with maize-colored straw hats—topping and cutting, stripping and bailing, but I knew none of them. All new faces had replaced the familiar ones that I could have spoken to by name. Thoroughbreds of Father's wistful dreams roamed the places where I'd previously helped the children learn to read, practicing on them my rudimentary teaching skills whenever possible. The young ones were gone now. The mighty oak under whose branches we'd sat was gone as well.

Robert Maxwell was holding his own, counting himself among the smattering of gentleman farmers who maintained their property with economically disabled and politically powerless black laborers. Hard times had deepened the dependency of the black folks, affording them little choice but to stay on as hired hands, working the devastated farms that brought in, at best, a piddling one-third of the revenue they had in the three years prior.

From outward appearances my father projected prosperity in the way he walked and the way he talked, but I suspected differently. The previous day I'd spent with him at Hillbound all but confirmed Father was putting up a front. He'd sold a portion of his beloved five hundred and sixty acres of burley tobacco farmland along with the forty acres of wheatland he had acquired when he married Francine Delaney.

Father was an imposing man, dark-complected with a full head of sleek black hair and a broad smile. Even at sixty he was straight backed and poised as we rode into the center of Elkton. Other folks, too, made their way into town for essentials. If any one of them owned an automobile, more than likely he could no longer afford to drive it. The depression had hit, and gasoline prices were high, so most folks came in carriages and congregated at the square.

A late-autumn breeze rippled the surrey's fringe that canopied above my head. Our ride into town in the splendor of this October Saturday was proving to be a chilly one. After two miles of the horse's clip-clop, we rounded the last turn. Straight ahead of us was the courthouse square. For a small town in Kentucky, the two-story brick building with its white clock tower stood modestly impressive.

Father halted in front of Jim Carver's Grocery and Hardware and stepped down from the carriage, leaving me perched on the seat while he hitched the reins to a post. No looks, no whispers indicated I had something to hide.

I held my head high. Even so, gossip's sting could prick without warning beneath my skin. I hadn't thought of the scandal in months, and it took a mere single night in Francine's presence to resurrect it. Her staunch ability to live with herself was not my concern—yet it was, and my urgent need to guard outcomes for my brother and the entire Maxwell family name had overtaken my restraint. The moment had crystallized in yesterday's outburst.

I wish I had said much more to Francine. Looking back, I wish I had said less to Father.

My two years spent away at Logan Female College and the subsequent two at Athens College in Alabama had solidified my ambitions and reshaped my less constructive attitudes as if they were a lump of clay. No longer the broken fifteen-year-old or the self-empowered eighteen-year-old, I accepted the hand Father offered to assist me from the carriage and grasped his fingers as my foot touched the ground.

"Sister would love some horehound sticks," I said, "and of course I want to see Jim, if he isn't busy. I'll pop inside and be right here when you return. That's all, Father. Nothing too long."

Father was quick to plant a kiss on my forehead. "Fine and dandy, Gracie, go ahead. Give my best to Jim . . . I won't go in this time. We should get us over to Millicent's house directly. I'll be across the street, but only for a few minutes. If you're ready to go before that, don't hesitate to send word," he said, nodding with a two-term-senator polish to a passerby.

The out-of-doors had a way of doing wonderful things for me. I breathed deeply the refreshing air as I waltzed toward my brother-in-law's store, my long coat fluttering behind me. Several of the town's men had gathered in front of Carver's Grocery and Hardware to exchange news of the day and toss about their ideas on how the turn of events might affect the nation. Most of them were nowhere near recovering income losses that supported their livelihood.

I gave them a passing smile and continued toward the store. My father's agenda was evident to me, and time wasted was intolerable. I had come to accept the vigorous manner that let his wishes be known.

Inside, a buzz of activity swirled about in immeasurable contrast to the motionless bystanders outside. I went straight to the candy counter without dilly-dallying. My mouth watered in anticipation of the taste of chocolate. "Glorious day, isn't it, Miss Baxter?"

"It is at that. And I'm just glad as I can be to have you visiting every now and again. Tickled pink, I am, you're spending another year nearby. Good thing for us folks here in Elkton that Russellville's just a hop, skip, and a jump away." A generous smile spread on her face. "So tell me: how's our young schoolteacher doing?" she said, squeezing her chubby hands together atop the glass case that covered the candy confections.

"Fine, fine. I haven't expelled anyone in the first two months of this term . . . and not anyone last year either," I said, grinning, briefly distracted by the appearance of a tall man warming his hands by the potbelly stove at the rear of the store.

Miss Baxter gave a jolly laugh to acknowledge my attempt at humor, and my glimpse of the gentleman ended.

"You're right. Russellville's not very far. And you haven't seen the last of me, unless I start spreading out like Sunday dinner on a picnic cloth," I said, realizing Miss Baxter resembled my remark. "Then I'd have to stop eating chocolates."

"Me too," she said with a never-you-mind gesture, relaxing her forearms farther across the counter. It was clear, she was in no hurry for my candy selection. "Your sister sure tries to keep everybody up to snuff around here. Got her own schoolgirl nowadays. That little Louise is cute as a pie. Second grade . . . Goodness, goodness!"

"I know. It's certainly amazing how time flies," I said, focusing on the candies." Point out what Louise would like, then the usual: three sticks of horehound for Millicent. Now then. Chocolate. Let me . . . um . . . decide between the—"

"Please excuse me for interrupting. May I offer a recommendation for the chocolates before you make your decision?" The smooth voice slid into our conversation like butter on a hot biscuit.

Surprised, I turned to find the tall gentleman from the back of the store standing next to me. Having captured my attention, he smiled a gorgeous smile that momentarily broke my concentration.

"The finest of the fine is right before your eyes—your beautiful eyes, if I may be so bold. I'm something of an expert on the subject."

Seriously? I thought. An expert on how time flies or chocolate?

"But first things first. My name is Simon Hagan."

After a slight hesitation, I gave him a brisk once-over during which time his smile never faltered. I'd not ever met a statelier man and maybe not a better-looking one. The weight of his gaze caught me off guard. *But only a little*, I told myself. I then recast my answer: "How do you do, Mr. Hagan? I am Gracie Maxwell."

Miss Baxter wasn't helping the situation's awkwardness. She no longer rested against the candy counter, but rather leaned in to hear what she could hear. Her mouth had dropped, and I warned mine not to do the same.

I tried to give as little heed as possible to Mr. Hagan's remark about my eyes and forced myself to look straight at him as he continued to speak of how glad he was to meet me. Perhaps he missed the cold shoulder that I thought I was presenting. He proceeded to select a bar of chocolate from the case with one hand, then gave coins to Miss Baxter with the other.

Father passed the window. A tip of his hat indicated he would just as soon be on his way.

I stood dumbfounded as Mr. Hagan handed me the chocolate bar.

Jim Carver's voice rose above others, dickering politely with a woman who had doled out produce and eggs for his consideration. Their transaction seemed to be coming to an end, and my brother-in-law turned toward us at the front of his store where Mr. Hagan continued to stand at my side.

Miss Baxter's smile was way too big.

Flustered by the simultaneous doings, I offered a quick thank you to the tall stranger, snatched the horehound that Miss Baxter had laid on the counter—forgetting to pay for the candy sticks—forgetting the candy treat for Louise—then darted straight out the front door without a backward glance.

"Gracie!" Father was waiting outside when I emerged. "Guess I should have come inside . . . I'd already unhitched us, though. Here, let me help you up. When you see Jim later today, do remember to give him my regards."

I hopped up onto the seat, and Father steered the horse around the town square, its hooves plodding noisily on the cobblestone street. The ride was quieted as the buggy rolled onto the dirt road leading to Millicent's house.

"Glad you didn't, Father. No need to come inside," I said without knowing why. "It will be a good visit with Jim tonight at supper."

He peered over at me. "You seem preoccupied, Gracie. Everything all right?"

I didn't look at him. "Of course. Just met a gentleman . . . He must be related to Mr. Hagan who got me my teaching job." Slightly embarrassed, still puzzled by my own doings, I held up the chocolate bar and waited for Father's reaction. "I believe he said his name is Simon. Yes, *Simon* Hagan."

"Ah! For sure. Simon's been away from Todd County for quite some time. Didn't realize he was back." Father shot me a suspicious gander, then signaled the horse to pick up speed, giving the reins some slack with a nimble foist from the driving whip.

The surrey's wheels creaked in objection to the horse's surge, and the forward jolt startled me. I wondered if the timing had not been right to exhibit the chocolate. "Oh, Father, he just happened to be at the counter as I was deciding. All of a sudden, he was there. He simply insisted on making this a gift."

"Hardly proper for him to cover your purchase of chocolate." Father glanced at the horehound sticks. "He didn't pay for those, too, I hope."

Realizing my predicament, I cut my eyes at him. "No. *Nobody did.* I got them for Millicent . . . I forgot to pay. Silly me! Mr. Hagan was just being kind," I said as we rolled up to the front of the Carvers' house.

"What's he doing now, anyway? Believe he had tuberculosis . . . although I could be confusing him with another of the Hagans. Geoffrey had six or seven boys and a couple or three girls."

"Heavens, Father! I have no idea. You mustn't go thinking poorly of him, though. And I can certainly fend for myself. I am twenty-three, not fifteen."

He stepped down from the carriage, hitched the reins. "Big family, the Hagans."

Millicent had not missed the sound of the approaching carriage. Oblivious to the October chill, my sister was out the door to greet us.

Father paused to serve up his customary greeting to her. I reminded myself not to compare its woodenness to the top-shelf affections he openly lavished on Francine, practically from the time of Mama's passing. The crater in my heart caused by his attraction had stubbornly closed, but having spent last night in my stepmother's presence, old grievances had threatened to undo family peace that time and my absence had afforded me.

Inside the short day spent in the country, I'd seen the signs that revealed my brother's discouragement. Hardest to take was seeing how Father regarded Henry with cool detachment. Witnessing my brother falter with every attempt to make a decision was more than I could stand.

Father offered me his hand to steady me off the carriage step.

Having squelched the bitter rise of contempt for the fresh evidence of Francine's power over Henry and the ease with which she dominated Hillbound, I rallied, grateful that Father had avoided either subject. Our arrival at Millicent's had interrupted the discussion of the Hagans. It had stilled, too, the recurrent rusty attitude of bygones that had no place in my reshaped heart.

Chapter 2

"**H**appy Birthday, Father. What a handsome sixty-year-old you are, too."

"And you're looking well, Millicent," Father said. "How's that Jim? In good health and prosperous, I trust. Haven't gotten into the store lately. I will. I will."

"Busy there, as you might guess. Ownership has its demands. Long hours, you know, but Jim's quite well. Do come in, both of you. Gracie, how radiant you look."

Father and I shed our wraps in the parlor before moving to the kitchen and seating ourselves at the table. A tea kettle gurgled on the stove. It had been awhile since the three of us had been in a room together when Francine wasn't close by. Even so, neither Millicent nor I would consider rehashing the past with our father.

"Sister! I have been dying to see you. Even in the short couple of weeks since I was here!" I was completely bursting at the seams. "You've been more than gracious. Jim too. I love being here."

Father seemed to squirm at the mention of my landing place being at Millicent's rather than my childhood home, but now was not the time to count the cost of treachery or calculate the price of greed.

"And where's our little Louise?" I gave Millicent a look, hoping the scars we'd endured were soothed by the salve our bond had provided, that our being sisters had helped us make it through the tumultuous years.

"She'll be along after church tomorrow. Gets to spend the night at her Granny Carver's. I wanted you all to myself for once! So now, tell me what's happened since I last saw you!"

"I'll visit only a short spell," our father said, perhaps sensing the urgency of our desire to catch up or, better yet, his need to attend his esteemed thoroughbreds. "Truly, I must be on my way soon. Gracie, however, does have a mysterious bar of chocolate . . . and, shall we say, 'lifted' horehound?"

He was amused. His inference that I had some explaining to do had Sister on alert.

Sheepishly, I admitted I'd come with horehound candy that I had not paid for and nothing for Louise. "But I do have a gift from a gentleman. May I emphasize 'gentleman'? Simon Hagan." I felt the color explode on my cheeks as I went to the parlor and retrieved the bar of chocolate I'd stashed in my pocket. I plopped back down at the kitchen table. "Happy to share this with anyone interested."

I continued. "You know the Hagan family's farm, Millicent. It's north, Father said. Half dozen boys, couple of girls, I think. Geoffrey Hagan married Zack Peterson's widow—"

"Yes, I know the connection. They're in the store, of course. Jim thinks highly of them, I'm sure," Millicent said.

"And there's more. The elder Mr. Hagan is responsible for my teaching job. Don't think the particulars of that ever came up for discussion. Otherwise you'd have known. He was on the school board, and I met him. Guess it's been three years ago now . . . the summer of '28. Mr. Hagan appreciated the fact that I was getting my degree from Athens College. Anyway, enough about me. I have him to thank for my first teaching job."

"Millicent's right, Gracie. Geoffrey Hagan's a well-respected man. I was merely teasing you a mite about the chocolate, odd as it is for Simon to . . . Well, anyway, a piece of news was associated with his farm. Interestingly enough, the skeletal remains of a Shawnee Indian turned up on the property. Been 'bout two years ago." Father relaxed with his account of the story. Smoke from his cigarette curled in the air between us. "My understanding's that it was discovered very much intact."

"That is fascinating! Had I been living here at the time instead of Alabama I would have been extremely interested! I'd love to hear more!"

"The find attracted a good deal of chatter through these parts, and—"

"Humph!" Millicent rolled her eyes indignantly. "Is there any possible chance of my getting in a word, edgewise or otherwise? Fine, fine on dead Indians. What about Simon Hagan?"

Apparently Father took the mention as his cue to leave certain discussions to the women. Draining his cup, he stood. "Listen, ladies, I'm gonna head on. Just making sure, now, your plan is for Jim to get you back to Russellville. Correct, Gracie?"

A fragment of his smile remained, clinging to the charisma that had him suited up for more important things than sticking around to talk with two of his daughters.

I shrugged and turned to my sister. "Will that work out for Jim?"

"Of course, and Father," Millicent said, "please let Francine know that we couldn't have come out last night even if she'd invited us to celebrate your sixtieth birthday with you."

Father looked deliberately at her and crushed his cigarette in a nearby ashtray, perhaps deciding he had misinterpreted the inflection. He pushed his chair from the table and smoothed his tweed vest as he stood. "Good to have you back, Gracie."

I kept my seat as if a weight held me there, simply stirring more cream into my coffee. After what seemed forever I raised my head to look up at him. "You'll always be my father. Always. It's just probably best if it don't go back out to—"

"Yes, I know," Father said, and his dark, lamenting eyes sought to pierce my thoughts with a constant glare. Then came his attractive smile. He bent over to kiss me on the cheek, and the few small lines in his brow eased and vanished.

I waited in the kitchen as Millicent walked Father to the door.

"Well, Gracie?" she said with him gone. "Was my sarcasm terribly unbecoming?"

There was not a reason in the world I couldn't speak my mind to my older sister, but moments passed and I did not answer. Her self-affirming nod said she was ashamed, but a twinkle in her eye said she was justified. Thick black waves in her hair framed the youthful face that held back a grin.

"Not really, but I think he's past our disapproval of Francine." I sipped the last of my coffee and gently set the cup down, part of me wanting to applaud her. The other part wanted the past to just heal itself, like a crab regenerating its lost leg. "There is a very high wall between me and Father. Rightly so. Maybe."

"How was it?" Millicent sat down across from me, her mirth diminished. "Being there again. Be honest."

"If you want my opinion, I don't believe Father could ever have calculated the cost. Seems to me he was blinded . . . incapable of knowing what diminishing returns lay hidden beneath the surface." I walked to the window, wiping away tears that brimmed from my eyes.

Being honest meant looking at the past, not running, not cowering, neither letting injustices destroy the essence of my core, nor come close to ripping apart the fiber of a family in the way Francine had Moe Lee's.

"I'm hesitant to ask again, but has anyone heard from Moe Lee?" I turned to face Millicent.

She was wagging her head. "Not a word that I've heard," she said, and my heart seemed to swell beneath the flattened hand I laid over it.

"You know my direction changed the day Henry told me Moe Lee and his family were run off the farm. There, behind the great white facade we call Hillbound, upstairs in my room, I made my decision to come here in the middle of the night. Remember?"

She hadn't forgotten. None of the Maxwells could have, and in my remembrance I still credited the episode with my calling to go to the mission field.

"It was a terrible time, Gracie. I'm so glad you came here." Millicent reached across the table and patted my arm. "And we've loved every minute you've spent. When you went down to that potter's house in Madison County that year—even then you could have been here with us if we'd only been aware of what was happening."

"I don't know what I would have done without you and Jim giving me a place to live. My having your home to come back to during those four years of college was so generous of you. And I'm sure Emma would have been glad to have me except for lack of space and the children. She's a wonderful sister, too."

Talking provided some relief. I smiled. "Y'all are bound to have seen it yourself, just how Francine's influence is trickling like a slow drip over a pile of stones, etching in Henry a visible erosion. That's just what occurs over time. Do you know what I mean, Sister?"

I gave her a little space to answer, trying to get my concern in the open before it burned a hole in my heart.

"Whew . . . I'm thankful you intended to spend only one night there," she said. "You're right, though, Gracie. But who knows if, given the chance, Father would roll back events and do things differently. She's pushed everything and everybody, starting with Father, and I suspect he will never give up his—what? Obsessions? Addictions . . . if that's what horses and betting are."

"I think you see it on a regular basis, in bits and pieces. But for me to come back and witness firsthand Francine's callous regard for our brother is almost obscene. The rest of it? Yes, most anything can become an obsession." I had to breathe deeply. "On that note, I do have to say things work out. Interesting, isn't it? Because it was that very trip to Madison County that gave me a new beginning. Actually, it instilled in me a confidence in God's grace and a way to climb to new heights."

"But who doesn't have the family celebrate a sixtieth birthday?" Millicent gave me a sly look that said we'd covered the rough spots on the subject of our stepmother. "Maybe she's just a teensy bit too young yet. You'd think she would enjoy having some folks around the place, and close to her age—like us!"

We both burst into laughter. I had to cover my mouth. Millicent wiped tears. A good laugh helped everything.

"We do have a lot of wonderful memories, Gracie, and a lot of goodness to carry us on," she said. "Things never stay the same, do they? Enough!

Tell what you think about Mr. Hagan. *Simon* Hagan. Might he be a very interesting topic?"

⎯⎯⫷⎯⎯

"Get in this house, James Carver! Gracie and I have bones to pick with you. Come sit at the table and start talking. We want details. Simon Hagan. Start at the beginning."

"Sister, please. You're embarrassing me." I couldn't fool myself. I definitely wanted to know what my brother-in-law had to say. "And I do need to apologize, Jim. I rushed out today without speaking . . . and I owe you some money, too."

"Ah, no worries. Millicent may put you to work washing dishes to cover for yourself." Jim laughed and gave me hug, then peeled off his jacket and hung it on the hall tree. "Would seem," he said, taking plenty of time to position his hat on the hook above the row of coats, "I'm getting caught right in the middle, aren't I?"

"Indeed! Spill the beans! Gracie told me she left him talking to you. Or starting to, anyway," Millicent said, dragging him by the arm into the kitchen. "Fess up."

I caught the wink he sent in Millicent's direction. "Stop it, Sister. There's probably nothing to tell. Is there?"

"So happens, young Mr. Hagan's gonna be working for me. I offered to let him take my old truck. Don't know how he was gonna get out to his homeplace without it, but he took it and headed out there." He took a seat, put his elbows on the kitchen table, and laced his fingers together. Millicent and I stood over him, waiting. "Come Monday morning he'll be back in for work. Been away from these parts for quite a while—ten years, I believe he said. Frankly, I didn't recognize him. Geoffrey's got six boys and a couple o' girls. Simon's the oldest of all of 'em." He laughed and started to fiddle with the corner of the stack of napkins in the center of the table. "Gonna give his folks quite a surprise, from what I understand. This is his first day back in Todd County. They don't know he's arrived. Other than that, I'm afraid I don't know much. Oh! Well, now, I guess I did forget this one thing, Gracie. As I mentioned, I don't know anything about Simon Hagan past the time when he used to come into the store for supplies . . . eighteen years old, probably. But—" He paused, long enough for me to squirm.

"Heaven's sake, honey. *What?*" Millicent yanked apron strings around her waist. "What?"

"Simon did ask if I thought it would be alright if he called on you . . . here at the house." Jim said. "He is most interested in meeting you. Again."

Millicent squealed.

"You told him I would be staying here?"

"I did. That's all I'm saying."

———

Millicent and I talked into the night before we finally pried ourselves apart. "Get a good night's rest," she said, following me to the small room, an enclosed porch that had become mine whenever I had a break from school.

"I hope I'm not wearing out my welcome. It is so exciting to think where I'll be this time next year. Well, really in seven months. Then you'll be rid of me."

"Don't be silly. You're always welcome here, and you know it. Now go. Sleep tight." Millicent closed the door. "A lot can change in seven months," she said from the other side.

I was too keyed up to sleep, so I sat instead by the lamp and scrawled some thoughts in my journal:

October 18, 1930

> *This is where I belong, back in Todd County, teaching the children until May when my world will broaden into a purposeful mission to places unknown. Every day that*

goes by, my commitment is confirmed, but I'm here at Sister's for a time—the closest thing I have to home. And with God's help I will overcome the loss of all I've held dear.

I will rise, forgetting those things which are past and reaching forward to what lies ahead, the upward call.

The hardest burden to bear is knowing Henry has been crippled, with no strength for living. Praying the viciousness that Father has directed toward Henry will stop—and that Henry will be embedded with hope.

Simon Hagan is the man I met today at Jim's. Nice gentleman. His wanting to call on me is a lovely thought. Very lovely.

It must have been sometime after midnight before I dropped off to sleep, having kept myself awake with vivid images of my previous day at the farm. And meeting Simon Hagan. Even as I buried my head in my pillow and lay in darkness in the room Sister had prepared, I could see the dreadful events that had altered the course of our family.

I could see, too, the tall figure of Simon Hagan.

With morning only hours away and a big day ahead, beginning with church, I rolled over and tried to get some sleep.

Chapter 3

Pumpkin-colored leaves, curled and crisp, rustled in flurries as the oncoming horse and buggy scattered them from the path in a gust of wind. I purposely kept myself turned away from my brother-in-law as he guided the horse through the wooded terrain. Emotions had run the gamut this visit and could have proved exhausting were it not for the spark of interest that had kindled for Simon Hagan. Talking to myself, I dabbed at the corners of my eyes with a gloved finger, trying to think more on him than the disaster taking place at Hillbound.

No doubt Jim has seen the emotion I'm trying to cover, I thought. *My overreaction has to stop! Henry will surely pull through this sour period.*

Jim Carver rode quietly beside me in the carriage that was taking us sixteen miles away from Sister's house to Russellville, back to the school-house where I would resume teaching tomorrow. Being a well-mannered man, Jim was not about to reveal he'd noticed the tears. He looked away as I regained my composure. He respectfully said nothing of Mr. Hagan, but Millicent had pressed through Sunday lunch with her questions regarding the man—ones that shouldn't expect answers to come out of our brief meeting. She had been satisfied to surmise that I had not seen the last of Mr. Hagan, and such was her forecast to me as part of her farewell. Jim had loaded the carriage with my bag. He and I had departed after church with a hearty meal of pot roast, potatoes, and carrots, bound for Russellville.

Perhaps a day will come, another day, when Mr. Hagan will call on me. With that revelation, I shifted on the seat and sat straight as an arrow.

17

"'She'll be coming 'round the mountain when she comes,'" I sang out, unable to stop myself from bursting into song as we met the winding road.

Jim turned toward me, trying to mask his astonishment, and we both laughed at my poor rendition. I couldn't sing. It didn't matter. I didn't care if I could carry a tune or not. My song was meant to recharge me and chase away the tears. It seemed to have succeeded.

Through the trees, I caught sight of the church's steeple, majestic and gloriously white, pointing out over the treetops as if suspended in midair. In the middle of autumn's splendid offering, I reflected on my fifteen-year-old self—a girl who had left following a Christmas service within its walls, having experienced what brokenness felt like.

Inside the doll-like structure, hope had become real, rising as visibly as the spire above the unadorned chapel where I had found it so many years before.

The buggy bounced unpredictably as it rounded the downward slope of the hill. At the next bend in the road, the familiar clapboard building, sitting regally in the clearing, came into full view.

Russellville was several miles ahead, and in a matter of a few minutes, Jim would leave me there to start a new day, early in the morning, in the two-room schoolhouse with the children I loved.

Chapter 4

⟡

The morning was an invigorating one—the beginning of a new day. A furry critter, most certainly a red fox, slithered into the nearby woods as I climbed the four steps leading to the schoolhouse that sat west of downtown Russellville on Boughey Street.

The final two weeks of October and the entire month of November had whisked past in an exceptional array of intentional activity, and once again visions of changing my little corner of the world had me riding high on ambitions. My commitments were going forward, and—Lord willing—I would take on the rest of the world come May.

A rigorous teaching schedule filled my daytime hours. Preparing myself emotionally and spiritually for the mission field filled my evening hours, but with December plans fully underway, I found myself eager for tomorrow's return trip to Millicent's home to spend Christmas in Elkton.

Henry was due to come for me in the morning, but until then I had an agenda to meet.

"*Humm-hum hum-hum* . . . looking above. Filled with His goodness, lost in His love. This is my story, this is my song, praising my Savior all the day long. *Hum-hum hum hum-hum*, all the day long—"

Arguably, wealthier areas touted more books and better buildings and equipment. And higher pay for my college degree did elude me, but it was the experience in these two classrooms that put a song in my heart. I pushed open the door in a moment charged with confidence. Both school rooms were empty, both freezing cold. Even so, it was going to take more than seeing my frosty breath in the air and a little chill to back me down. Grabbing the bucket, I dumped chunks of coal over the existing weak glow, as many as the potbelly stove would hold.

Lesson plans that I had bundled yesterday were stacked at the corner of my desk; the black-handled school bell sat on top. *Were it not for Mr. Geoffrey Hagan and his enthusiasm as school board member to have me teach in Todd County*, I thought, *and the timely meeting when our paths crossed, I might have stayed in Alabama.*

I removed my gloves and ran my bare hand across the cold surface of the chalkboard, then picked up a piece of chalk and wrote *MERRY CHRIST-MAS* in bold letters across the top of the board. Hugging myself like a bear that had lost her cubs, I walked briskly past the two short rows of desks into the next room and wrote the same Christmas wish on the chalkboard.

"Thank goodness I made that commitment," I said aloud, stuffing the potbelly stove in there with coal as well.

"What commitment, Miss Maxwell?"

Startled, I turned to find one of my fifth graders. A blue scarf, worn but patched, wrapped her head, and a too-large-for-her plaid coat was tied at the waist with a cord. Having come from one of the many depression-hit households that had embraced a new level of frugality, she stood looking up at me. *And existing*, I thought, *perhaps unwise to the world of adults, carrying on with life as close to normal as possible, with parents keeping up appearances during a very bleak period in our American history.*

"To be here with you! *You* and the other bright students in this very school. Y'all are going to do great things one day, Elizabeth Ann." I gave her a hug. "Your whole future is ahead of you! Do you know that?"

"Yes, Miss Maxwell. You've told us. So it must be true." Her appearance was fresh faced, and my having taught her for the last four months indicated she had a mind like a sponge.

It was Elizabeth Ann and the thirteen other children—those from the four first graders and four third graders to the three sixth graders and a seventh grader to the lone eleventh grader—whose passion for learning had, in a short time period, affirmed and likewise justified my decision to return to my roots. Gaining experience and maturity for what lay ahead for me after this initial year of teaching was essential. More important, my having taught the Negro children to read and write at the tender age of fifteen—giving them an eye to the world outside Hillbound even when my love for them exceeded my expertise—had set in motion my life's course. Not everyone who heard the inspirational speaker at Athens' campus had responded the way I had. Not everyone had pledged two years of their future to become a missionary.

"Good morning, Miss Maxwell." Betsy Sue Samuels laid a greeting card on my desk.

"Merry Christmas, Miss Maxwell," Clara Ridgefield said and handed me an apple, one that looked like she'd possibly polished it on her sleeve on the way to school.

Gradually the coat hooks became overloaded, the desks filled with jabbering students. I settled the younger ones into their reading lesson and proceeded to the room where the older students were, as it appeared, keyed up with excitement for the upcoming two-week vacation. I caught a glimpse of the paper airplane Ronald Birch hurled through the air. It landed in Molly Jane Foreman's long curls. The laugher immediately ceased as I entered.

Momentarily displeased, I decided the best approach was to set aside the airplane incident. Instead, I removed my coat, hung it on the back of my chair, and went to the blackboard, my back to the students.

"Miss Maxwell?"

I turned, chalk in hand, and came to an abrupt stop in my arithmetic quizzing. My face was set into a pruney scowl that threatened to be permanent.

"Yes, Philip?" I said, acknowledging the raised hand of one of my sixth-grade pupils.

"Your dress is not zipped."

I took a moment to gather my wits about me. "Thank you, Phillip," I said, putting on my coat, then slowly fastening its hooks. "Question: if my coat has seven buttons down the front, two on each sleeve, and one on each pocket, how many minutes will it take to button my coat if it takes thirty seconds per button to button all of them?"

The sixth graders looked at each other in dismay. Some began counting on their fingers. After a delay, one hand went up.

"Yes, Charles?"

The seventh grader was smiling as he stood. "Six and a half."

"Ah-ha," I said with a lip smack and a victorious laugh. "*If* my coat *had* buttons, your answer would be correct. It only has hooks, though. You may be seated."

The arithmetic lesson brought cautious laughter, and curiosity had the younger children peeking at us from around the doorframe. We all joined in the gaiety, and then it was back to business.

I walked to the front of my desk and sat on its edge. "We'll be out of school for a little over two weeks, boys and girls. That's going to give you an opportunity to read a good book . . . and there are many, *all kinds*, to choose on the shelf in the other room. Consider the one you take as if it's a Christmas gift and savor it. Then bring it back so it will be there for the next person. Alright. Now, in the few hours left, let's get busy and wind up this school year with a bang."

Accounting for the cheerful intermission and tidbits of giddiness that seemed to be unusually prevalent the entire day—not to mention the absentmindedness that had begun it—I put blame on the fact that upon my arrival at Millicent and Jim's house tomorrow afternoon, Simon Hagan would be coming for tea. The desire that typically preoccupied and drove me to create a positive change in the public-school systems and equality among school districts would simply have to wait until I returned on January 5. Meanwhile, having had Elizabeth Ann zip my dress, I finished up the last day of the 1930 school calendar, rang the handbell, and hugged the students as they filed out. After smothering the coals, I walked three blocks in the blustery wind to Mrs. Martin's boarding house where I lived.

Chapter 5

———⚮———

As I eagerly watched from the window in the parlor at the boarding house the next morning, it was all I could do to contain myself. I hoped to spot my brother coming up Boughey Street in a buggy, but he was not. Tardiness was easy to predict where Henry was concerned, but of all times for him to be late, this should not have been one of them.

My rather large suitcase and one small bag sat at the edge of the porch. I stepped outside one more time into the invigorating air to get a feel for the weather and evaluate the potential for snow flurries. Frothy clouds hovered in shades of gray.

"You're letting every bit of heat out of this house. For Pete's sake," said my landlady, "come back in here right now, or I'll have to raise your rent!"

I knew she was joking, but I apologized, anyway, and stepped back inside the cozy confines of the hallway of my boarding house.

"Your brother's going to show up any minute. Why don't you seat yourself and relax?"

I'd no sooner plopped on the petite settee in the parlor than here came the familiar sight of the carriage, its fringe swaying, the horse's head bobbing. With blinders on its eyes, the horse looked neither to the left nor the right as it trotted down the road.

I was already out the door, and at Henry's command, the old filly came to a halt out front. The recognizable figure of my older brother was perched high on the bench.

"Morning, Sis," he shouted over horse's snorts.

"You-hoo! Don't ya be forgetting these suitcases. Merry Christmas now!" With a wave, Mrs. Martin was back inside before Henry had jumped from the carriage to the ground. He tied the reins to the post then walked toward me with a boyish grin, pausing to wrap his long, lanky arms around me. Deep eyes gazed at me from beneath a well-worn hat situated atop his boney forehead. He smelled of old straw and stale beer.

"Thanks for coming. Thanks for getting an early start. Ah! Fresh air! Cold, fresh air," I said with every indication of enthusiasm I possessed. "I simply love it."

"Yep. Did at that, Sis. It was barely light." He snugged me in with heated bricks at my feet and after tucking the luggage in place, handed me a blanket for my lap." "You're looking well."

He settled himself on the bench, reins in hand and with the whip poised over the horse's rear end, gently tapped her. "Step up, ol' girl."

"It's going to be a good Christmas," I said as the horse began walking. "Emma goes to a lot of trouble for all of us. You know how she is. And this year little Louise must be very excited . . . looking for Santa and all." I turned to see if I was giving Henry something to smile about. "Hope Emma's children are going to let her hang onto the anticipation a few more years, don't you?"

"I enjoy it, Sis. No doubt about that." Henry swallowed hard as a gust of bitter breeze swirled in our faces. He reached over and pulled my scarf higher over my mouth. "You're a pretty girl, Sis. And you'll get married. Be gone for good then. Hillbound's never been the same without you."

"Now, Henry, we have to look on the bright side, don't you think? Besides, marriage is about the last thing from my mind. One day, of course. No time soon. Will you join us for church tomorrow?"

"Nah. You did the right thing by Moe Lee's children—all those colored children, Amos's—teaching them to read and write when you had the chance. I should've never given you a hard time about it."

"Goodness! Those children were my inspiration. Without them I might not have gone into teaching or the mission field. We have to work with what God puts in our path. He'll mold raw materials into something beautiful . . . if we let Him."

Henry mulled over the suggestion. Part of me wanted to say more, to find a way to paint a picture of him with a wife, children, maybe. Managing the farm, tapping his natural wherewithal as a farmer, making Hillbound thrive once again with tobacco—completely restored as the tobacco farm that our father had squandered in his counterfeit trade for race horses, gambling, and glitz. I could feel myself relishing the savory wintry morning, soaking up in my memory the smell and richness of tobacco crops, reaching out to the touchable Maxwell legacy that Henry so tentatively held onto.

Either deep thought or melancholy had set in. It was hard to tell, but after a long silence Henry's shoulders straightened and he gave a little giddy-up to the reins. "You got a suitor coming over to Millicent's? It's what I heard."

"Oh. Well, sort of, maybe. Simon Hagan's coming for tea. That's all. I'm looking forward to finding out about him, anyway."

Henry's head lurched backward in a burst of laughter. Hearing him joyous again was the music to my ears, even at my expense.

"Not funny, Henry."

"Don't know if his brother ever played football at the high school, but he was sure enough there before I had to quit. I was a good athlete back then, Sis."

He turned to see if I agreed. Inwardly, I agreed that his talent, too, was lost when trades were made: trade for Henry's labor over Henry's education. But I gave him a sincere and affirmative nod. "You have all kinds of talents, and don't ever forget it."

"He probably would've played after that . . . ol' Alan. Alan Hagan. Yep, would be Simon's brother. Wonder whatever happened to him . . . And now that I'm thinking, I believe he died somehow, a few years back." Henry rambled on, seemingly in need of someone to talk to, and I was content to let him speak his mind as Trojan Girl trotted us past field after field and the grassy broadleaf weeds that had sprung up along the road and in between the stubble of harvested wheat.

But the mention of Mama never came up, and I let the subject be.

Chapter 6

The carriage headed up South Main Street. I was inside Millicent and Jim's house before Henry rode out of sight.

"Are you just about frozen? Here," Millicent said, turning me around, "warm your backside. Give me your coat . . . all this extra . . . and thaw out! Why didn't Henry come in? He should have. I mean, he's been out in the cold for hours!"

"Stubborn. What else? I think he was a little bit insulated, if you know what I mean."

"No! I don't want to hear it." Millicent put up a hand to ward off the mention of alcohol. "Is he going to Emma's Christmas Day?"

"He promised. But I guess I didn't even bring up Father and Francine. Should I have?"

"Probably not. Emma's planning on everybody! Father won't disappoint her . . . awkward as that's gonna be."

Millicent and I gave each other knowing looks. With no further speculation about what to expect come Christmas Day, we moved into the kitchen.

"I didn't give you much of a chance to get warmed up," she said and busied herself with uncovering the shortbread while I tinkered with the tea kettle. "It's fine, fine," I said.

But it wasn't—the expectation was too high to contain, and practically at the same moment and without warning, we both squealed like stuck pigs.

"What time's he coming?" I carelessly twirled myself around between the washbasin and stove, teapot held high in the air.

"Oh, dear!" Millicent was coy. "You are expecting someone?"

"Sister!" I brushed by her as Louise came bounding into the kitchen.

"Well! My favorite second grader, right here!" I squatted just in time for her to come flying into my arms. "And tell me: what is Santa bringing you?"

Dark-brown hair spiraled in curls over her shoulders. Her smiled showed the loss of two front teeth. "Flossie Flirt," she said and skipped away.

"A doll, of course. The thing says 'Ma Ma,'" Millicent whispered with a wink. "Alright. Now, Gracie Mae. Mr. Hagan will be here about four o'clock. That is if Jim lets him off. Ten after, maybe. Your cheeks are still nice and rosy from the out-of-doors. That's good."

Whether they were bitten by the cold ride from Russellville or the rip-roaring fire in the fireplace in the living room, by the time Simon Hagan arrived they were completely flushed. I could feel it.

Millicent and even little Louise had made themselves scarce. I heard the knock on the door and took a deep breath. One last peek in the mirror, one last twist to the notable black curl at my left cheek.

"And a good afternoon to you, Mr. Hagan. Do come in."

Hat in hand, it seemed his head narrowly cleared the door frame. "Gracie Maxwell! So good to see you again. Jim's done me a big favor, I'm sure, arranging this time."

"May I take that for you, and your coat? It's lovely to have you visit. Please, have a seat. won't you?"

"You were in quite a hurry to leave his store . . . on our meeting—"

"Oh, that!" My face couldn't have gotten any redder. Convinced it was trying, I sat in the chair next to the maroon mohair divan where he settled. "I'll pour us some tea. Cream?"

"Yes, I think so." He laughed. "If you are. I've not had much tea in my lifetime. This is a real treat, and I've been looking forward to getting to know you. So this is also a treat. I'd like to think I masterminded our improbable little meeting at the candy counter. However that happened, I'm glad for it." He smiled. A charming smile, bold, warm, confident.

I was quite sure he was not about to melt right into the wool rug on the floor at Millicent's house, as I was. *Suave. Gallant*, I thought. *Cheeky.*

I took a sip of tea. He did the same. "I've been interested to know about the Shawnee Indian that was found on your family's farm. What can you tell me? "

"Not much. I've been holed up in Albuquerque, New Mexico, for a while. Before that I was in Detroit for close to eight years. Sorry to say, and as much as I have to catch up on happenings here in Todd County, I haven't been back here but twice in ten years. My dad's probably the expert on the Indian you're referring to. But you're a teacher. I'm impressed with that. A very high ambition."

"Well, it is and one that thrills me to no end. This is my first year, although I've taught a Sunday school class at Logan College and the Negro children to read and write. High school girls, too, over the years I was there. You have no way of knowing this, Mr. Hagan, but your father was responsible for getting me the job I have in Russellville. I'm indebted to him," I said and passed the plate of shortbread.

"He's something, alright. I'm proud to call him my father. And it's hard to believe all that he's accomplished with a third-grade education. School board member is only one of them." He paused and grinned. "Actually, my dad did tell me that about you. He thinks very highly of you, Gracie . . . if I may call you Gracie. And please, try calling me Simon." He lit a cigarette and returned the lighter to his vest pocket.

"So, Albuquerque. What on earth took you there?"

Simon stood up, walked to the fireplace. He ran his fingers through the waves in his hair, and I thought I would faint just as little Louise pranced into the room. "Try calling him Simon, Aunt Gracie," she said, giggling.

Simon tossed his cigarette into the fireplace. "And who's this?" He lifted her with a brisk swoop, both of them laughing.

"Louise Annabelle Carver."

"Well, Louise Annabelle Carver, I'm Simon Newton Hagan. It's a pleasure to meet you. I have a brother just about your age. Seven. Am I right?"

"Yes, sir. What's his name?"

"John. We call him *Big* John. Know why?" Simon acknowledged Millicent with a head nod as she entered the parlor.

"Bet it's 'cause he's big!"

"Mr. Hagan, so good to see you. Now, Louise, we have things to do for supper. You're welcome to stay." Millicent directed her invitation to Simon.

"Thank you, but I'll visit just a while longer and not interrupt your evening meal. Glad we've had the chance to chat at the store, though. I might not've been here today without your help."

I cut my eyes at Millicent. She and Louise skedaddled. "You were just going to tell me about Albuquerque, Mr. Hag— Simon."

He pursed his lips in an ah-ha moment. "Good. Very good." He sat back down. "Oh, that's a story. Version one is that I did some acting and attended the University of New Mexico to become a doctor."

I scooted to the edge of my chair, set my empty cup on the table in front of me, all ears.

"Version two, and the beginning of that story: I had tuberculosis and went from Detroit out there to a sanatorium."

"That must have been horrible. I'm glad you're well. But you're smoking?"

"TB's an infection. I'm certainly over it. But, yes, I did start back smoking."

My mention had made for an inopportune little lull in our conversation. Simon smiled and cocked his head in a most attractive way. "You're my envy, Gracie. Wish I could've continued college, but the depression seemed to take the air right outta my sails. Who knows . . . maybe one day?"

"Never give up. You know, it's been my vision to help others, particularly teaching them, since I was quite young. I believe God's set me on a path. Currently, that desire has me going to the mission field. In May. How about you? What will you be doing, now that you're back? Working for Jim? Or are you staying?"

"Let's see . . . that was three questions in one. If I'd had plans to leave, I would have changed them by now. Having met you, I mean." Simon's big brown eyes were deeply inquisitive if not dejected. "The mission field? Somehow it has a far-away ring to it."

"Africa. The Sudan," I said, unapologetically. "Yes, pretty far."

"*Gosh!* It's the other side of the world! Tell me you're kidding!"

It was plain to tell he hoped I was.

"No, I'm completely serious. Big jump for a girl from the backwoods of Kentucky, isn't it?" I watched his reaction, knowing he'd seen much more of the world than I, realizing his dreams, too, exceeded the boundary lines of Todd County. "I've been coming back to Elkton for brief visits during my four years of college. I am very familiar with pupils in poor rural areas and how they—and those I've seen in Alabama— have to make do with what little their school districts can put together. Standardization is happening, but it's still in infancy because of federal bureaucracy and government legislation. I want to help make a change. But about three months ago something altered my direction—again. You see, I read a novel called *In His Steps: What Would Jesus Do?* It's written by a man, Charles M. Sheldon. I may have a yearning for the spectacular, I don't know. But I read that book about the same time I heard an inspirational speaker talk about the intense need in the Sudan. It prompted me to rethink where I was going from here. And it anointed me with the freedom to leave."

Simon's face had turned blank. The shortbread he'd picked up was still in his hand. "Gracie." He faltered. "Gracie, I think that is tremendous. You have me wanting to hear every detail, " he said and laid the cookie on the saucer. "Partly, I'd like to change that vision and keep you here for selfish reasons. Frankly, I'd like to court you. But I am aware enough of God to know not to try to control what he's got His hand on. That's been too much, in my experience. Doesn't make me not want to see you again, though." He settled back on the divan. "Betcha Big John—and he's my half-brother, by the way—can tell you all you want to know about the Shawnees. Dang! If I promise to brush up on my history, may I call on you again? If I get down—"

"No, don't. Please!" I'd stopped him in the nick of time from getting on his knees in his gray flannel trousers. "I would like that, Simon."

"Then it's settled. No, wait. Guess it's not exactly settled. Where . . . when can I reach you? I'll telephone here? I'll come here . . . I'll go there," he said with a stagey wink.

"Come over . . . for dinner." Millicent arrived, unannounced, wiping her hands on her apron. "Excuse me. I was sure you were about to get away before I could invite you. Christmas Eve. Here. I'll talk to Jim. Y'all could cut us a tree, get it in the truck after work, and come on over. That's a nice arrangement, isn't it? You are still using that old truck from time to time, right?"

Simon looked at me. I looked at him. He smiled, I smiled, and we both nodded a yes.

"Well, thank you very much, Millicent. Jim does let me borrow the truck . . . in exchange for Hannah's canned goods. Which means I then trade in on chores for my stepmother. It's high finance, but with gasoline being such as it is . . . Yes, it works."

"Some of us will decorate the tree," Millicent said, her personality bubbling, "and Gracie will cook."

I registered a look that did not include a smile.

"It's been my pleasure, Gracie. And I'll see you on Wednesday evening."

With our goodbyes said, Simon slipped on his overcoat, set his fedora at a rakish angle atop his head, and was out the door.

"*Sister*," I said with an accusatory inflection, my back to Millicent, my shoulders arched like a predatory cat's before I turned around.

She conceded with ridiculously raised eyebrows. Her tongue clucked. "That's why the good Lord gave us sisters."

Chapter 7

A strangely wrapped gift sat suspiciously tucked beneath the bare Christmas tree at the Carvers' home on the night before Christmas 1930. Jim and Simon had wrangled the fir inside and stood it on the cross-member wood base that formed an *X* nailed to the trunk. They both backed away from the masterpiece and proudly huffed at their accomplishment.

Christmases past conjured up memories of the happy occasions of Mama with her beautiful dark hair twisted in a tight knot at the nape of neck, her contagious smile that lingered still as a reminder of her kind spirit. The love she'd had for me and Emma, Henry, and Millicent had shown in the way she prayed with us at nighttime and tucked us in with a kiss, read poetry to us, and made sure we appreciated literature and respected people of every description.

The vision of sacks of candy in knitted socks that hung from the mantle in the drawing room at Hillbound as Santa's surprise for her "wonderful babies" and the kiss she had for Father as she encircled his waist with her arms caused a lump in my throat.

Then came the flood of memories of joyous laughter and the abundance of simple things in the summertime—food that grew in the garden and glorious flowers that flourished in beauty beside the picket fence before gracing our home because Mama insisted, and the natural goodness that fell from the sky to water the crops and nurture life as I knew it.

Plans to decorate the tree had been at Millicent's command, while the kitchen duties were mine. It had been a test, and I knew it. Either from God or from her. In any case, the dinner was a disaster. Yet Simon managed to find a lovely way to compliment the lumpy mashed potatoes, and Jim suggested the fruit salad was the freshest anywhere in Elkton. Louise discovered the biscuits were in fun shapes, nice and hard so she could engage them in play and other creative antics. Berry jam helped the cause.

There was hardly a way to ruin the ham, but I found it. Dry as it was, "Simply delicious" seemed to be the less-than-truthful reassurance handed down. I wasn't buying it, but neither was I going to leave the table in tears. *Merely a test*, I reminded myself. We still had dessert to go, so hope abounded.

As for the tree, garlands were strung and homemade ornaments hung, and when it came time for the star, there was none other than Simon Hagan qualified to place it on top of the tree. No need for a stool or a tiptoe. At six foot three, he could manage. And with a magnificent smile, he did.

Little Louise was ecstatic. "It's so pretty. Will I leave cookies for Santa Claus? And milk?"

And our answers were exuberant, perfect for the child in every person in the room.

"What's for dessert?" Jim said when all the hoopla had settled and the fire was dying down. "Want another log on, Millicent?"

"Oh, I think so. We'll have cake and ice cream and sing a Christmas carol or two and call it a night. Miss Louise, I think you should run on to bed since Santa will be watching for little girls who are sound asleep. And tomorrow's a big, big day. So fun, too, at Aunt Emma's. Let's go say prayers and tuck you in. You've had candy canes—a wonderful dessert—so come along, sweetheart. Tell everyone nighty-night."

"Merry Christmas, Mr. Simon. Will you be here in the morning?"

"No, honey. I'll be with my family, but I'll be wishing that Santa Claus arrived down the chimney and was very good to you. Did you remember the cookies and milk?"

"Mother! No!" Louise gasped and was off to the kitchen in a flash.

Simon had saved the day, and my dessert cake was not the worst of the dinner. We finished it with the help of hot coffee and afterwards a quiet verse of "Silent Night." My verse was extra quiet.

"I have a small something for y'all to share," Simon said and walked to the Christmas tree. The gift was wrapped in butcher paper like the kind used at Carver's Grocery and Hardware for raw meat. "It's just a token of my appreciation, but it's sincere. Here, Gracie, you open it."

He handed the lumpy package to me and took a step back while I opened the biggest assortment of chocolate I'd seen—short what the candy case held at Jim's store.

"My goodness! I do love chocolate. Look, y'all."

"She does love chocolate, Simon. We do too."

I stood and passed the package for Jim and Millicent to see. "Thank you so much, Simon. I'm afraid I don't have a gift—"

"Tell you what. I was not at all expecting a gift. Being with your family is gift enough. Come, take a short walk with me. It's a beautiful night. Cold, but I think we can brace for it. Just really quick."

Millicent made a beeline for the hall tree and returned with our outerwear. We bundled up and stepped outside into a starry night. Simon was a head taller than I, and looking up at him I almost lost my balance.

"Watch out there!" He caught my arm and held it. "See, I've saved your life. How about returning the favor by going out with me on Saturday night? I could teach you the Charleston. Or maybe you already know it?"

"A little, but I'm not a great dancer. You're the actor. I imagine you're a great dancer. And I've already heard you sing . . . 'Silent Night.' You have a nice voice."

"Guess I can cut a pretty mean rug, as they say, but let me, and I'll teach you. We could be an attraction come New Year's Eve." He looked over at me, checking, I supposed, to see if I caught that he'd asked me to go out on two upcoming evenings. "Would you consider it . . . them . . . those." He laughed, apologetically. "Look, Gracie, the thing is I'd be honored to take you out if you'll go. And this may sound terribly forward of me, but it would be nice if we could squeeze in church on Sunday. This Sunday. Can you tell I'm trying to make the most of the time you have here? It's so short." He was breathless, either from the cold or the lengthy invitation.

"That's very nice of you, Simon. And thank you, too, for the wonderful chocolates." I was ever so comfortable with the name Simon, and I felt quite stunning myself, clinging to his arm under a spectacular sky.

"Simon . . ." I could feel his arm stiffen as if he were about to hear unwanted news.

"You need to understand that I have very high aspirations. Becoming a missionary is not a calling I'm taking lightly."

"Calling? As in a voice from the blue—"

"You're not taking me seriously. Perhaps you have plans, too, once this economic depression ends. Go back to school? It's difficult nowadays to get an education, but you could do it. Your father's certainly in favor of higher education."

"He is. Definitely. He's worked hard to get what he's got. I know that better than anyone."

We'd reached the end of the block. Simon walked us around the street lamp. Slowly, we were making our way back. The cold seemed irrelevant.

"Dad owns two thousand acres, and his farm is self-contained. The man deserves a lot of credit. I sure as heck don't expect to lean on him. Never have, Gracie. Never will. My brother Raymond and I are working on the particulars of opening a tire business together."

I felt Simon relax. It was all I could do to keep up the pace. Thankfully, his stride slowed.

"Want you to meet Raymond. He'll be at church on Sunday. Would you at least promise that one? It would absolutely make my Christmas."

Millicent's house was just a few feet away. The evening was about to end, and nothing about me was anywhere near ready. "I'd love to do that, Simon."

"So, are you saying 'love to do that' as a yes to learning the Charleston on Saturday night, Providence Methodist Church this Sunday, and New Year's Eve next week?"

Simon looked like a puppy awaiting a treat as we stood on the last step back at the house. I couldn't help but laugh out loud. "You're funny." I let go of his arm and took hold of the doorknob. "Alright, then. I'd love to do those things."

Simon was beaming. "Merry Christmas, Gracie. I'll ring you up on Thursday." He tipped his hat and waited on the step until I was inside. After I'd waved to him through the glass frame in the front door, he turned and walked to Jim's old truck parked at the curb.

Chapter 8

I awakened to the melodious sound of a familiar carol coming from the radio in the parlor at Sister's house. It couldn't have been much past seven o'clock, and the morning after Christmas was pushing its way into my room by way of the fresh fragrance of cedar. It came past the door that creaked as it opened, wafting over to the very spot where I had been sleeping *ever* so peacefully, enjoying the luxury of extra time beneath warm covers with no responsibilities to roust me out of bed.

"Aunt Gracie?" The whisper worked itself into my dream the way that voices and events do, and I rolled over with the images of Henry and Father outside on the porch at Emma's house, smoking their cigarettes, puffing black curls into the air, arguing about nothing. And Francine was whispering to my eldest sister in distasteful tones, a witch-y finger pointed in vigorous gestures at Emma.

"Aunt Gracie, wake up! Don't you want to talk to Flossie Flirt?" Louise, unrestrained, stood by my bed. Her new doll was propped up beside me.

I stretched my mouth wide open in oversized yawns and forced my eyes to open, blocking the glare of a sunbeam forcing its light through a slant in the window blinds.

"Good morning, Louise!" I sat up in bed and pulled my robe from the bedpost. "Of course! May I please talk to your cute doll?"

"Oh, Aunt Gracie, she's *much* more real than a doll! Flossie Flirt says 'Ma Ma'! Why are you still in bed?"

"Louise, honey! We were going to let Gracie sleep. Remember?" Millicent chastised from the doorway.

"I need to be up anyway," I said, hoping to reassure them both with a theme of forgiveness. But having turned in late last night, tied to the emotions of yesterday's family gathering, reminiscing about the good times and anticipating the future, reflecting on the uniqueness of the single Christmas spent down at the potter's house and recounting the changes in my life since that time, it was a wonder I'd slept a wink. And I'd dreamed of food but woke up hungry.

Breakfast made me grateful for what I had, but I prayed with a deep awareness that went beyond the oatmeal and butter on the table in front of me to the many hard-hit people adapting to new economic circumstances. To the people whose lives had made a difference in mine. To the Willoughbys—Marcus and Lucy and Chester—whose home was open to me when there was no place else to go. To the opportunity for education when all around the living conditions had worsened and farmers had come to the brink of losing their land in these difficult times of our nation's depression, hard times. "Amen," I said aloud.

"You always pray by yourself so long, Aunt Gracie?"

"I'm not alone, honey. God's beside me. Listening." I tried to grab and tickle little Louise, but barely got my knuckles to her ribs before she skipped away. "Guess Jim was out early this morning," I said to Millicent.

She sat down at the table, coffeepot in hand. "I thought yesterday went well. Emma makes it all look so easy. And Henry was pleasant. Certainly avoided Francine, it seemed."

"Yes, it seemed so. Did you think my dinner for Simon was perfectly horrid, Sister? *Did* you?"

"Cooking takes practice, Gracie. It was fine. Fine. You know Jim's going into the store no matter what. I doubt many folks will be in, but who knows?"

"Simon, maybe? Was he going to work today? I didn't think to ask him, but he is going to telephone me today. I know so little about him, Sister. It might not be right, after all, to see him too much . . . with my leaving in

May and all. I've promised to be with him *three* times in the next several days. What do you think?"

Millicent stirred her coffee, poured in a dribble of cream, and slowly stirred again. "I'm not one to stand in your way. Africa's a mighty long way away and—"

"Oh, but I'm not referring to my leaving. There's no question about my going where I think God can use me. I'm trying to be like clay in His hands, trying to let Him shape me as He sees fit . . to help the people He wants me to help."

"I know, Gracie. I know your heart, too, I think. But it is . . . *interesting* that the two of you have come back to Todd County pretty much the same time. Simon's a good man. Good family. Good sense of humor. Very handsome. I'm just saying, you can be clay in God's hands anywhere." She offered a warm smile, and her sisterly advice felt sweet. And then she laughed out loud like she loved to do. "You don't have to be *foreign* clay!"

The telephone rang two short rings, loud and clear from the nook in the hallway.

"Something to think about before that telephone rings off the hook and you go changing your mind about seeing him," Millicent said with a prissy little simper. "That's going to be for you, Gracie. Why don't you go ahead and answer?"

It rang again before I could get there. "Carver's residence," I said. "Gracie Maxwell on the line."

"Go ahead, Mr. Hagan," came the operator's reply.

An awkward silence seemed liked forever, and then I heard Simon's familiar deep voice, first in the form of a cough, then a huff-laugh. "Gracie! Please excuse me! I have a small, unanticipated audience for this call. Let me turn myself around here and see if I can duck behind one of Jim's storage boxes." I could hear rustling in the background. "I do apologize. And I'm afraid I am gonna have to be rather brief."

"Hello, Simon. I hope your Christmas was good . . . with your family," I said, trying to alleviate some of the awkwardness of our conversation's beginning.

"Gracie . . . "

Uh-oh, was a thought that entered my mind, followed by, *He's cancelling*. It was the kind of bad-news inflection in his hesitation that might've stopped my heart had he not immediately continued and the awkwardness returned as quickly as it had departed.

"Yes! Yes, a wonderful one! Could not have been a better time with family. Just almost everyone was there for the reunion. Don't even think I can count that high, there were so many. But listen, I want to hear all about yours when I come for you on Saturday. Turns out there aren't a lot of places in Elkton where I can teach you the Charleston, though. And nothing like there is in Albuquerque, unfortunately. So, would it be alright if—"

"Of course," I found myself saying. "Come here and I'll try fixing—"

"No, I won't have you going to any trouble, if you were going to invite me to dinner. This was going to be such a good plan: first a dance lesson, then I thought of a movie, but there's not one anywhere within miles of here. But, Gracie, this just has to work. Hannah, my stepmother—and you're going to love her—Hannah's going to fix one of her great meals for us. There's room in the parlor to dance and a Victrola. You can stay overnight in my sister's room. Then, there you are: Sunday morning and Providence Methodist Church, very close, just on the south end of my dad's property."

I guessed he'd paused to take a breath. All I could hear was snickering. Either from the party line or in the background at Jim's store, but Simon has his agenda and he was sticking to it.

Millicent and Louise had come into the hallway, and I was making *go-away* faces, batting the air to emphasize the imperative.

"What do you think?" It was almost a whimper. He'd definitely simmered down, sounding more like an insecure twelve-year-old than the tall, confident man of two nights ago.

"Well . . . I think let's plan on it," I said. "What time will you be coming by for me?'

"I'll be there at five thirty with bells on." The relief in his voice was palpable. "Actually, I'll be in Jim's truck, so more of a rattle. But I'll see you then."

I hung up the receiver and pursed my lips—lost in speculation over my impulsive agreement. "That should not have happened," I said, my finger still tightly hanging onto the hook.

Chapter 9

⚛

If my coughing fits during most of Friday hadn't been warning enough, the next day confirmed the inevitable fever. Saturday morning I was tucked beneath the bedcovers with a cool compress on my forehead. Millicent's telephone call to the Hagan household had served to pass along my disappointment and sincere regret for having to cancel my visits, both for dinner and the promised visit to Providence Methodist Church.

She plumped my pillow and handed me a cup, and I sipped a warm concoction of honey and lemon juice. "Simon sounded positively crushed, Gracie. But there will be other times." Her sympathy showed.

"Well," I said, coughing, "we've carried on a lot for having only been face to face one time . . . and two brief other times. Simon had a little cough too. Must have caught a bug on our Christmas Eve walk. Guess a cold wind got us."

⚛

"A cold wind got us, I guess," Simon was saying on the other end of the telephone line. "But I feel one hundred percent. I hope you do, Gracie. Hate to think I brought this on by taking us on a walk."

I couldn't keep myself from smiling as I pictured him hiding behind a large barrel of some sort at Jim's store, a graceful hand bridging the gap between the receiver and his mouth. "Oh, don't go thinking such a thing.

And I'm fine. My fever's been gone for two, three days. I'm very sorry about dinner and all. Please, I hope Hannah understood. And I'm glad you're feeling well."

"Would you believe I have a new plan?"

Millicent was right about his sense of humor. It perfectly complemented his charm, but the thought of a new plan put me on guard. I bit my lip.

"We still have New Year's Eve tomorrow. Now, I know, I know. There's not a great selection of places to celebrate, and Hannah has whatever epizootic whatever we had, so I won't suggest coming all the way out here again—not yet, anyway. But it's gonna be a nice sunny day. I've asked Jim to let me take the afternoon, and if you'll let me, I'd like for us to go on a ride."

With no chair nearby, I yanked the carpet runner over to my feet and used it to pad the spot where I was about to sit on the floor. I tilted my head against the wall, the telephone base in one hand, the receiver in the other.

"A ride on a sunny day," I said. "The last one of the year. Any place in particular in mind? Gasoline's high, though. You know, driving is such a frill these days. But it's a lovely thought, Simon. You could come over for hot chocolate instead, and—"

"Ah! Not to interrupt, and I do apologize, but what about taking a ride out to the country, maybe past your homeplace? Or there's also Pilot Rock. That's a bit farther to get to, but the view of scenery there is truly spectacular. Might be too cold for that one, and we don't need another cold wind, do we, now that I'm thinking . . . Umm—"

"Your homeplace" had come through the telephone wires, resounding in my head like drum beats from a distant parade. Inwardly, I recoiled like a child needing to cover her ears.

"You've probably already figured out that I really just want to be with you, Gracie," he said. "Hot chocolate would be nice, but let me get to know you. Why don't you show me where you grew up? It's only two or three miles out there, isn't it? Maybe we could stop in and say hello to your dad."

I could hear in Simon's pause a deep breath of satisfaction.

He chuckled. "Ah, yes, and this does go back a way, but I do still recall the day I saw him ride onto the grounds outside the church where we went at the time. Mr. Robert Maxwell had the only automobile in the county—close to it, anyway. Running for Senator, he was, and had everyone's attention. I knew right then and there I'd own a Model T one day. Fact is, Senator Maxwell might have been the biggest reason I went off to Detroit."

"To Hillbound? Um. Out to my old homeplace? Tomor— Tomorrow afternoon?" I felt goofy for saying what I'd said and for stammering the way I had.

"What do ya think?"

He sounded cautious now, so I stood up and tamped down the over-sized wrinkles in the rug that my wiggling on it had caused. I glided my fingertips slowly down the length of the telephone's cradle, then up and back down, trying to fashion in my mind an excuse for not wanting to allow Mr. Simon Hagan to take me from this secure present moment, to prevent him from touching anything in my past—the places I'd left behind. Simon had no way of knowing I'd put Hillbound's shaky foundation behind me and exchanged it for higher ground, or that the dark thread in my life might unwittingly be revealed in riding past the two-story clapboard house with its white picket fence, seeing the old barn, seeing the tobacco fields lying frozen in wait for spring, or seeing from Allensville Road the horse stables in the background. In my mind, I grasped for words, for some purposely offhand joke over the accolades Father had earned in Simon's eyes.

Still . . . The chance of old wounds reopening loomed as a very real possibility, but I asked myself what threat of harm, what unreasonable power, should be able to keep me from returning, *ever*, to Hillbound? I felt fragile, with more than enough reasons to cower at the thought.

Even so, I let them go. New resolve had me agreeing once more to Simon Hagan's wild plans before I hung up the telephone and sat down again on the floor. I leaned my head against the wall, crossed my legs, and began in my memory to walk through the backroad of my memory, through seven years of reasons to cower. Reasons that I had let go along the long journey away from that place and time.

Chapter 10

Back in time

August 1922

For the daughter of a gentleman farmer, summer days in 1922 lazed by in idyllic enchantment. Slivers of August sunshine cut between tree branches and lay in wide beams across the faces of four children who sat cross-legged at my feet.

The afternoon heat wasn't bothering any of us, and the Kentucky sky was as cloudless as any I'd seen. Nothing but my mother's illness ruffled the tranquil state of my mind. I shifted my position on the ground beneath me, straightened my back against the sprawling oak's mighty trunk, and continued to read aloud from the book that lay flat on my lap. Leafy shadows layered in clusters on its pages.

The abundance of tobacco cultivated on my father's vast acreage yielded affluence sufficient to suggest I might perch my bottom on a princess's throne, fleeting as the notion was, but when it came right down to it, the place called Hillbound was simply home to me and home to the colored folks who worked it, and they outnumbered the white folks who lived within its boundary.

I caught sight of Moe Lee coming up from the fields that nestled themselves through the rolling Todd County countryside. His straw-capped head bobbed into view over the crest of the hilltop, and the meadow echoed his song.

It was not a coincidence that he'd arrived, as it was his children who sat before me, listening with rapt attention as I read to them an episode of *Five Little Peppers And How They Grew*. Twelve-year-old Enoch sat beside me, squirming on the hard earth, his curious eyes feasting on the book's pages. His older sister Celia's gaped wide as saucers. Her hair jutted from her scalp in a random array of short, stiff braids. Little Bessie rocked on her haunches, hugging bent knees with skinny dark arms. She paid no attention to her papa, and Bertha mimicked Bessie. The four of Moe Lee's children huddled like open-mouthed baby birds awaiting a worm. Not a peep came from a one of them, and I pressed on with the story, this being day four of its telling.

The same number of days had passed since I'd turned fifteen, and as magically as a caterpillar changing into a butterfly, I had succumbed to maturity. Whatever had befallen me was instant, and whatever was significant about being fifteen had slipped out of nowhere.

Moe Lee kept coming, his familiar scarecrow build and quick, gimpy walk entering into full view. He was heading in our direction and sang as he came, "—constant Friend is He, *oh, oh-oh*, His eye is on the sparrow, and I know He watches—" The closer he got, the wider his smile. Chiseled white teeth protruded from the coal blackness of his beard and face.

"Afternoon, Miss Gracie." With the back of his hand, he pushed the hat off his forehead and wiped sweat from the brow over his marbled eye. Skepticism shone in the good one.

I waited for him to assess the situation while my instincts told me that I was trying his patience. His children sat quietly, and Moe Lee repositioned his hat.

"You be fillin' their heads, Miss Gracie," he said.

Despite his soft voice, the loud warning was there. Had it been the first time he'd aired concern I would have brushed it off, but his disapproval was dropping in with a noticeable regularity. Kind as he was, I felt the scolding.

His dim view of my teaching was matched only by Henry's, but as far as I was concerned, both were unreasonably afraid of what other folks thought of the Negro children learning to read and write. My mind was made up about such things—maybe ever more so, now that I'd become fully blossomed and adult. With my two older sisters having married and gone, it fell to me to complicate life at Hillbound, so whether or not Henry stopped saying I was too big for my britches, I was determined. Moe Lee would have to have been blind in both eyes not to see that I was going to teach his children.

There was no reason for me to tiptoe around the fact they looked to me for life and were as eager to learn as I was to teach, but he didn't see it that way. Neither did Henry. But reading to Moe Lee's youngsters sparked my existence. Teaching them set it on fire. Not that it was a waste of time, either, for the children were more than people to be with. I'd had enough of the veil of curtsy with a half-smile from naysayers, and no second glance to the "depravity" of the colored folks because of their dark skin.

Even so, unspoken rules—*felt* ones, hateful ones that kept them from learning—hung over my head like a dark cloud.

Aggravated, with storybook in hand, I scrambled to my feet and planted them on the ground in solid defiance, as if there were a snake to kill. "Nonsense! Celia and the rest of them," I said, spewing the words, "why shouldn't they read? It's not fair. This is my father's land. I oughta be able to do as I please. Oughtn't I?"

Moe Lee positioned his head at a quizzical angle, obviously startled at my outburst. "Yessum. I ain't agin' it, mind ya," he said in a reverent tone. "Guess I best be goin'. Was jus' lookin' out fo' the chil'ren, Miss Gracie. Be goin' on up to the house now."

But I wasn't about to let things go. I handed the *Five Little Pepper's* book to Celia. Time and use had limbered its spine. It fell open in her hands. Celia flipped to a new page, and the children gazed in earnest at the colorful pictures.

"Begin with 'Mamsie,' and sound out the words," I said, pointing her to the first sentence, not missing that Moe Lee was getting away from me. "Celia, you can do it," I urged before turning. "Wait!" I shouted in Moe Lee's direction. "Wait!"

Ox-stubborn as he was, and despite his hobble, his stride increased.

Little Bessie hunkered down as I dodged her and ran after her papa. I stopped in the shadow of his tall figure—obstructing the way—and struck a resolute pose. "Listen to me, Moe Lee. Those children are bright as buttons. They should know how to read. Write too."

I swatted the lock of black curls that had fallen to my forehead. Hot moisture had built up and dampened the collar on my middy, and I waited, huffing, while he studied me with his good eye, not backing down. And nothing about the half-hearted kick he dealt a nearby dirt clod changed my disposition.

"Yessum, Miss Gracie," he said. "Guess it's plain a'nough. You's taking over as the lady of Hillbound now 'at Miss Annabelle's got a sickness." Having mentioned my mother, his lower lip tightened. His words poured out like spilled molasses. "Now 'at you've turned fifteen and all. And yessum," he said again, tipping his hat, "you is Lady of Hillbound now."

I took an immediate liking to his words. The title slid into place in my head, and the sound of it rang in my ears. Even so, I viewed my situation with little pride, warding off haughty comparisons to the ways of others, because Moe Lee's pampering was as apparent as a mother cat toward her newborns. I was used to it, but concerning his own condition, I knew little—not why he limped or what had happened to his eyes, the left of which was gone. Such subjects had a way of not coming up, and until now I'd been sensible enough to keep my questions to myself. His and his brother Amos's jobs centered on the comings and goings at Hillbound, and they worked alongside the sharecroppers and hired folks, seeing to it that the Maxwell family experienced a well-run household. Father wouldn't have it any other way.

Moe Lee cleared his throat. "Mine is good chil'ren, alright," he said in a dither. "They is. They like what you be doin', teaching and all." His chest swelled beneath the bib of his overalls. "It's jus' some folks don't take kindly to us a-learnin'. You knows it by now, Miss Gracie."

He repositioned himself, shifting weight from his left leg to his right, while I absorbed the reality of what he had said, not now wanting it to be truth any more than I had in the past.

But it was, and the claim nagged me, like the buzz of a bumblebee threatening to land on my neck. I bristled.

"'*Some folks*' indeed." The townspeople. White people. The *some folks* who congregated in Elkton's square on Saturday mornings, the *some folks* who dawdled on Sundays outside the door to the clapboard church and cuddled up and let their opinions air themselves with a predictable frequency. Confident folk. Adult folk.

Their opinions should be none of my business, but they were. "Never mind '*some folks*,' Moe Lee."

He answered with a look. Caution clouded his good eye, alerting the very heart of me that pushed me to teach children some folks wouldn't, that probed reasons for why they were not present when it came time for church.

Moe Lee looked long and hard at me, as if he might read my mind if he didn't let up, and I thought of one particular Sunday when Father and I had gone to church. I remembered with great clarity the half-baked smiles on the faces of those adult who had wanted to keep me from speaking my mind about the colored folks whose existence went no farther than the farms they worked. Only an inkling of an excuse had presented itself in my understanding that day when Father's Model T rolled away from the white-steepled building. The talkers were still talking, and I, with new insight, had sat on the carriage next to him, groping with injustice for the first time.

We'd come up from the south, away from Mt. Zion Baptist Church, and turned onto Chestnut Lane. It had been springtime, a mild day when the sun was not shining and the air was damp with more oncoming rain. Father was preoccupied, I'd supposed, with the lingering halo of handshakes and back-slapping. The fact that he was now Senator Maxwell, not Robert Maxwell, had flurried the crowd.

We had ridden for a stretch, past the places where Negroes milled between their shabby dwellings. Others had gathered with no sign of making ready for anything—not church, not a ride in a carriage. Not a one of them hurried inside to avoid the start of raindrops, and the scene stuck like a drab pastoral painting before my eyes. Moe Lee's children, his brother Amos's children, and Pete's and Lucien's, and the adults too—all the assortment of similar folks who had hired on with limitations that contained them, made them different. Moe Lee and his kin and others like him who worked on the farms nearby. I saw on that day the difference, and a one-sided view of fairness began to fester in my mind.

I glanced at Father to see if he noticed it afresh—in the event he ever had before. It appeared he had not. The wail of a distant train broke the unusual spell of silence that had fallen between us. He steered the automobile to the left, making the turn that took us off Railroad Lane. The final half-mile to home stretched out before us.

On that very morning, when rain-soaked fields waited for the earth to dry, something moved in me: I felt the hidden striving beneath the weight of featureless soil—miles of it—ready to be tilled and seeded, and in that instant the unsettling urge sprouted in my imagination, as real as the early daffodil that poked out its head from a grassy clump by the side of the road. *If I could teach the children, those who stood near their shanties and watched as Father and I rode past*, I thought, *then their minds like ready soil would be awakened.*

That was the last time we had gone to church. Mama was frail, Father was now Senator, and no one prodded us to go. I wasn't sure I belonged there, anyway, but the thoughts of having been there had spun me full circle and reconfirmed my convictions.

"Are you scared for me to speak up . . . help your babies . . . give them a chance to learn?" I didn't wait for Moe Lee's response. "Leave it to me. Never mind '*some folks*,'" I repeated.

He nodded a yes, but his shoulders drooped.

"Henry . . . hum. Henry—" Moe Lee looked in the direction of the house. His bony fingers raked his beard. "Henry done told me he be needin' a word with yore daddy. Having to do with the new filly, I guess. Told me to come along, seeing as how I knows a little somethin' 'bout horse ills and all."

That took the cake in my estimation. I all but stamped my foot. "Henry's *always* needing a word with Father. And if it's not one thing, it's another. Listen to me: if I'm like that brother of mine when I'm seventeen, just shoot me." I skirted my way around him in a huff. "We don't need two Henrys around here."

"Yessum. You gots a point." A twinkle slipped from behind the dark lashes of his seeing eye, and he turned away.

"Then go on, One-ey—" It was a slip of the tongue. Midway in my abandoned habit of calling him One-eyed Moe Lee, I caught myself and decidedly said to him instead, "*Moe Lee*, don't forget to have that talk with Amos. His boys could come over tomorrow, in the afternoon. No reason I can't teach his at the same time as yours."

"Yessum, Miss Gracie. I 'spect Amos . . . I 'spect he'll listen."

Weakly delivered as it was, Moe Lee's answer satisfied me. Off he limped toward the house, lifting tuneful words toward the sky as if he were seeing the future and was duly convinced God's eye was on the sparrow. If his melody bespoke a gospel truth, I had no idea.

"You'll see," I shouted to him with yet another stab at bolstering my intentions to teach his children. "And one day when they can read and write, you'll be glad."

I pointed to the four of them for emphasis, not needing to interrupt the session that was yet underway beneath the gigantic tree, then began wondering instead, as I watched Moe Lee slowing down beyond the patch where watermelons grew, why I'd never asked the personal things: his birthday, his favorite dessert, and whether he dreamed at night. And inquisitiveness as always began stacking itself like mystery books in the corner of my mind.

"I'll be up directly to check on Mama," I yelled, certain that he had to know he'd not heard the last of me this morning.

He hesitated long enough to glance back at me, then veered off to where Odelia was hanging laundry on the clothesline, and I made my way back down to the tree where the children sat, wondering as I went why I'd never squeezed such juicy morsels as favorites from her or any of the others on the farm, either. Nor had I considered what caused Moe Lee to come to Kentucky from Virginia with Granny Maxwell and the rest of my family.

I kept my eyes on Moe Lee as he sidled up to the clothesline post and leaned against it. Sheets hung on a wire strung between it and another post at the other end. Odelia was unaware of his presence. Either that or she had chosen to ignore him.

Moe Lee and Odelia had a different marriage, one that Father called *common law*. For the most part I'd not thought to concern myself with how Father would describe them if they had been white folks. But they weren't, and I wasn't sticking my nose in where it didn't belong. What did interest me was how Moe Lee was now shielding himself from Odelia's view, thanks to the strutting peacocks in the yard and the drying overalls on the line.

Without looking in his direction or bending her knees, Odelia reached low inside her laundry basket, the way I'd seen her do dozens of times.

I glanced again at the children and discovered Bessie, too, was eyeing her ma and pa with a smile that stretched over a new tooth. It peeked out from dark-pink gums. The other two children continued listening to the story that fourteen-year-old Celia read, not seeming to care that she timidly plucked the words one by one from the page. When Celia came to a stopping place, the children gleefully clapped their hands.

"Excellent, Celia! What good students! Here," I said and reached to take the book from her. "I'll take it, and tomorrow we'll come back to it. Your uncle Amos's boys might come too."

`The children quickly got to their feet and scampered off, running like sheep down a hill. The dog was egging them on, and I could see no benefit to ending the chase.

I began the short walk up to the house. Unnoticed by both Moe Lee and Odelia, I neared the overalls that dangled from the line and stalled there, out of Moe Lee's sight. His full attention was on the stern-faced Odelia.

"*Psst!*" I said to him but got no reaction.

Odelia was pulling a bed sheet from the basket at her feet when, without warning, Moe Lee seized her from behind, encircling her bosoms with his long arms. She dropped the sheet. Impossible as it was to free herself from his grasp, Moe Lee burst into head-thrown-back laughter, and she did the same. As quickly as if nothing had happened, he let go, and Odelia returned to her laundry. She wrangled the sopping sheet loose and whipped it in the air with a flick of her wrists. The billow of pure-white cotton gave a loud pop of surrender and unfurled like a flag on the Fourth of July. In the blink of an eye, she had it pinned to the line and was bent over for another, and Moe continued up to the house, a song on his lips.

Amused, I watched him amble off. Not a half-minute had passed before I caught Odelia peering at me through the gap between the corner of one sheet and another.

"Hidy-do, Miss Gracie," she hollered above the squeal of penned-up pigs.

"Wonderful day!" I hollered back with a passing wave.

Hot as it was, even so, I would have preferred being outside over most other choices. Rainbow-colored hollyhocks that blossomed in the side yard gave me a good excuse to linger. Had I not planned to see Mama, I would have hung back to enjoy their scent before going inside at the back of the house, but I traipsed on up, and the kitchen's screen door snapped shut behind me. The sweet smell of stewing fruit hung in the air.

Clarice was stirring with one hand a pot on the woodburning stove. The other was braced on her hip as if her back's support depended on it. Her dark face glistened from the steam. "Miss Gracie," she said, not missing a stroke and not turning toward me. "Hidy-do.

If she said anything more I didn't notice. Henry's voice boomed nearby. Down the hallway, the door to Father's office was slightly ajar. Moe Lee was standing, barely inside, and Henry stood to the left of the giant rolltop desk. He wielded an accusatory finger in midair.

Aiming to get my two cents in with Henry, I rapped on the door, easing it open with the back of my wrist.

"— and upstairs at this very minute she—" Henry's rant trailed off with my intrusion, but the scowl he directed at our father remained. His hand pressed hard on the desk's surface where a small bouquet of flowers lay.

Father's dark eyes were piercing and his mouth was molded shut.

Moe Lee looked as if he might at any moment crawl beneath the desk. "You'd better go," Henry said to him in a breathy voice. "We'll talk later about the filly." And Moe Lee turned to leave, bumping my shoulder in his awkwardness. He nodded apologetically and limped toward the kitchen, hat in hand. Without my ever having entered the room, Henry shoved the office door closed with a loud smack in my face, and behind it his forceful voice did not let up.

"Humph!" Being able to teach the sharecroppers' children was just as important as anything else around here, I told myself. "Humph," I repeated. "Henry's just plain rude!"

Muttering to myself, I left them to their arguing and tromped off in the direction of the morning room. I expected Mama to be sitting up when I went in. Instead, she appeared to be sleeping, tangled in a wad of blankets at the edge of the bed, borrowed from Millicent's room upstairs. A fire smoldered behind big brass andirons. Given any slight move on her part, she would've fallen on the floor in front of it.

How she could sleep through the ruckus down the hallway was beyond me.

I laid the *Five Little Peppers* book on the mantle where multiple other books nestled in a row, and I crept to the side of her bed. The room was stale with stingy, stifling air to breathe, and the odor—soured and strong—hovered like a mixture of medicine and decay.

"Good morning," my mother uttered in a raspy voice from beneath the covers.

"But . . . it's afternoon already, Mama. You've been cooped up for days in here! Let me open a window. It's sunny. The birds are singing!" I made a start to pull back the curtain.

"Honey, don't." She coughed and rolled onto her back. "Light . . . no. My eyes." She coughed again, loose and rattling. "Put another log on, would you? I'm cold. So cold. Maybe close the door."

Clarice reached it before I did and stepped inside. Before she gave it a hip shove, I saw Father in a brisk climb, heading up the stairs.

Liquid sloshed inside the bowl Clarice carried on a tray. "A bite to eat, Miss Annabelle. Hot peaches. Gots to eat so you gets yore strength back."

Mama's head wagged—feebly—indicating no, yet Clarice kept on walking, swinging the tray.

"It looks good," I said energetically and took it from her before tidbits of peaches swam from the bowl.

Mama's raised hand told me not to bring it a step closer.

"Now, Miss Annabelle! We've done moved you down de stairs till this illness be gone . . . jus' so's I can make you eat." Clarice said, backing me. "I didn't move in dis house here fo' no reason. I needs to see that you—"

Mama's moan was unsettling. Everything in me wanted me to cover my ears, and Clarice gave me a frightful look. With no choice, I handed the tray to her and went to the fireplace as Clarice left the room with the unwanted food. Stacked sycamore logs lay in a bucket on the hearth. I promptly chose one and nestled it in the smoldering embers, then crept to Mama's side as light flared from the awakening flames. I tried to ignore the knot in the pit of my stomach but couldn't keep myself from gagging on the wet slime that rose at the back of my throat. I despised the illness and balked at the sight of my mother's suffering.

"Let me prop you up, Mama. You'd be more comfortable. Don't you want fresh air?"

"Fire's fine. Fine, ladybug."

Her name for me had enfolded me in a sweet balm of tenderness when she hovered over me as a child. Now it was I who did the hovering.

Week after week had erased Mama's sparkle. Wrinkles layered beneath her sunken cheeks. Her eyes, once clear and blue, were now clouded and gray. The skin below them hung in dark pools. I looked away to avoid showing her my dismay. *She'll get better*, I reminded myself. *Tomorrow she'll turn a corner.*

The bed creaked as I sat down on its end, trying to imagine how she could be fine without sunshine, fine without the laughter of children, fine without the songs of the Negroes or the sound of harvesting equipment or the noise the animals made. Staring off into nothingness, I longed for her to be up and moving, walking with me to choose hollyhocks, arranging them in a pretty vase on the sideboard.

"No one knows, ladybug. I might not get upstairs to my bedroom. Ever," she said, as if she were reading my thoughts. "Have you homework?"

"No, ma'am. Not in summertime," I said, respectfully. "I'm teaching Moe Lee and Odelia's children, though. Maybe Amos and Clarice's will start in, too, if Henry'll stop being so mean about it. Moe Lee's going to talk to Amos, and I'm seeing to it: all the Negro children are going to read if Moe Lee will stop being all worried. It's silly. Why can't they be taught?"

"My ladybug . . . growing up so fast. Beautiful."

"I'm not beautiful, Mama. I'm just me. And why Henry won't stop pestering me about it?"

She attempted a smile. It didn't get past the twitch that tugged at one corner of her mouth. Her chest rose and sank, barely moving the covers that lay over it. "Cautious, persnickety like your father . . . and Robert hasn't changed—"

Her eyes closed, and for a moment it seemed she'd dozed off. "—in all the years," she said overtop a wince. "Teaching's good, honey. Don't give up. I'll speak to Henry."

It was clear enough I had tired her.

"I'll fetch some cold water and a cloth for your forehead," I said and went to the washstand. But the pitcher sat empty. "Let me go fill this, Mama, get Odelia to change your sheets."

"Don't." She tried to lift her head. "Don't leave. Henry—" It was all she could do to draw her arm from beneath the blanket and motion me over.

I crossed the room and sat down beside her, half on and half off the bed, smiling to keep myself from staring, terrified by how pale she'd become.

"He wanted your father . . . earlier." She spoke no louder than a whisper and wriggled her hand into mine. The delicate gold ring Father had given her for their wedding dangled on her finger. Slowly, I turned it, gazing at the familiar circle of pearls that formed a tiny flower. Its ruby center caught the firelight.

Mama watched me spin it around. When I stopped, she spoke. "One day, ladybug, you'll marry."

The thought irked me. "Boys are mean spirited, Mama. That Freddie Hudson! He pulled the wings right off a beautiful butterfly and then—" I took a deep breath. "—and then he put it on a rock and laid a stick across its little body so it would die. *In the hot sun*." I was more irked than before by the telling. "I hate boys!"

"Don't *hate*, honey." Mama looked helpless, and I continued to hang on beside her—too near the fire not to notice its stifling heat—when out of nowhere a ruckus commenced in the front hall. Noticeable footsteps descended the stairs, coming from the bedroom area above. Father's voice was more than loud enough to get my attention, but I was too riled to care.

"Trying to impress me. That's it! And I hate Freddie Hudson for it. And now Henry! Henry just aggravates me. And he puts Moe Lee up to tormenting me!"

If I hadn't worn her out earlier, it was clear that I had now.

"Gracie. 'Tormenting'?" She mustered a pitiful expression: something between pursed lips and a grimace.

I let go of her hand and stood, wishing I'd kept my mouth shut. "Never mind. Father will get after Henry. I'll make him."

"Henry was here . . . earlier . . . to find him." Her breath was shallow. Her words painstaking. Creases formed in her brow. "I haven't seen Robert. Not lately." She began to cough. "A woman's voice . . . a dream? I don't know. I'm confused and a bit dizzy. Go, honey. Enjoy the sunshine."

I gave Mama a peck on the cheek and hurried to investigate, hoping to talk to Father before he left the house. I pulled the door open with a reckless yank and he was there, three or four steps up on the stairs, rapidly coming down. Henry, midsentence, was looking up at him from the hallway. Stair spindles separated them.

"—needs to leave," Henry was saying in a peculiarly low, hostile voice.

At the sight of me, silence dropped over the hallway. Father and Henry stood as rigid as iced-over sticks in a pond. And across from them our neighbor lady, Mrs. Delaney, stood near the front door. At the sight of me, she looked astonished. I must have looked the same.

The threesome glared at me, making me feel quite unnecessary. Henry reached behind my back to close the door to the morning room.

It took a moment, but Mrs. Delaney stepped toward me, prettier than I remembered from the few times I had seen her in the year since she and her husband purchased the Peterson farm next to ours. She batted heavy lids over dark-brown eyes. "Gracie, how nice to see you again," she said, extending her hand after apparently giving it some thought.

"Why, hello, Mrs. Delaney. I had no idea we had company," I said, thinking about how different she appeared from the woman I'd twice met at the Peterson's old barn. A thick, blond hair braid, apparently loosened by her energetic handshake, dropped from the others that wrapped her head like a crown.

Father moved off the last step with a hasty stride and rested his hand on the newel post. "Yes. She came with flowers to give to your mother, but—"

"*But*'s right." Henry chimed in. An expression of displeasure clouded his deep-set eyes. "*But* unfortunately, she felt . . . faint . . . took ill. Suddenly, as a matter of fact. *But* she seems to have recovered. Indeed, our company was just leaving."

My brother's slow, easy grin might have spread across his face on another day, but not this one.

"I might ask you, Henry," Father said, his head cocked in a manner that seemed to follow his election as senator, "precisely why we have both you and Moe Lee present in the house at this time of day, anyway?"

I watched Henry's face turn hard. He squared his shoulders. "If I'd been given the chance to mention during our little chat in your office," he said, directing an intense glance at Father, "I'd have let you know. The filly is in pain. A mean rash has cropped up just above her hooves. That, sir, is why I happen to be here—to locate you."

Henry looked in Mrs. Delaney's direction. "We need an expert to attend the rash as soon as possible. I'd appreciate it if your husband could swing by. Take a look. Perhaps at his earliest convenience."

Even on the August day at hand, I felt the chill that crept through the entrance hallway.

Father nodded in agreement. "Well, then. It would be a good idea, Francine, if you'd ask Felix to come by. His evaluation would be of the utmost importance where my filly's concerned."

"Well, Mrs. Delaney," Henry said, "let me see you to your carriage and—

"I'll thank you, Henry, to leave that to me. Do believe I can manage our neighbor's buggy." Father turned to Mrs. Delaney, presenting a radiant face to replace his scowl. "Let's not stand here." He nudged her elbow and guided her to the front door. "I'll be to the stable for a look-see at our Trojan Girl's rash," he said over his shoulder. "And you, son, can go back over there now. Maybe mind the business that is your concern."

I recognized Father's tone, reserved for the hired hands and the Negro folks who worked on the property. It sent a shiver down my spine, but Mrs. Delany smiled up at Father.

She took a step toward Henry. "I'd be happy to send my husband your way. Always want to be a good neighbor, you know."

If she'd become smug I couldn't be sure, but an air of some sort had me looking to Father for an answer. He lit a cigarette and inhaled with a degree of showiness. Slowly, the smoke streamed from his nostrils as he smiled at me. "Why don't you get the flowers from my office, Gracie, and see to it that your mother gets them."

"You don't seem all that ill, Mrs. Delaney," I said, piping up with the opportunity to give my opinion, "but I'm happy to take them. I hope you feel better soon."

"Actually, Father," Henry said, and his manner was unbecoming as he mirrored Father's loftiness, "seems fitting you'd want be the one to let Mother know about our neighbor's visit. But I'll take the flowers to her. Gracie probably needs to go read to Moe Lee's young'uns."

Delighted as I was by my brother's suggestion, it caught me off guard, and before I could muster a smile, he was off in a twit at full speed past Father's office. I made my way back to the kitchen where Clarice stood near the sideboard, shucking corn. Without a word, she moved to one side.

"Mama's pitcher needs filled. Would you? And some cold water?"

The screen door slammed shut behind me, and for whatever reason Moe Lee was not far from the other side of it.

"You know, don't you? Whatever's going on, you know. Henry was in there, trying to get rid of me. And I'm not the least bit fooled by his change of heart. He's treating me like a child," I said to Moe Lee.

"You is right. Guess he needs to know you is Lady of Hillbound now."

Chapter 11

⁓⬥⬥⁓

I t wasn't the step from the landing at the back of the house that tripped me. Rather, it was the huff I exerted, hoping to propel myself as far away as possible from the odd gathering of adults in my home. The resulting unladylike leap should have embarrassed me. Clumsy as it was, it didn't, and Moe Lee rushed to keep me from falling.

"Easy goin', there, Miss Gracie. You be breaking a' ankle if you ain't careful."

"I'm fine. Fine. Galloping like a horse doesn't become me, I suppose," I said, ignoring the matter. "But my book's inside now, and I'm out here."

He glanced back at the house, as if it were a puzzle to work, then gave up. "Looks like the chil'ren is gone on, anyway. Want me to round 'em up again?"

"No, we've had enough for today. Besides, I've been banished. You too. Can't go back inside, can we?"

"No'am," Moe Lee said, scratching his throat, "I jus' do as I's told."

I hesitated on his remark. It pointed to Father owning him, as if he were a cow in the stall or a sheep in the pen. I detested the claim the Maxwell's held over his head. What if I told him the ridiculousness of such a mindset this many years after the Emancipation? If Father knew my thoughts he'd have a fit. Even so, I intended to tell them to someone on the subject. If not today, another.

"According to Henry, I'm now being encouraged to teach. And I have your blessing as well. Is that it?"

"Yessum, Miss Gracie. I believe so." He offered the head nod I was accustomed to."You'll tell me, won't you? What was Father—"

"I gots to be a-going, Miss Gracie." He turned in the direction of the barn. "Yore pappy, he been managin' a plateful these days, now 'at he's a senator and all." The words tumbled over his shoulder and he kept on moving.

"But wait! Henry's being so strange," I said. "And you're bound to know it too."

If Moe Lee was in hearing distance, he didn't let on. He limped off, not listening, not making an effort to help resolve the problem at hand, and I was left to unravel this latest confusion on my own. Tears tried to spill over the rims of my eyes, as if the slightest thing could keep them coming, and I was annoyed at something I couldn't put my finger on, longing to be heard, to have my questions answered, my heart understood as Moe Lee always had, because he was like family.

"Miss Gracie!" Odelia called from across the yard, still pinning laundry on the line, and I could see her sulking beneath her bonnet.

It took another of her shouts to move me. I wiped my cheek with the back of my hand and began walking in her direction. Odelia, too, was like family, along with the other sharecroppers, and not their work-worn faces nor their gnarled hands made them any less endearing. They lived in their squat houses on our property and came down the lane in mule-drawn wagons. Once the work was done and the crops were in, Father paid them in cash, gave them enough to keep them from walking off the place for reasons other Negro folks around Todd County had. I'd never thought of Moe Lee and Odelia or Moe Lee's brother, Amos, or any of the others as poor, but they were. Their houses were different. Their clothes were different.

"You be needin' to slap yore self outta somethin' now, Miss Gracie?"

"No," I said, shaking my head. "No, but Mama's bedding . . . It needs changing. She's not well today, and . . ." I paused, screwed up courage to say what I didn't want said. "And she's not getting any better, is she?"

Odelia stacked the last of the laundry baskets and straightened up with a groan. "Miz Annabelle, she have her bad days o'right. Weak as a kitten . . . I gets her up direc'ly. We kin go for a stroll after it cool down."

"Good." I blinked hard to block the sun's glare, turned, and headed to the side yard. Steering clear of the house and deep in thought, I rounded the corner. Not a breeze stirred on these long days of summer.

It took nothing more than the whinny of the carriage horse out front to distract me. The horse kicked up its hooves, carrying Mrs. Francine Delaney away at a pretty good clip. Father stood for a moment by the side of the road, waving.

With her out of sight, he sauntered along the length of the picket fence and stopped to scoop a handful of rocks. Tossing one to the side of the road, he entered the gate just as I caught up.

"Well, now, Gracie! Where'd you come from? Thought you were going out back to teach the—"

"That's a beauty," I interrupted.

"The mare . . . yes. Yes, she is at that. Shame that one's not racing. Pity. Reduced to a carriage horse. You been here long, honey? Standing here?"

"No, sir," I said as we strolled toward the house. "And why, all of a sudden, can I teach the children when before I couldn't? First Henry, now you? If there's no reason to keep them from learning, can you tell Henry to never mention it again? He's still at the house, I think.""Later, honey. Some things you won't understand till you're older."

"What, for instance?" I hurried to keep up with him, not wanting to miss a word.

"Lots of things, Gracie. Lots," he said and pitched the last rock. "I'm pleased with your interest in horses, I mean."

"I'm afraid I'm not, not really. But they are beautiful. And they take you where you need to go. I'm writing in the diary you gave me, Father. What a wonderful birthday gift! I can almost feel like I'm talking to a higher power when I write."

"Good. I thought you'd like it. Perhaps you'll go with me to the Derby next year. It's a sight to behold. Yessiree, a spectacle!"

"Maybe, Father, but right now, I just want to teach, the best I can. Watching horses race around a track is . . . I don't know. That's for you and Mr. Delaney."

In the length of time before we lost sight of the path to the stable, my brother came into view, headed there, and Father, pestered by a fly, stared after him. "Sure expected Henry'd show more admiration for Trojan Girl. But we do need a farmer, now don't we? Just hard for me to not be caught up in the whole thoroughbred plunge," he said and slapped at the fly with disgust. "The Delaneys live so close, not to mention that their connections with racing are nothing short of remarkable. Miss Francine . . . why, she's an expert horsewoman. I'll have her demonstrate for you—"

"Father, honestly, I have other interests. What about Mama? Will you look in on her now?"

He was silent, and we walked for a bit without speaking, then climbed the steps and crossed the verandah, making our way past empty rockers on the porch. Boards creaked underfoot, and I could tell by his shuffle he was frustrated with the subject. "Later, honey. Right now I need to change clothes and go on down to the stable. Talk to Henry about the filly."

"Will you talk to him? Please? Make him stop fussing at me."

I entered the house ahead of Father, and the quarrel in my head continued in full swing. The door to the morning room stood ajar. It was plain to see Mama was asleep. Father took hold of the handle and pulled it shut.

"Wasn't Henry surprisingly sharp with Mrs. Delaney?" I asked in a whisper." What possible problem could she have caused, bringing flowers to Mama?"

He looked at me from the corner of his eye. "None, really, honey. Pay no attention to him. You go on and teach the children." Father sounded a bit intolerant. As a further matter, it was the way he searched my face that bordered on mysterious.

He gave me a quick kiss on the forehead. "Henry's just being a brother, concerned, I suppose."

Maybe I'm going be like you, Father. Not a senator or involved in racing . . . but in other ways. I do plan to see the world, you know. And I'll surely go to college. Mama says I'm pretty. Am I, Father?"

"Simmer down, Gracie. You'll wake your mother. You most certainly are! Why don't you check on her? Henry's waiting for me at the stable, probably put out with me by now. You're a beautiful flower, honey. Would you excuse me?"

He brushed past me with something other than his immature daughter's comments on his mind. I wasn't sure he'd actually heard all of what I said. Carelessly, the back door slapped itself shut with a bang.

It left me standing alone in the entry hallway, wanting to go in and find Mama was miraculously no longer sick, wanting Father not to leave her to fend for herself. *How could a silly illness tell you how to spend your life?* I considered my own good health, knowing I'd always and forever have energy to pull back the curtains, throw open the windows, and never, ever have to lie in a bed or be cooped up in a dark, dingy room.

Henry had left the house in a huff, saying bad words and lots of them. He had appeared to be at the end of his rope. He was put out, alright— so much so, in fact, that I was certain he was outraged—and long before Father would have had a chance to reach the stable. Doubtless, Father had other things on his mind too. *It could be the issue of the thoroughbred at the stable with a rash or a different thoroughbred or politics or the random other distractions that make him the man that he is*, I thought. *He's my father, well-deserving of my pride in him if only as a respected landowner. And Senator Maxwell!*

But everything inside me fought unwanted feelings of being in his way and being held at arm's length in the nine months since the election in November had gone his way.

I went to check on Mama, flitting off in my imaginary world of teaching an endless circle of children in my own backyard. Enthusiasm for living above mediocrity kept me going. Some days it was all I had, and most days it was all I needed.

Hoping the conversation outside her door had not disturbed Mama, I slipped inside the morning room where she lay sleeping as helpless as a wounded rabbit, and I sat down by her bed. Mama moaned when she felt me beside her. Part of me wanted to tattle on Henry for saying bad words, but in the light from the dying fire I could sense her pain. Her forehead dripped with perspiration.

Daydreaming, with nothing else to think of, I assured myself I'd never marry a farmer or be told what to do. And I'll never kill chickens or cook carcasses or scrub pots and pans. I might just someday live in Lexington and shop in the stores with Mama again, and love the parcels loaded under my arm.

Lady of Hillbound, I thought, with no reason to speak aloud the beautiful name.

Chapter 12

—◦〜◦—

I propped a sheet of music on the piano rack in front of me and sat down on the three-legged stool. For several minutes, I fiddled with its fringed edges, entertaining myself with the grand notion of making the beast produce some nice sounds. Mama was still sleeping in the morning room across the hallway, giving me excuse enough to put off practicing until later. So, there I sat, swiveling restlessly on the velvet-covered cushion beneath my bottom, then got up and went to one of the drawing room windows at the front of the house, prepared to see the blue sky beyond the cover of trees.

My morning had begun with all the promise of a typical Saturday and freedom from chores, including the added ones since taking up the slack due to Mama's illness. Through the open window I could hear chirping birds, and in the out-of-doors was the plentiful smell of a world afresh.

On the horizon, the sun was rising like bread dough on a warm windowsill, beams streaming across the immensity of Father's tobacco crops and merging with the Delaneys' wheat farm that separated our property from theirs. Row after row of fluffy green clumps—burley tobacco in August—and late, late red winter wheat on the property lines of the Maxwells' and the Delaneys' awaited the harvest.

I gazed to the east beyond to the farm that sat next to ours: the old Peterson place where the tornado had swept through in the spring. It had already been two years ago, 1920, but I could still hear the howl of the tornado wind, feel its whir, and see the trees bend. I envisioned the devastation that had claimed Mr. Peterson's life. What was left of his young family had now moved on to a farm several miles up the way.

Today, inconsequential slopes in the high country to the north meandered from the base of the mountains, looking like mounds left by misplaced trinkets beneath the covers on my bed. No indication remained to bespeak the tragedy save the ridge where downed trees had been cleared and—in the spot where the old one had been—a new barn raised. Father had coveted the land, but Zack Peterson's widow up and sold it to Felix Delaney. Word had it someone alerted a relative in Madison County regarding its availability, and much to Father's chagrin, Hannah Peterson's forty-acre wheat farm slipped through his fingers.

I walked back to the piano, sat on the stool and cupped my hands over the keys. As much as I loved the slick sensation of my fingers on the ivories, I lacked a smidgen of Beethoven's enthusiasm for dogged dedication, and practicing was a nuisance. Maybe if I could sing.

Birds outside seemed to warn me against it. I reflected instead on how Mama had exercised her opinion to Father, for all to hear, about the lost Peterson property. Somehow she'd managed to make her comment to him sound respectful. *"You don't need forty acres of wheat fields to add to your holdings, dear, no matter what you want to believe. You've got politics now. Not to mention the extra task lately, Robert, of bringing on so many more Negroes to tend the crops. And what about that prize horse of yours?"*

They were wasted words. The wheat farm went to Felix Delaney and his wife, Francine, and Father's five hundred and sixty acres of tobacco land sat below the timberline without the benefit of Father owning Hannah Peterson's parcel.

I wasn't given to meditative periods. The pursuit of the meaning of life or the loss of it, perhaps, but with the distant sound of the machine threshing wheat, the recollection of the twister departed as impolitely has it had arrived. In the meantime, I asked myself why I shouldn't take in the coolness of the morning before it was swallowed by the heat of the day. Given little reason not to, I popped up once more, left the fringe jiggling on the stool, and went straight back to the window. Not that I didn't love the *ping* and *pong* of a melody under my strokes, and the *tick-tick* of the metronome as I learned a new piece. I did. But being held captive in the drawing room, tethered for the length of time it took to play "Für Elise" over and over, was pure torture. I'd have preferred to be alongside the sparrow on a nearby tree branch—if only to imitate its voice.

I watched toward the other end of the branch as other birds intruded, and without reasoning they all flew away. *Never fails*, I thought. *One tiny change and the flock follows. Mama's in bed all day. Clarice takes over and gives me chores, even expects me to do them, and Mama has changed. Father's busy with horses. Busy, busy. If his becoming a senator isn't changing everything, then Mama's illness is. I'll be glad to get back in school.*

Through the rippled distortion of a different window, partially closed, I caught sight of an approaching automobile. The stately black Model T motored down Allensville Road, drowning out the noisy churn of the distant threshing machine. I pulled back the curtain to get a better look and watched as it came past hearty tobacco mounds. Having come around the wheat fields, the automobile hastened down the road where travel had packed two parallel ruts into the dirt. It pulled up next to Hillbound's white picket fence and came to a halt. Mr. Delaney's familiar pale features, roasted by the sun, shone from behind the windshield. Because his wife's horse-drawn carriage had only yesterday been on the road, going the other direction to home, I enjoyed twice the curiosity that I'd had in days, particularly on Allensville Road.

He shut off the engine and lost no time in getting out, unlatched the gate and walked toward the house, stepping on the random stones that made a pathway beneath mammoth walnut trees.

Certain Mr. Delaney's business was with Father—the horse's rash issue, I assumed—I let the window curtain fall back into place and darted past the drawing room's huge double doors, down the corridor past the curving staircase to Father's office on the left. I found him sitting at the rolltop desk behind a curl of smoke. He slicked his jet-black hair over one ear with the palm of his hand and, after crushing his cigarette, stood up with a smile at my announcement that Mr. Delaney was coming up to the house.

"Ah! Wonderful! Perfect timing," he said, leaving his office.

I followed him through the hallway as he went to answer the knock at the front door. Sunlight poured through the windows above it and reflected off the cranberry-glass lamps on the hall table as if their bubbled globes held a thousand tinted eyes.

Father opened the door with a ready handshake for Mr. Delaney. "Felix! Kind of you to stop by. Please, come on through. Filly's got us a bit worried. We'll head down to the stable the back way. You as well, Gracie."

I didn't detect that he was joking. I thought of Mama. I thought of the piano. The ticking metronome. Father approved of my interest in the filly, slight as it might be, and it was his approval that lit up my life. Besides, it was beautiful outside. "Let me speak to Mama and then come."

"Might've been here earlier but it was pert-near sundown yesterd'y by the time Francine told me 'bout the problem. Thought I'd stop in on my way to town. Happy to give an opinion. Probably gonna need an expert, though. That in particular's why it's hard to breed fine horses in these parts." Mr. Delaney said.

"Todd County's as good as any, Felix. And you do have a vested interest, ya know," Father was saying as they continued toward the kitchen and out the back door.

Quickly, I tiptoed to Mama's door. Convinced she was still peacefully sleeping, I left the house and ran past screaming peacocks to catch up.

After the unusually rainy summer, the sun seemed to have doused our Todd County flatland with brilliance. For as far as I could see, the rooftops of the hay barn and horse stable appeared to be aflame in every imaginable shade of orange. The pasture was lush green, and beyond to the south stretched the lone railroad track as it snaked through the fields.

The muddied distance to the stable had firmed up in the last two days of dry weather, and the ground was solid underfoot. The men were crossing the exercise ring where Henry had Trojan Girl in a workout. The dirt track, laid out in recent months, was to the far side of the stable.

The complex of barns and sheds clearly showed Hillbound was a working farm, owned by a country gentleman, and a thoroughbred horse meant necessary hired hands and black folks to manage what Henry had passed off. For them, the day was in full swing.

Felix Delaney's anticipated visit was surely a relief to Henry, but Henry could be a serious sort and didn't seem to take too kindly to the chipper tone in Mr. Delaney's voice.

"She's suffering, Mr. Delaney," Henry said, unsmiling. "Suffering bad. A skin disorder of some type."

"Well, then, let's see if I'm able to relieve your concern. We'll take a look."

Henry led Trojan Girl by her bridle to the stable. It was new, and the stalls were pristine, built for Trojan Girl and the others Father had talked of buying ever since he and the Delaneys traveled to Louisville last May for the Oaks, then the Kentucky Derby the next day. Father had come home smitten with the idea of breeding thoroughbreds. In the months since he had built the stable and track. Most recently the exercise ring while Trojan Girl stayed on at the farm that the Delaneys now owned. Her move over from the old Peterson place last month had given Father time to establish the right environment. The interruption of a hard winter and the lateness of the Delaney's wheat harvest due to the rain had been factors that somehow worked in everybody's favor. Except for a muddy spring, I'd adjusted to all the newness.

The three of us matched Henry's every step, wordless. He swung open the stall's door and let Trojan Girl inside—the beautiful bay's black tail swishing against sweating hamstrings.

"The rash cropped up about midweek," Henry said, pointing to the filly's leg. "I noticed yesterday how much worse it'd gotten." He seemed worried, bearing the weight of responsibility. Whether it was compassion for the horse or fear of Father and the frightful possibility that Trojan Girl was in serious danger, I wasn't sure.

Father was listening, smoking a cigarette, and Moe Lee ambled in at the far end of the stable, hesitating only long enough to drop off watering buckets.

The other horses in the stable—Char and Gray Mare, who pulled the plow hooked up to the buggy—neighed in protest at the disturbance.

Henry bent over beneath Trojan Girl and lifted the lower part of her back leg. The horse's beet-red rash was awful. I gasped.

"It's troublesome alright. Rain rot. All over here." Mr. Delaney ran his hand upward over the bumpy spots of festered skin. "Both legs. It's all this wet weather we've had causin' it."

"She's been seen to . . ." Henry stared in. "I've taken good care—"

Mr. Delaney shook his head. "Not much you coulda done—"

"No, no. Quite the opposite." Father stepped in, a scowl on his face. "You should've known what to watch for. This is a prized animal here, and she's your responsibility. May not be thrilled about it, Henry, but that's it. Your responsibility—not to train her but at least to have the good sense to keep her healthy."

Father had struck a harsh note that put Henry on notice, had him staring at the base of the stall. Mr. Delaney motioned for silence. His fingers darted like a butterfly. "Horse's skin is vital to the animal's survival. The skin is subject to attack in various ways, infectious bacteria to biting insects." His mouth was going nonstop, doling out instruction. "This is a fungal infection, much more common in wet, humid climates. Most likely the fungus lives in the soil. This could have lived in dormancy within the skin for some time. It probably became active when the skin was compromised . . . high humidity, high temperatures we've had. The fungus just seems to have set up shop on the animal's legs."

With a suffering filly on his hands, Henry couldn't have looked more guilty.

"If anybody's going to make this a suitable place for thoroughbreds, it'll be Sammy. And a trainer, of course. You've had your cap set for that day alright," Mr. Delaney said to Father with an all-knowing look. "I just don't want you to count on me one hundred percent. I'm still mulling over the idea of our partnership on all this. Francine, of course—you know all too well her enthusiasm for it."

"Yes, and I expect things to change once we get another filly in here."

Father spoke with confidence. "That's certainly gonna happen before the end of the year."

"But if I'd known—"

My brother's attempts to defend himself were met by Mr. Delaney's quick interjection: "This is a prize horse, Henry."

Father was pacing. "I'll say it is! She cost me a pretty penny, and I expect a return on the investment come race day."

"You'd do well to periodically examine the animals for rain rot, Henry. Not just this gal, but all your livestock. A visual evaluation won't get the job done, especially during the wet winter months coming up when the horses have a full coat of hair. It'll take a hands-on examination. That's the most effective."

Mr. Delaney glanced up to make eye contact with Henry. "See these bumps along the back and crop? They're typical." He rubbed them with the palm of his hand. "See how they come free?" He stood up. "Those are my thoughts on the subject, but you need to take a culture. Have it tested in one of those laboratories in Nashville or closer. Treatment of infected animals is relatively straightforward. Pick up a disinfectant that contains a cresol or copper salt base at the apothecary. Apply it locally to decrease the spread of infection. Still, nature's best cure for rain rot is a warm sun and dry weather . . . like we've had the last couple of days."

Father had apparently had enough of the discussion of the filly's dry-rot condition. He butted in. "Trojan Girl, simply put, is a finer horse than Nancy Lee. If a filly like that who won the Oaks last year can win, I know this one can. I've seen her training right here—" He whirled his arm in the direction of the dirt track. "—and I have a winner here! I feel it. I wish I could get her over to Sam's for him to take a look at her run. She can win the Oaks. I'd wager that."

Mr. Delaney looked at my brother as if he were sizing up a stalk of tobacco. "Henry here can take care of the farm. He and the Negroes practically have full charge of it already, don't they? That's seems like where he needs to be. Farming. Adding thoroughbreds . . . Well, I'm afraid the vision you have is far and wide too big, Senator. With all due respect, it isn't realistic. I've said it before: we're too far from Louisville to own a competing thoroughbred or ever hope to train one and race it in the Derby."

Father didn't seem to have heard a word Mr. Delaney said. "You're right, Felix! Makes sense, and we'd need several more hands tending the horses. I plan to get whatever it'll take. It's no secret. My eye's been on your brother's filly for months. Free Rein. The bloodline's good. What'd you think it would take to own her?"

Mr. Delaney was a wispy man, his laugh quiet and short. "Dollars? Be serious, Senator. There's not only the responsibility of caring for a thoroughbred but the logistics of getting her to the races."

"Frankly, it seems like a cockamamie idea, purchasing another thoroughbred." Henry chimed in—quite boldly, I thought. "We're giving up valuable tobacco land for horses."

"I'll thank you to keep out of my decision to buy horses or not, to partner with Felix here or not, Henry," Father said, and I wished I'd stayed with Mama. "Certainly I can't do it alone. I'll have to hire more Negroes once more horses are being purchased. My money hasn't come from farming, anyhow, and ever since the war, farmers aren't having it so good. Their farms are failing; machine costs are going up. These aren't the best of times, son. Fortunately, my money's come from my father owning slaves in Virginia. Sometimes you have to step out and make the money that you do have work in your favor. Realistic or not, I will own a thoroughbred that qualifies for the Derby."

Henry couldn't stand it. "Seems like you're trying to make Hillbound a farm that's more about horses than tobacco."

"I'll be going into town now," Felix said. "I'm sure Trojan Girl will get past this little setback, but it's just a minor example, though. You could be faced with injuries and heat exhaustion. Both are common. Emergency veterinary care would be essential when it does. Most farms have basic vet facilities. You don't—we don't. I think we should give up this idea of breeding. It's why I gave up the idea myself and started concentrating on wheat farming. We're just too remote, Senator. There're a lot of risks involved. You could always keep your horses elsewhere."

"That's absurd. Why would I choose a farm other than Hillbound. Why, Felix, would you bring up such a thing when we're knee-deep in putting together a partnership of our own? Didn't count on you for backing out on me. And don't you forget, I still have several items to get from you—bridles . . . incidentals."

"I know. I know. And Francine sure loves the partnering idea! She didn't expect not to be involved in horse racing either. That's for sure. Don't know how I got away with buying a wheat farm in Todd County. Guess she's not so happy with the move now that it's more about farming and less about horses."

"This would certainly all be up Sam's alley, wouldn't it?" Father was edgy.

Mr. Delaney seemed to be eager to leave. "My brother's definitely the one you need to be with, alright. Sammy's been at it since he was a youngster. Me, I'm content with my wheat crops. I was lucky to get this farm when I did."

Henry just stood there, holding the door to the stall, studying the hay on the floor. I tried not to let on that I'd noticed how disgusted he was. Father's grouchy edge bothered me and Henry seemed lost in some far-off details that eluded me. I couldn't help but notice that Father was indifferent to him.

"It would be a game changer to get a trainer. You've set your cap for Luke, but I'm not so sure that's gonna fly with Sammy."

"You'll come 'round, Felix, once we look into the eyes of those splendid animals. Yessiree. And I'm thinking of bringing Gracie along. She and Francine can do all the shopping they want." Father gave me a side glance and a wink. "We like to keep the ladies happy, alright."

Henry appeared strained, his jaw set.

"As long as Francine can go into Lexington and spend time shopping . . . well, she's happy as a clam. Keep her away from children, though. Wants nothing to do with them."

Father took a deep breath and wrangled his head and neck beneath his collar. He found the comment amusing and produced one of his broad smiles to prove it. Henry did not.

Felix didn't miss a beat. "Racing is still in my blood. No doubt—"

"Remember now, none of this would have happened had Zack Peterson survived the tornado of 1920 or had his widow not remarried and sold the farm. Yeah, you were lucky indeed. I had my eye on it, as you well know. You kind of bought that land parcel out from under me."

Father sounded jovial, but I knew how angry he had been when the Peterson's farm sold very quickly without his knowledge.

"Now, now, Senator. Timing simply had it that the Peterson place came available when I was ready to get out of Madison County. Farming's perfect for me."

"So our trip's still on." Father looked relieved. "You're just overthinking things."

"As I said, best be going."

Nothing more was said, and Henry avoided me, looking first at Mr. Delaney and for a second at Father, then away.

Chapter 13

———

I boarded the train behind Mrs. Delaney, knowing the minute I set foot on the bottom step of the L&N in Guthrie that the trip to Lexington held adventure. I hadn't been on a train since a year ago with Mama, going to shop in Nashville. School had not started, so taking three of the few remaining days before it did meant I wouldn't miss the beginning of my sophomore year.

The Delaneys seated themselves side by side, leaving the leather bench that backed up to theirs for Father and me. We'd settled in only seconds before Father turned around, his neck craned, talking to them. Mrs. Delaney was facing him, lapping up Father's every word.

Within minutes we rolled out of the station with the rhythmic beat and push of the train's momentum as it picked up speed, and everything in sight whizzed past like a dizzying parade. The adults could talk of nothing but the partnership, and I drifted off to my own world of amazements.

Before I could imagine, it was 4:10 p.m. The train was right on time. Civilization began to appear. Through the blur of cornfields and silos, houses began to take shape until, with a mighty *whoosh*, the train pulled into Lexington's Union Station and rolled to a halt past a flash of awaiting faces. Among eager bystanders stood a small Negro man, obviously on the lookout for the likes of us.

I wasn't sure my presence with the adults had thus far added much, if anything. We'd left Henry cooling his heels back at Hillbound. Everyone around him was aware that Henry was nothing close to a horseman and had every intention of continuing his life as a farmer. According to him, a satisfactory workhorse was good enough.

Father's spirit was not, however, dampened because he and Henry didn't share the same regard for racing horses. It was simply one more of the things that had changed in the last two years. With both my sisters having married and gone to live elsewhere and Mama's illness, Hillbound was not the same. Millicent lived in a house on Main Street with her husband, James Carver, who owned the local grocery and hardware store. Emma had married a tobacco farmer, Elmer Rivers. They lived on a respectable tobacco farm outside Guthrie.

Mr. Delaney shouted to the man who came running toward us, waving his cap, and we weaseled our way through the crowd. Mrs. Delaney looked stylish in her low-waisted maroon dress and bell-shaped hat slung low over her forehead.

"Been expecting you folks. Be driving you out to Cloverdale. Right this way."

He led the way to the waiting automobile, and I wedged myself between Mrs. Delaney and her husband on the back seat. The convertible top was already arranged in neat folds behind ours heads, and the black man tucked our valises in at our feet. Father got in the front with the driver, Carl, and we were off, down the road to Cloverdale Stock Farm.

"A'course, Mister Sam's out to the stables. He's been a-waitin'."

Mrs. Delaney adjusted her hat and fidgeted with the purse on her lap and spent the few miles' ride out to Cloverdale gazing at the scenery or glancing at Father. He couldn't sit still, completely absorbed with the prospect of owning a thoroughbred, convinced he could qualify in a matter of nine months for the Kentucky Derby. His eyes darted from her to Mr. Delaney. I noticed them but had no intention of missing the view of the vast open pastureland with its rambling white fences. It extended beyond where I could see, then tapered off into a thin line in the distance.

The afternoon sun cast long, distorted shadows ahead of the automobile as it rounded the bend and came to a stop some distance from the stables. An attractive and rather large home sat off to the side. A wiry young fellow came to greet us.

"Luke, my man! Buddy!" Father stepped from the automobile, strode over to the guy, and landed a hand on his shoulder. "Taking care of that champion filly of mine, are ya?"

"Yours? Is it?" A hearty voice thundered from inside, and a tall, robust man followed it out into the open. His eyes darted from one guest to the next like flies at a picnic, and a nonstop smile spread across his face. Straw-colored hair poked from beneath his wide-brimmed white hat. A mole the size of a pea perched itself in the middle of his left eyebrow.

I knew immediately he was Mr. Delaney's brother. The likeness showed in identical smiles with an outcropping of pearly white teeth. Beyond that, he and the Mr. Delaney that I knew were Mutt and Jeff.

"Welcome to Cloverdale. Welcome, Senator! Pleasant trip, I hope." He extended an enormous hand toward my father. "Glad to have you back on our famous Lexington soil."

Mrs. Delaney stepped from the automobile, a spritely hand outstretched, expecting the assistance her brother-in-law offered. His smile lingered but its dazzle was gone. "Francine," he said as if her name weighed a ton and dutifully removed his hat.

"And who might this lovely young lady be?"

He was looking at me, otherwise I'd have thought he referred to a galloping horse in the background. Cloverdale was breathtaking with spire-topped stables and miles of white fences. My wide-eyed admiration had to be completely apparent. "Your place is beautiful!" I said with a broad sweep of my arm. "I'm Gracie. Nice to meet you, Mr. Delaney. And that's my father," I said, nodding in his direction. "I think he's trying to make me a horse fancier."

"Delighted you've come, Gracie. But most everyone calls me Mister Sam. Call me Mr. Delaney, and not a soul will know who you're talking about. Only one Mr. Delaney. That would be Felix here." He gave his brother a handshake and a half hug. "The wife's expecting y'all at the house for dinner. Have no idea what the fare is. Now, shall we take a look around? We've expanded some since your last time here, Senator."

"I'll say!" Mr. Delaney piped up, "and it's an impressive place alright. Too bad Paw didn't get to see what you made of yourself. He'd never have put you in his will," he said with one of his quiet laughs, "knowing you needed nothing of his holdings."

"You've had your good fortune, too, Felix. Understand you've gotten yourself a nice spread of land in Todd County. Doing what makes you happy."

Mrs. Delaney looked uninterested in the exchange going on between her husband and brother-in-law, but neither had I seen Mister Sam give her the time of day once past his initial hello. In his eagerness, perhaps to show us around, Luke was dancing an impatient jig, a side show all to himself.

"Best decision of my life—second only to marrying Francine. Guess I'll always wonder how you got so caught up in horses at such a young age. Waco was a good place for potters and preachers. That and a few farmers like me and Papa, but you made your move to Lexington at the right time. Me, at fifteen, sixteen, whatever I was, too young, I guess, to consider such a thing. It's still appealing to me, though. Otherwise, I wouldn't be here except for the horses, racing, breeding—everything you're doing. Just more of a farmer when it comes down to it. Francine's not as happy about that as I'd hoped." He gave her a knowing look. "She's mighty keen on the partnership with Robert."

Father was bursting at the seams. "It's a fine place at that. Fine place you have here, Sam. Very impressive. Good to see you again. And you're looking well," he added, "but what say we see that redhead of mine?"

Mister Sam laughed aloud. "Hey, now. Not so fast, Senator. We've a mite bit of talking to do. No guarantees of ownership just because of your little jaunt to Cloverdale."

He turned toward a sprawling group of stables. "I'm sure y'all are weary. Let's take a quick walk through, and then you can rest up a mite before dinner. We have a full day tomorrow. And I hear your womenfolk are going into town in the morning. Not any better place to shop than Lexington. That's what the wife tells me, anyway. And she's got the goods to prove it. This way," he said, and Luke herded us after Mr. Sam like sheep to the pasture.

The dirt track for training and exercising was off to the left. Men led some animals by the bridle and rode on the backs of others. The breeding stables were so perfectly kept they could have been the inside of a home except for the scent of fresh hay, and we walked down the corridor with the stately heads of beautiful horses looking at us.

"You deserve all the success in the world," Mr. Delaney said, gently goading his wife along while he addressed his brother. "You've done mighty well, Sammy."

Luke went on ahead and stopped at a stall near the far end. We watched as he led the stately chestnut filly out to the common area and strutted her in circles.

Father was beaming. "Just look at the way she lifts her hooves. Y'all! The way she cuts her eyes, the way she holds her head!"

"If I didn't know better I'd think we had a love affair going on, Senator. She's had her run for today, but tomorrow's another day. Luke here is an amazing handler. Got all it takes to ride this lively girl too."

"Francine," Father said, "What'd think of her? Felix? Free Rein's quite an animal, don't y'all agree?"

Mr. Delaney's interest in the thoroughbred was clear enough. "She's breathtaking, alright. No doubt about that. Just hope you're not making an awful mistake taking her from here."

Father wasn't sidetracked by our neighbor's comment. "It is *we*, Felix. *We* are taking this fine animal."

Mister Sam's pride in the animal was showing. He gently cupped the palm of his hand over the horse's nostrils, then ran his fingers through its fiery red mane.

"Why, I think you've got all it takes to make her a Derby winner," Mrs. Delaney said, her admiration for Father showing. "There's no reason your place can't be a breeding stable same as here. Smaller perhaps, but every bit as viable. Just because Felix might be getting cold feet, not any reason you should, Robert." She placed her hand briefly on his arm before turning to our host. "I don't know which I'm more excited about: a day in Lexington or seeing these unbelievable thoroughbreds, Sammy.

You'll promise to let me see each one up close tomorrow after Gracie and I return, won't you?"

Mister Sam had stopped smiling. He stepped in front of his sister-in-law and led the horse back inside the stable. "Luke, why don't ya go ahead and give Free Rein the feed for tonight. We'll be back around nine in the morning. Plan on running her through her routine for Senator Maxwell."

Mr. Delaney shot a worried look at his brother. "Sammy may have other plans, Francine."

"Not at all. No reason the ladies shouldn't see a few of the geldings make their run. We'll save it for your return, Gracie. We'll make a horsewoman of you before you leave here." He gave me a wink.

I smiled back at him as Father pulled me off to the side. "Gracie," he said, "I think you'll find Miss Francine to be a very agreeable companion. She knows all the best stores, I suspect. So take this, and I'll bet you you'll find the latest ladies' fashion are quite to your liking." He handed me a twenty-dollar bill and planted a kiss on my forehead.

"But Father, I'd really rather stay here at Cloverdale. Do I have to?"

"No buts about it. Now, shall we catch up with the rest and see what's for dinner?"

With the meeting ended, we made our way back to the automobile and headed up to the house.

Chapter 14

⟨decorative divider⟩

It was late afternoon of the following day when Mrs. Delaney and I returned from our shopping trip into Lexington where popular styles outfitted every mannequin in every department store we entered. Thanks to Mrs. Delaney, there had been several dresses in the store window that had us browsing the racks for the perfect beaded sheath for her and a simple tailored middy with a pleated skirt for me.

The thrill of a town larger than Elkton had been sufficient to hold my attention. Lexington's colorful store windows, packed streetcars, scurrying shoppers, and the latest in ladies' fashions had me captivated, *almost* ready to ditch my subdued wardrobe for one with beautiful modern clothes and head-turner hats. Never mind that I was barely fifteen.

According to Mrs. Delaney's suggestion, it was in our best interest to expand our Elkton-sized fashion sense. The saleslady had seemed very much aware of our intrigue but had proved less than exuberant about having to hold dress after zany dress with complementary accessories against my figure. I was not, however, prepared to consider more than a single school dress, nor to be eyeing one or the other of the slinky straight dresses she selected for me. With no place to wear it, I refused to try on either of them, but that didn't keep us from giggling at the future possibility of revisiting some options at a later date. *Or with Mama*, I'd thought.

The saleslady did provide both Mrs. Delaney and me with amusement with her uppity attitude that changed when Mrs. Delaney began making her own selections with a flair that showed off her enviable figure.

Mrs. Delaney's dress and accessory purchases were brought to the counter for wrapping, as was my selection of a knee-covering pleated dress with a tailored middy top. With packages in hand, Mrs. Delaney and I left Burton's Ladieswear Store.

We returned to Mister Sam's Cloverdale Stock Farm in a mild state of exhaustion to find a small crowd had gathered to watch the horses exercise. Were it not for the exhilarating sight of them in motion I would have been less than energized, but there was plenty of excitement—something about watching a thoroughbred canter, something about his walk, his gallop.

Inside the complex of stables, Mister Sam was talking to Father as we entered the office. Father was more than attentive. Mr. Delaney was chewing his fingernails. None of them seemed to take much notice that we had joined them.

"The value of an unquestionably good horse is enormous, Robert," Mister Sam said, "and it's certainly been seen what handsome prizes are offered for competition. Of course, if and when you choose to withdraw Free Rein from the track, she could easily secure a large income for you as a broodmare."

"I'm well aware of that, Sam. But you've put an uncommon price on her head."

"And why not? I raced the filly in her first four start of her two-year-old season, and while none of those starts has showed quite the potential she's shown here in her workouts, it's there. I'm a breeder, Senator. I know a good horse. She has a heart as big as her ability. Free Rein could come back and take the Derby."

"This is your venture, Robert," Mr. Delaney said, glancing at his wife. "Francine has a good deal of respect for you, Robert, but I've got my concerns. Same ones I had when I made the decision to go back to wheat farming and leave the horse business to the Lexingtonians. Granted, you didn't think much of my selling Trojan Girl, did you, Francine?"

"You're such an old fuddy-duddy," she said with a dismissive air. "Maybe if we put it between us—together—join forces to create a breeding farm, partner the way Sam and Mr. Fillmore have. Personally, I love the idea of partnering, Robert." She gave my father a wicked little wink. "I'll have to work on Felix."

Mister Sam stood up, a bit on the defensive, inches taller than his younger brother. "As you are certainly aware, Trojan Girl's a great filly. Homebred—born right here at Cloverdale. Nothing here but purebred, fleet-footed thoroughbreds. You've started well, Senator. Y'all's decision."

"They're hot-blooded animals," Father said. "Known for their agility, speed, and spirit. If they prove differently, they're sold. That's all there is to it. My place wouldn't be any different than yours in that regard."

My father was in control. I could see that without a speck of training. I guessed that Mr. Delaney was a sure connection to strike a deal between his brother and Father to purchase Free Rein, but Father seemed perfectly capable of managing without our neighbor. He was proud of his growing reputation as a horseman, having had Trojan Girl place in Louisville at the Kentucky Oaks only three months ago, and his clout had him coming off a bit cocky. Watching him deal with Mister Sam was stunning.

"Perhaps I'm somewhat closer to being persuaded, but a venture like this is gonna require a whole lot of cooperation all around." Mr. Delaney looked directly toward his older brother and shook his head. "It's just that if we purchase Free Rein from you, a trainer's an absolute necessity. Unless there's some sort of partnership that includes you, I'm simply not willing."

"Everyone here stands to make money, Sam," Father said with certainty. "I've been the master of my fate thus far. Wouldn't you agree?"

I kept quiet, focused through the open window on the horses, intrigued as I was by how they ran but listening with both ears to the goings on.

"But in Todd County? Not realistic. We're 150 miles or better from Louisville. I know. Believe me, I *know*! I've been on the fence with this thing all along. It's no secret, and y'all have been persuasive up to now. Sure, the horses can transport in a train car. And there are trailers. The logistics, though, make it impractical. Seems rather foolhardy to me, Robert. Sorry. The whole thing does. I'm backing down. Count me out."

Mrs. Delaney turned to her husband, a look of disbelief furrowed her brow. "Well, Felix! Do I have a say-so? Or am I just a fly on the wall?"

"Be sensible, honey. We'll talk more about this later. But my mind is made up. It's too big of a risk. We all know, don't we, Robert has a bit more resources than I'll ever hope to have. That's the bottom line. I don't want to be indebted to my brother . . . or the Senator here."

Mrs. Delaney turned away from Felix and gazed at Father as if he might possibly rescue her from the ridiculousness of her husband's poor judgment.

Mister Sam's enormous smile spread across his face. Unseemly as it was, his obvious approval broke the hostility, and Mr. Delaney looked relieved. Father was surprisingly restrained with only a grin suggesting his satisfaction.

Mrs. Delaney was the only one not smiling. She swished her thick blond hair as if it were a horse's tail and brushed by her husband with a look that could have seared a spot right through the side of his face.

"Felix, I respect that about you," Mister Sam said, still displaying his pleasure. "So,

Senator, I do believe my dealings are solely with you, and my little brother Felix here can be the best ol' wheat farmer Todd County's ever seen."

Father stood as straight as a walking stick. I was sure his aspirations for the Kentucky Derby were set higher than high. I did my best to smile. "We already have a nice track, Father, and Moe Lee's pretty good with Trojan Girl, isn't he?"

Father disregarded my question. Mister Sam, though, gave me a nod. "You've got a point there. Like I said before, Senator, your girl's got a head on her shoulders." He stopped short of glancing in the direction of his sis-ter-in-law who was in a march out of the stables. "Not so with every young lady," he added. He and my father headed off, down past the row of sables, toward the opening at the end.

If Mr. Delaney had any further thoughts on the subject he kept them to himself. From my point of view, poor Mr. Delaney's other decisions had landed him in the ditch.

I ran after Father. "Can I watch? I won't get in the way. You won't even know I'm there. Promise!"

Mister Sam stopped, waited for me, then spoke to Father as I caught up to the both of them. "If you want my opinion," he said, "there's not a reason in the world she can't be in on the deal. Who knows? Gracie might, after all, be the best one to partner with."

It was Mister Sam's diplomacy that I liked. That and his courteous way of making me feel important. "We all know I haven't done anything to merit such a recommendation, Mister Sam. But I'll be happy to let you build my confidence," I said and extended my hand as if I'd made a bona fide business deal. "You're very kind. Thank you."

"I didn't bring you along just to shop in Lexington, honey. I'd be delighted if you'd get up to your neck in this sport."

Mr. Sam gave me a smile and a nod. "Well, alright, then. We'll work thought the financial aspects of the filly's future and then get Luke to come join us. You're not going to be able to make a good start without him. Felix was right about that, and Luke's young. One of my best handlers, but I'm willing to let him go. Got others."

"That's what it's all about. I'm prepared to hear what kinda figure you're thinking, Sam."

"I'll get straight to the point. You're as aware, as I am, Free Rein comes with a pedigree that's impeccable: sired by Star Shoot out of Lady Sterling. And you've got to be willing to pay for it. I won't mince words, Senator, you might as well be paying with one of your—"

"I think I get your drift." Father glanced at me and continued. "I almost captured the Oaks with Trojan Girl. Seems I've got the knack for horses. Feel like a natural. With Luke, we can have a champion, I'm sure of it. My sights are set on this three-year-old chestnut filly! Not a stallion. Not a gelding. And I'll be taking her to the Oaks next May."

"One thing at a time. I can't sell Luke." Mister Sam looked intently at Father. "I hope you didn't come here thinking anything other than asking him what he wants to do. If he isn't interested, I'd advise you to rethink this deal. You might have a knack, but you'd darned well better understand it's gonna take a whole lot more than that. Winning the Kentucky Derby is the greatest accomplishment in thoroughbred horse racing.

With all due respect, Senator, you must know you've got to qualify first. Saratoga, Grand Union Hotel Stakes, the Hopeful, Sanford Memorial, Travers. Somewhere along the line, you've gotta score, and score big."

I wasn't sure if he was lecturing Father. I sat still.

"Forty-five hundred, Senator."

"Poppycock."

I felt dust in the heat of the August breeze that floated past the stable's opening.

"Racing's making a huge comeback. You know that as well as I do," Mister Sam said in a rapt tone. He threw back his head and laughed. "And you're no fool, Robert. Senator. You know what caliber of animal we're dealing with here. It's a lot about control and pride of ownership. Am I right? Why else would we stick our necks out?"

Father peered out to the track, not saying a word.

"I could always manage your racing interests … keep her in my stables, especially if it doesn't work out with Luke. Leave out the burden of keeping Free Rein in Todd County. Horse racing's a sporting diversion for you, Robert. You're a landowner, a large one at that, and Kentucky is a hotbed for enthusiasts of the sport. Kentucky's strengthened its reputation for raising blood horses. Man o' War—"

Father waved his hand as though he'd heard enough.

"Frankly," Mister Sam said, changing the subject, "I'm glad to see Felix bow out. He's a good man. Not the best choice of wives—that's between you and me, of course—but I care about him. Good thing you came along and took Trojan Girl off his hands—for a price, I'm sure. He'd a-kept her a buggy horse. Unbelievable."

Mister Sam laughed, and by this time Father had loosened up as well. "I like your style, Sam. I do like your style."

"Sure didn't take you long to find out that thoroughbred of Felix's could outtrot anything in the neighborhood. Don't believe he's cut out for any of this. You on the other hand—I'd be willing to bet on you. And that's what it's gonna come down to, isn't it? With the state legalizing on-track betting, they've simply given us a popular new source for state revenues. Tip of the iceberg! Bookmaking has its pitfalls, though. Just look at what happened at Travers Stakes last year. That betting scandal may never be lived down. But hey, it's part of the risk, isn't it?"

Father turned and in a swift move extended his hand." Forty-five hundred. Got yourself a deal."

Mister Sam grabbed Father's hand, and his smile spread from one ear to the other. "Contingent, my friend. Contingent. Let's get Luke and go back to the office."

I stood up. Father and Mister Sam did as well. The real reason for our coming to Cloverdale was ending in a moment that had me aware of the powerful transaction Father had made. I was proud of him and eager to know his thought about Mama's reaction to such a big deal. He followed Mister Sam out, lagging behind to let me catch up.

"Will Mama be pleased, Father?" My eyes searched his for a positive answer, but he avoided my gaze.

After several steps away from me, he lit a cigarette. "Think nothing of it. Annabelle's in no condition," he said and blew smoke into the air.

Chapter 15

Mrs. Delaney wore one of her new frocks for the ride home. She boarded the train in a blue silk dress patterned with large rose dollops and a vibrant blue cloche to match. If her agenda had been to rekindle her husband's interest in breeding horses, the trip by all accounts was unsuccessful. If, however, her agenda had been to return to Todd County with the latest in fashion, then she had, in my opinion, succeeded.

Father seemed to appreciate her stylishness and graciously carried a share of the excess baggage.

I closed my eyes and laid my head on the back of the train seat, reliving in my mind the rainbow of gaiety that had absorbed me. Shopping the downtown department stores of Lexington with Mrs. Delaney had been like colorful turns of a kaleidoscope. Picturing myself as one of the ladies in their finery—sashes tied on their hips and a fling in their skirts, smoking their cigarettes, sporting their sassy new looks—fit nicely with the name Lady of Hillbound.

The day had spun my world around, and the thought of Carver's Grocery and Hardware or McCurdy's Textiles in downtown Elkton with its lackluster offering of calico had me hoping for another trip to Lexington. Or Nashville with Mama, for I'd been to a place wider than Allensville Road and looked to buildings higher than my house and formed ambitions broader than my backyard—bountiful and rich, far-reaching and fierce. I would want to write of the fantasies in my diary. And whether or not I even liked Mrs. Delaney or the fact that she and her husband had taken more than their share of Father's attention.

Grasping for the bag at my feet, I placed it on my lap and pulled out the small velvet bag from the inside pocket. It was not something I'd share with Father, who sat next to me, and certainly not Mrs. Delaney, who sat behind me. As the train roared over the tracks and into the countryside, I felt the shape of the brooch I'd bought for Mama, allowed my fingers to trace the ridges of the filigreed fan, then returned it to the pocket of my bag.

I must have dosed off. Father's voice gave me a start. He was turned in his seat, eye to eye with Mr. Delaney. "Luke caught my attention as far back as a year ago. He's a natural, and small enough to jockey. Why, he began as a stable hand at fourteen, mucking out yearlings' stalls for fifty cents a day. Now that he's eighteen, he's handling the horses with impressive expertise. It'll be because of him that I'll qualify this horse."

Mr. Delaney squirmed on the train seat. "You've gotten quite a prize, not only in Free Rein, but now in a trainer. Better you than me. Don't much see how you wrangled that deal. Guess most everything can come at a price. You've got the golden touch."

"What's your opinion, Francine? Luke was pleased to negotiate. He'll be training Trojan Girl starting in October, then Free Rein once the Dade Park race is over. We'll get Free Rein over to Hillbound around Christmas."

"You. Not we," Mr. Delaney said.

"You've managed to get yourself a beauty, Robert," she said, ignoring her husband.

I could see even through my closed eyelids that she doted over the wonderful decision Father had made. And I could somehow feel her distain for how silly her husband had been to balk at the chance to partner with the wise Senator Robert Rutherford Maxwell.

"Training bill at fourteen hundred dollars . . . twenty-four hundred dollars for the pair once Luke takes over with Trojan Girl . . . Got myself a good rider."

A nauseating feeling had presented itself at the back of my throat. I opened my eyes and looked at the ceiling to steady the whir in my head and take my mind off the train's motion as it bounded the curves, the engine, and the awkwardness of the conversation passing over the seats. And Mrs. Delaney's cigarette. The push Father had given me to connect me to her had been uncomfortable at first, but then the shopping had been fun.

I wrestled with the lumpy train cushion and talked to myself. *Just because Mama happened to be sick at the moment didn't mean I needed a substitute.*

Ashes fell from the cigarette Mrs. Delaney dangled in the air, and Mr. Delaney seemed to fume for most of the train ride back to the L&N at Guthrie, although no one was carrying on a conversation anymore.

The *clang-clang* of a bell as it crashed on my ears all but took my breath. It was followed by the continuous loud horn as the train approached the station. It passed the cross tracks and came to a heavy, smooth halt.

"If anyone's capable of pulling off a win with this horse, Robert, it's you," Mrs. Delaney said to Father as she stepped away from the train and a porter hauled our baggage and her packages through the station. She kept up with Mr. Delaney and Father.

But Father was on the lookout for Henry, agitated that my brother was apparently not there, waiting at the station.

———⟶

The Delaneys' hired hand, Clancy, waved to us as we approached the station's entrance and rushed to pick up their baggage.

The immense L&N locomotive blocked the view of the road north where Henry would be driving Father's Model T if he had been anywhere close to coming to pick us up. For sure, he was not. It didn't seem to surprise Father that Henry was not on time. He tightened his grip on the handles of his alligator valise and huffed.

"What'd you expect, anyway? It's Henry."

It wasn't clear if Father was speaking to me or to the Delaneys or to anyone who'd listen. We were spent. It was late in the day, so Henry's tardiness posed a dilemma. Father hated wasting time. Had it not been for the attention he was getting from individuals who recognized him, he would have been even more riled up. As we waited outside for the train to clear the tracks, admiration for my father was everywhere. I was not alone in my pride for him. Mrs. Delaney seemed to enjoy the wait, if for no other reason than to bask in the adulation.

"I'll be around in the next few days. Still have those few items for Trojan Girl yet to get from you, Felix," Father said as his parting words to the Delaneys once they were able to load up and leave.

As soon as his audience departed, his mood soured like milk too long in the heat. Henry was not coming down the road on the other side of the tracks.

"Take a seat, Gracie. He'll be along any minute. It's a rotten shame he can't be on time." He glanced toward the Delaneys, their backsides visible as they headed off with Clancy.

We chose a bench and sat there with our backs against the building. Father seemed preoccupied. "And Felix, of course. I'm afraid he lost his nerve. Hate that he reneged on our vision. Too bad. A fool. Had a good opportunity too." He forced a half-hearted laugh. "We might've made a good partnership. But that's neither here nor there, is it?"

I scooted farther back on the bench and reached inside my bag, gently pulled out the small bag containing the gift for Mama, and once again loosened the drawstring that gathered the folds of velvet around it. The delicate fan-shaped brooch fell into the palm of my waiting hand.

"Look at what I bought for Mama."

His brow furrowed. A faraway look in his eyes said he was not really listening. The transaction with Mister Sam to purchase Free Rein and bring Luke to Hillbound had, up to now, been sufficient to hold Father in a mood of expectancy. It took the reminder of Mr. Delaney's defaulting and Henry's being late to change everything.

I could see that now was not the time to show Father the brooch. I put it back in its pouch, slipped it in my bag and held tightly to the handle.

"Free Rein is beautiful, Father. Will I be able to ride her?"

I was not to know his answer. Just then the Model T came into view and Father was on his feet. "'Bout time," he said.

Henry parked the Model T and was all apologies, stumbling over his feet to help us with our bags. Afterward, the twelve-mile ride home felt like a long one. Mama, I felt sure, would love the brooch, never mind what Father had not said.

Chapter 16

⚜

With August coming to a close, I'd wrapped up my summer reading to the children. As far as I could figure, Henry's lull of supportive complacency had disappeared as quickly as it had come. Even so, inspiration had blossomed in the children over the last weeks and had begun to unfold like crocuses in springtime in spite of the one bootstep that would quell them. Henry's.

The heated days since the fanciful trip to Lexington were harbored in my memory and on the pages of my diary. The new dress Mrs. Delaney assured me was perfect for the first day of school had been just that, and my wearing it as a witness to my shopping excursion with her made me wish I'd taken her advice for another one for this second day.

At breakfast, Henry's nose was bent out of shape over something. It was hard to keep track. In any case, I kept my attention pretty close to my grits. The day's labor had begun, and in the distance the sound of the steam-powered threshing machine hitched to a tractor whirred as it moved across the Delaneys' field. I finished eating, took the dishes to the kitchen, and in my walk to Bledsoe's Creek School held thoughts of returning to the two rooms sitting on a knoll surrounded by beautiful green fields.

I walked on Allensville Road alongside the waving shafts of wheat, then turned on the path next to the grist mill. The mile-long walk along the creek bed took the most of my time. The smell of drying leaves in my path was pleasant enough.

I was early to school this morning. The single room was empty except for the woodstove used in wintertime. The floorboards creaked as I entered through the big wooden door. The two-seater desk where I put my books and lunch on the shelf in front was aligned with fifteen or sixteen others.

Before long the schoolhouse began to come to life with most every aged student, from first grade to eleventh. There were friendly faces and happy chatter. Energetic younger children bounced up and down on the five or six steps leading up to the large square room. Four windows provided as best as possible a cross breeze for the sweltering days that were bound to occur for the rest of the month.

School gave us one of the few places to gather and meet people our age or those close to it. Several of the older boys wouldn't be attending until after the harvest, establishing that girls would outnumber boys in the upper classes. Jean Morgan was among them as a tenth grader like I, and she was closest to me as a friend. Even so, I'd seen her only once—aside from yesterday's return for the first day of school—since midsummer. Impatient, I went back outside to wait for her.

Two eleventh-grade girls were the oldest students. Autumn's beginning session didn't include a senior, not unless a new family had moved into the vicinity over the summer. But no word of such an occurrence had spread. I greeted the twin Daniels girls as they ran up the grassy embankment and eagerly watched for Jean to appear from the direction of the tree line at the rear of the school.

In another minute I saw her coming in a fast walk across the yellowing grass. She waved back at me, and we were soon talking before we could actually hear what the other was saying over the loud rumble of the nearby harvester. I caught sight of Miss Avery trudging across at a rapid pace from the opposite direction, clutching an armload of books in her arms. Jean and I both rushed to help our teacher.

It was precisely nine o'clock when Miss Ida Avery rang the bell. The first fifteen minutes were set aside for all classes to join together in prayer and devotions, and when the roll was called each student present recited a Bible verse from memory. I glanced at Jean with a devilish smile. Mama wouldn't have wanted to know that Father had let me and Henry skip church or that Father wanted to have me believe it was because she was sick. He'd taken to going in the automobile to churches north of us to talk to his voters. I was convinced in my heart by his actorly behavior when he returned that he was happier glad-handing over worshiping any day.

Even so, I knew my Bible verse when the time came. I got up from my desk and stood beside it. "Jesus wept."

The others in the class snickered.

"You can do better than that, Gracie Mae." Miss Avery twitched her nose and mouth like a large rabbit. Otherwise, I was sure she would have at least smiled.

"Yes ma'am. But, *Gracie*, please. Just Gracie." I sat back down without looking at Jean.

My having to answer all the questions yesterday for all the lessons just because I was a tenth grader had seemed a bit unfair. More was expected of me, and church was not so important. Bible verses weren't either.

Lunchtime came, and Miss Avery motioned me to wait. She pulled me aside as the other students filed outside and looked at me with kind eyes until the last one was out of sight. I expected her expression to change—perhaps her chubby hand might take the paddle from her desktop and apply it to my backside—but she continued to gaze with kindness. "You're a model for the younger students, Gracie. As one of the older ones, you know that." Her smile pushed hard against oversized cheeks, and for a split second her straight little teeth showed like a row of corn between them. "I haven't seen you in church since spring. Everything alright at home?"

Laughter coming from the out-of-doors kept me from caving in. I swallowed hard. "Mama . . . Mama's just real sick," I said.

"*Quite* sick, Gracie. Well, I had heard that. I'm sorry. All the more reason to learn those Bible verses. Run on out to lunch now."

I went back to my desk and took the lard bucket Clarice had filled with sausage biscuits and apple butter and headed outside. It was easy to spot Jean seated on a slope outside the schoolhouse steps. I plopped down next to her.

"Did you get into trouble?" Jean peered at me overtop a fried chicken leg. Her brows arched in half moons over clear-blue eyes, and she waited while I got myself settled on the ground and pulled out a biscuit.

"Heavens, no! Miss Avery?" Starved, I wolfed down a bite and peered back at her with my own clear-blue eyes, chewing madly as I laughed. "She's too nice to get *really* mad. I mean, *mad*-mad. But I guess I'll have to memorize a longer Bible verse for tomorrow. Do you like homework, Jean? Like English and history lessons? 'Cause I do."

"Nah. I'd just as soon skip it all together. But my papa says I have to learn. And that's that. Your papa's probably the same, I'm guessin'. Mama's got another baby coming this winter.

Just told me last night. I don't know why girls have to go to school anyway. We're just gonna have babies and be mamas," Jean said with a degree of surrender, then chomped the last bite off the chicken leg.

I watched for a moment, considering her reasoning, while the others played Crack the Whip. "I'll be a teacher one day. A real one in a real school somewhere. That means I have to stick to learning, doing homework. I love teaching children too. But I wish you lived closer. I have Henry at home. But he's a *brother*." I forced my lips into an exaggerated downturn and held my nose. "And Moe Lee is my friend. But no girls. You could come spend the night again, maybe. Like you did that one time. We wouldn't pick strawberries but we could ride horses, maybe."

We both agreed the suggestion was marvelous as we gathered our lunch belongings and pushed ourselves up from the ground.

"Ten minutes, students!" Miss Avery's announcement sent me and Jean flying to join ourselves to the end of the Whip line.

The school day ended. Jean went her way, and I went mine, walking back up the side of the road, absentmindedly moving toward home, looking across to where Mt. Zion Baptist Church stood in the clearing. Another quarter mile and I was way past the mill when I saw Moe Lee coming down Allensville Road. I couldn't imagine the reason. He seemed to be running as fast as his limp would allow.

"Accident, Miss Gracie. Bad one," he shouted from a distance, slowing himself down and completely out of breath. "Mr. Felix . . . he done been kilt. He fall from the loft. Yore daddy—"

Moe Lee choked up. He tried to speak again as I ran to him, but he was unable. He straightened up by pushing his hands on his knees, but still, his words were completely garbled. I dropped my books and grabbed his arm, and he began limping. Without trying to talk at all, we limp-hopped and ran as best he could till we got close enough to the house. Moe Lee was balancing on his own, so I left him to fend for himself.

Frantic, crying, doubling over with a side ache, still I picked up speed and took off for the last few remaining feet in the direction of the house. Henry came into view as I darted toward the kitchen door. I shouted back at Moe Lee: "Where is he?"

Moe Lee was staggering to catch up. "He dead, Miss Gracie."

"*Father's dead*?" It came out at the top of my lungs and echoed across the meadow. I clomped both hands over my ears, too scared to want to hear another word from Moe Lee.

The peacocks scattered in every direction, and Henry, sauntering up from the stable, broke into a run.

Out of my mind, I rushed up the back stairs, tripping over my feet, screaming, and lunged at the door handle.

Chapter 17

———⟪⟫———

I'd barely gotten inside the house. Moe Lee came tearing up the back
steps, close on my heels.

"No! No, Miss Gracie!" He rushed inside the kitchen behind me.
"It's *Mr. Delaney*," he said, gasping for air. "Mr. Delaney's the one be dead!"

Odelia and Clarice stood by the stove, wringing their hands. Their faces
were scrunched in agony.

Henry burst through the back door, pushing it with a thrust enough to
send it smacking against the wall behind it. "What's happened?" He rushed
at Moe Lee, then stopped short as Father came walking down the hallway,
stone faced and ashen.

I ran to him, savagely threw my arms around his neck as slobber and
tears slid from my mouth and eyes. "*Father!*" When I finally released him,
he was solemn, unsmiling.

Henry's dark eyes were wild and glistening. He looked at Father as if
he were seeing a ghost. His mouth dropped open, but no words came out.

"He fell. Felix fell from the loft," Father said as Moe Lee wagged his
head in remorse.

Clarice slipped past us and was off down the hallway, going to Mama's
room I supposed. Odelia went too.

"You were over there?" I asked, panting. "When it happened . . . you
were there?"

"Yes. I was. Unfortunately, there's more."

107

I braced myself, holding to Moe Lee for support. He felt trembly, weak beneath my grasp.

Father stared down at the linoleum floor and continued, monotone: "I'd gone over to their place for fly masks. For the horses. Felix was in the barn loft, pitching wheat sheaves . . . down to the feeder."

We all looked at each other in dismay while Father stopped to clear his throat. "Made a misstep, that's all. Misstepped and fell headlong. Struck his head on the cylinder. Felix was drawn into the thing running at full speed.

Moe Lee's head dropped to his chest. Except for his rattled breathing, the kitchen was dead silent. Outside the peacocks screamed.

"What should we do?" I asked, looking to Father for an answer.

"I'm going into town to get help for Francine. Clancy's with her now, but you can imagine . . . She needs more than a colored man trying to—"

"What about Mother? Does she know?" Henry was incensed.

"Of course not, idiot." Father said, frustrated and sweating. "You tell her, if you think this is something she needs to hear.

I covered my mouth and ran past Henry, back outside.

The air was stifling with the smell of more rain on the way. All I could think of was the trip to Lexington with Mr. Delaney, so alive. Nothing could have suggested he would be gone in a matter of days. And Mrs. Delaney, so stylish and pretty . . . with a nice husband now dead.

Death, I thought, *is supposed to take the old folks, sometimes the mean when it's their time, like Granny Maxwell because she was both. But never the young and nice.*

My high spirits had all but vanished, and I felt ashamed for having allowed such a despicable thought about Granny Maxwell, fleeting as it was.

I walked down the way to where I'd dropped my books, picturing the last time I'd seen Mr. Delaney when he and Mrs. Delaney had left the train station after our trip to Lexington.

It helped to visualize a world beyond this moment to that day when he was happy and gay, full of life, or even roughly and courageously arguing his position regarding a partnership with Father. *Either way*, I thought, *his last days of life came without warning, and now what? Mrs. Delaney. Who* *does she have now, with her family somewhere else in Kentucky? Things change.*Clarice poked her head outside and searched with her eyes from the back stoop until she saw me walking up from afar. She hollered to let me know Mama was awake.

One day they're here, next day they're gone. Millicent and Emma, married and gone. Not so final as death but far different than when they were near, every day, here at Hillbound.

I breathed deeply the misty, hot September air and in the eerie quiet of the approaching evening realized how important the present was to savor. And I, at barely fifteen, was not too young to understand.

Chapter 18

⸺◦⟢⟣◦⸺

Mt. Zion Baptist Church was packed with more people than I'd seen on a Sunday morning. Mrs. Delaney sat alone on the front row as six grim-faced men carried the wooden coffin down the middle aisle. Father was one of them. Henry was another. Not a head turned.

Strangers to these parts filled the various other pews. As far as I knew, I'd never laid eyes on them, and there were others. I'd only in a quick moment looked behind me to see who they were.

Walking in very measured steps was Mister Sam. He was a somber version of the jovial man I'd met at Cloverdale Stock Farm less than two weeks ago. With hands folded in front of him, he stood for a moment at the side of his brother's coffin, then sat down across the aisle from us with his wife, whom I'd met at Cloverdale.

Two men followed behind him. The younger one carried a Bible. Both men seated themselves next to Mrs. Delaney. Otherwise, not a body moved till the family had taken a seat, and Father was the last after Henry to sit. Henry was on my left. On down the pew were my two sisters and their husbands.

"Chester Willoughby. That's Mrs. Delaney's brother," Henry said in a whisper to me and pointed to the older man. "Marcus next to him. That's his son."

Mrs. Delaney bowed her head, dabbing with a handkerchief beneath the black netting on her hat. She remained facing the front where the preacher spoke in glowing terms of the too-soon-ended life of Felix Harmon Delaney.

At one point he stepped down from the platform to shake hands with the family—the Delaneys and Willoughbys—and continued to speak to those gathered, extolling the deep significance of family. Then he turned and went back to the simple wooden pulpit atop the platform and referred to his notes.

The September day got hotter and hotter until, with a final amen, we all stood and sang "The Old Rugged Cross." There was little to say as we filed out of the church and the six men stayed behind to carry the coffin.

Sobs and sniffles were heard as the procession passed and the coffin was lowered in the freshly dug earth. I listened along with everyone else as the younger Mr. Willoughby—Marcus— read from the Bible. He sounded comfortable enough, handling the Good Book, but I was distracted by the fact that he ended with "Jesus wept."

The crowd seemed to find its own natural way of clustering, with the women folk moving toward the tables where an abundance of food had been spread. The bowls of potato salad and green beans that Clarice had made sat near to the end. I went and uncovered them for the line that was forming.

Father stood off to the side with Mrs. Delaney's brother, Chester Willoughby, giving an account of the accident to the all-ears people standing close by: "It was well after lunch. I might have gone into town for the fly masks, but Felix had made it clear he expected me to take what rightfully went with Trojan Girl. That was some of it. Fly masks, bridles . . . I had no idea where he was when I got to the house. Guess I did, actually. Made sense he would be threshing wheat. Crops being as late as they are . . . And so he was."

Henry was taken aback. "Oh, I don't recall you mentioning that."

"Of course, I went to the barn to find him and track down the fly masks in particular," Father said, frowning, obviously incensed that Henry had uttered a word.

Mr. Willoughby didn't speak. His son seemed to be headed in our direction.

"No. I meant that you went to the house first."

"Yes, I went to the barn for equipment, getting the last of the things, you know. Bridles and fly masks . . . that sort of thing. It was just easier to go up to the loft and talk to Felix rather than shout over the noise of the machine."

It was men talk. I couldn't tolerate the details, so I continued past them to speak to Moe Lee, who was talking to Clancy. Both leaned against the fence, out of the way of the white folks, quiet, perhaps listening to the conversation between Father and Henry. And there were other Negro folk standing around, afraid maybe, to bring up the subject.

"A shame," Moe Lee said as I walked up. He nodded at someone apparently coming up behind me. "Darned shame, it is. Farm accidents is all too common. Shore wished this had no part in yore young life, Miss Gracie."

"Miss Maxwell?" The voice was masculine.

"Yes," I said with a hasty turn to the person who had read "Jesus wept" from the Bible. The young man was a rather serious-looking fellow with sleeked dark hair like Father's, a high forehead, and very full lips. I'd already decided he was likable, judging only from his selection of Bible verses, and I'd decided he was older than Henry, perhaps twenty. He acted mature. *But it could have been the Bible thing,* I thought.

"I'm Marcus Willoughby, Francine's nephew. From Madison County."

My instincts told me he was a little nervous, walking over like he had, introducing himself like he had. He was attractive, and that spoke for itself. No instincts necessary.

"I know. I'm very sorry about your uncle," I said. "You read the Bible real well—quite well."

"That's very kind of you." He smiled and showed off his nicely positioned white teeth. "'Jesus wept.' It's the shortest verse in the Bible, in case you ever need a short one."

"I know," I said, checking to see if anyone was paying any attention to us. One by one, the Negroes began moving away from us.

"You do?" Marcus seemed a bit taken aback, but he was all smiles.

I looked past him in hopes at least Moe Lee would stick around, but he limped on off without looking back.

Noticing we were more or less standing alone, Marcus seemed more comfortable talking to me. "I started reading the Bible after my mother passed away. It's been just over two years. I've read it through twice already," he said.

"Oh, I see. Well, my folks and I haven't been going to church much lately. My mother's sick." Suddenly, it seemed like I was alibiing. I shrugged my shoulders, mainly because I had nothing else to do with them. Covering for being a slacker of a church-goer made me feel awkward. "Father goes all around to churches, but it's to see his voters." My comment hadn't served to smooth over one thing for me.

"I hope she'll recover soon." He seemed pleasantly sincere, like warm mittens on a wintery day. "Madison's a good ways away, three hundred or so miles away. My dad's a potter there, an *expert* potter. I can say that . . . he never would. Takes the clay and forms it any way he chooses. It's his hands that shape and reshape it as he sees fit. And he turns out some really beautiful stoneware pottery, like his father before him. I do some because I'm saving for college. Asbury next fall. Planning on being a preacher for the most part."

"I can see you as a preacher." I managed a smile. "Maybe we should go on back. I need to help with the food."

"Hope you don't mind if I say your eyes are . . . so blue! Forgive me. Just don't think I've seen eyes bluer than the sky itself."

I laughed out loud. "They're blue, alright. And yours are . . . what? Army-blanket green. Now that we've got the eye colors down, I'd better scoot."

It was a comfortable laugh between us. Spontaneous. I liked it.

Mister Sam reached for a plate about the time I got to the tables. He stopped to acknowledge me with huge smile. "Gracie! How's my favorite horse gal?" And without warning I got a hug from him, as huge as his smile.

I wanted the perfect sympathetic words to say to him, but without any experience, all I could think of was to tell him I was sorry about his brother's death. "He was so nice, Mister Sam. And I'm fine, thank you."

"Me too," said a perfect stranger. "Guess there'll be a reading of the will, but now's probably not the time to talk of it. My condolences, Mr. Delaney."

I didn't recognize the man who said it, but tacky as it sounded, I guessed it was part of dying—who and what was left behind.

Mister Sam hid from the stranger the fact that he rolled his eyes in disbelief, but it was for sure he wanted me to see. "I'm sure he would've left everything he had to Francine, sir. Who else? Not me."

I shrugged, not knowing anything about who talked about wills or when, and Mister Sam and I gave each other ghastly looks. "I'm really glad for the chance to see Cloverdale. I hope I'll still get to visit there even though—"

"I hope you'll come anytime, Gracie. Please consider it a personal invitation, and don't let Francine overawe you. She can do that. You're much too special. Be careful."

I didn't wait for the conversation to end. I shook Mister Sam's hand feeling like I needed to run. Father was not in sight. I began the walk toward home, alone.

Chapter 19

"Good morning, Mama" I said in a chipper tone even though Friday's funeral yesterday had left me less than exuberant. I eased into the morning room, dim and lighted only by the fire that Clarice had just stoked.

"Miss Annabelle's had a right bad night. Might want to leave her be. For now, anyhow." Clarice propped the poker on the hearth and scurried from the room.

The curtains were drawn. Mama was bundled as if it were the middle of winter. She struggled to raise herself on an elbow and forced a smile.

I plumped the pillow beneath her head, then settled on a tufted chair next to her. Hollyhock clippings sagged their heads in a small vase on the table beside her bed, and the fan-shaped brooch sat in full view on top of its black-velvet bag. It wasn't clear to me what she knew of Mr. Delaney's accident or the funeral, or any of the recent happenings since the day I'd presented the gift. Bringing up recent tragedy didn't seem right. Mentioning Marcus Willoughby made no sense at all.

She stretched out her hand for me to take. "The fan is dear to me, ladybug. Such a beautiful gift."

"How are you feeling?"

"A little stronger," she said, but her eyes were dull and spoke otherwise. "Maybe Clarice would help me take a stroll with you later on."

"I don't know, Mama. What if you fell?"

"Nonsense! I could use the fresh air. So this afternoon? I'll wear my brooch. Have you plans for the day? Anything exciting?"

"Practicing piano, I guess, now that you're awake. And Father's going to town, so I'm going. I'll read to the children when I get back." The thought made me smile. "Alright," I said.

Promising didn't feel like the perfect answer, but upon hearing it, she relaxed on the pillow.

"Shall I read Robert Browning?"

"What's my favorite saying of his?"

"'Best be yourself, imperial, plain, and true,'" I quoted from memory.

"That's it . . . A good one." If she could have appeared to be pleased, she would have, but perspiration beaded over her lips, and her eyelids drooped. "That's probably enough for now, ladybug."

"Can I get you anything?"

"Maybe just let me rest up."

Her dark hair accentuated how pale she'd become. Fitful sleep was usual now, almost every night, and she tired easily.

"We'll walk later on," I said.

She didn't respond, and I quietly slipped out, knowing I would be waiting to practice piano.

Father and Henry were in the drawing room with sections of the *Todd County Standard* open on their laps. They sipped coffee. Father was dressed to go into town. Henry was in overalls, hair uncombed.

I went in and quietly sat on the piano stool, my back to the keys.

"Yes, here it is," Henry said and proceeded to read aloud: "'A frightful accident occurred on Tuesday, September 5, leaving one, Felix H. Delaney, dead.'"

Father set his cup down with a plunk, sloshing coffee onto the saucer, and jumped to his feet. He circled 'round where Henry was seated and hung over his shoulder, and Henry continued to read. "'As near as we can learn, the tragedy happened as follows:

Mr. Felix Delaney was engaged in threshing wheat at his farm off Russellville Road, the machine being set in the barn. He was stationed in the barn loft to pitch the sheaves down to the feeder. While engaged in his duties he made a misstep and fell headlong from the loft, his head striking the cylinder, which was running at full speed. He was instantly drawn into the machine, head first—'"

Henry glanced at me and then at Father. Father punched his shoulder. "Read on."

"'—and in less time than it takes to tell it, his head and upper portion of his body was reduced to a shapeless, unrecognizable mass by the teeth of the cylinder and concave.'"

"That's disgusting," Father said, slick-smoothing his hair back, and the pomade glistened from the stroke of his hand. He lit a cigarette and flipped the lighter shut with a smack.

"'The deceased was 31 years of age,'" Henry said, continuing to read. "'He leaves a wife of 5 years, Francine Willoughby Delaney, and one brother, Samuel Delaney of Lexington, Kentucky. No children.'"

The room was silent except for the rustle of the newspaper being folded. That and the ever-present scream of the peacocks outdoors.

Henry laid the paper on the divan and stood. "The Petersons' old place sure seems like it's ill fated. As for me, I'm trying to make something good come out of this. Gonna be hard, though. Don't see it. Just don't see how—"

"My close-mouthed, un-opinionated son has suddenly become a little chatty. You best mind your business, son. That usually seems to keep one out of trouble."

Henry leaned heavily against the chair's back cushion and with his right hand gripped and pulled on the back of his neck as if he needed a moment to gather his wits about him. "So, you were discussing horses in the loft while Felix was pitching wheat?"

Henry wasn't given to disrespectfulness but I heard a touch. I bit my lip and gave him a weak frown.

"Of course! What new horse owner wouldn't want to know answers to—" He stopped mid-thought. "Gracie, we're going into town right away. Why don't you plan on meeting me outside. I'll be at the automobile shortly."

Henry looked like a sheep caught in the thicket. He'd impressed me as such for the last couple of weeks. His concern over the filly and the added responsibilities of his attempting to manage Hillbound seemed nothing in comparison to the weight of antagonism that Father had recently been doling out. The distasteful attitudes passing between Father and Henry bothered me. And now this, where Mr. Delaney's death covered us like a dream. A very bad dream, impossible to shake off.

Father's suggestion for me to meet him at the Model T was a clear dismissal. Whatever else he had to say to Henry he did not want me to hear. I left them and wandered out to the verandah so they could do their bickering alone.

And I, Lady of Hillbound—although perhaps that designation had not yet taken root—walked to the automobile, opened the door and sat on the front seat in the company of my own churning and pent-up emotions, incapable of sorting them out by myself. My newfound consciousness was doggedly accompanying me. Whether or not emotion defined my being a fifteen-year-old remained to be seen, but it somehow wanted to nest itself in my daily living.

The hand sewing I continually neglected—that I hated with a passion with its stupid stitches on warped fabric . . . The piano practice I avoided whenever possible . . . I considered how much I'd rather choose to do any of it over being a witness to the pain I was seeing in Henry's eyes.

Chapter 20

Moe Lee had the Model T cranked up. Father came out the front door, across the verandah, and down the front steps. He was upset. Given the heated conversation he'd just had with Henry only minutes ago, his frown was not surprising.

He wore a stiff collar with a tie tucked neatly beneath his waistcoat. Father generally had a polished look—even without a smile—and the contrast of the white paper of his cigarette always managed to set off his strangely handsome appearance.

Henry came out the back of the house and charged past the stable. By the time Father reached the automobile, Henry was seemingly bent on catching up to the hired hands who were nailing uprights in place on the little house being built for Luke.

"It's really coming along, isn't it? The house," I said, hoping our conversation could be about anything other than Mr. Delaney's accident or his funeral.

Moe Lee stepped to one side as Father redirected the automobile with a smooth twist of the steering wheel, then pointed us toward Allensville Road.

"He'll be here late next month, so the fellas do need to move right along on it. Yessiree, small but adequate for Luke. Guess he's gonna bring a woman too. Bertie, or Bonnie. Something like that. And let's not forget Free Rein is coming."

"I do love going into town. And there's nothing I'd rather do than see Sister . . . unless it's reading to the children. I plan to do that when we get back. I can hardly wait to see Millicent, Father. Will you be long?"

"Do have to talk to my constituents, of course. Just part of my job to know public opinion. But I should think you'd find plenty to do. Maybe find a book for Moe Lee's brood."

"Are you making fun of me? It feels like you are, Father. Isn't it silly that Moe Lee thinks they shouldn't be taught?"

"It's not Moe Lee. It goes deeper than that, Gracie. But on our property, with our folks, I say you can do what you want. It's important to you."

"Where were Moe Lee's folks from, Father?"

"Now that's an out-of-the-blue question. Heck, my father owned his folks! And Moe Lee was a feisty kid, apparently. A little too much for his own good, maybe."

"What happened to them? And what happened to Moe Lee's eye, anyway?"

"Oh, I don't know all the story, Gracie. Too long ago and not very relevant. Suffice it to say his folks, all except Moe Lee and his brother, were long gone by the time we moved here from Roanoke County. Those two came with us. My father died in Virginia. That was in 1896." He swerved to avoid a rut in the road. "I was twenty-six then. Your mother and Emma—a baby then, of course—and Granny Maxwell and I came to Todd County. I was my father's only heir. No sense staying when I could make a new life for myself . . . But enough about that, Gracie. Just hope you'll be enthusiastic about horses. I hope you'll learn to ride. Like Francine. She's an excellent horsewoman. Perhaps she could teach you to ride side saddle."

"Mrs. Delaney isn't going to take the time to teach me. Besides, Father. She is not my type."

"Oh, ho! Exactly who is your type? You're a young woman and needing to know some of the finer things in life."

"Mama would be the one to teach me, I'd think. Don't you?"

He looked away as we turned onto East Main and passed Latham Funeral Home. Straight ahead was downtown Elkton. "So I've heard," he said and tossed his cigarette onto the side of the dirt road, then drove in silence for a moment.

I could feel the knots in my tummy, gripping, like a bird clinging to a branch. "You hardly *ever* see her, Father."

His lips tightened. "She's ill, Gracie. I don't think you can expect much where your mother's concerned. More or less bedridden at this point."

"She's misses you. I can tell."

"She's sick, Gracie," he countered. "Sick. And she's not going to get any better."

"She *is*!" My chest pounded. I gulped for air. "She said herself that she's feeling stronger. She *will* be able to go up and down the stairs again and not have to stay in the morning room. We're taking a walk when I get back."

He pulled to the space in front of Carver's Grocery and Hardware and didn't look my way. Without a word he shut the engine down and stepped from the Model T. "Why don't you go to Carver's, and I'll catch up with you. I need to stop in at the postal office—just chew the fat with a few folks. I'll join you there before you run out of things to do."

Already the townsfolk were looking in his direction, most dressed in overalls with a worn look, but he carried himself with the properness befitting a senator. His dark eyes seemed to pierce right through their glances with a meaningless glare.

I went inside to the bustle of comings and goings. The bells jingled on the door as I shut it behind me and went straight to the rear to speak to Jim. He'd been married to Millicent for a year, and every day without my older sister was awful. She and Emma, the eldest, were my world.

Jim was busy but always eager to say hello. He walked toward me with his tight smile and an inquisitive tilt to his head. "You're looking well, Gracie. And what brings you into town on this fine Saturday morning?"

"Nothing out of the ordinary. Just always love riding in with Father. We'll go over to the house and see Sister. Or is she out and about?"

"Don't think so. She's quite the homemaker, as you know. Told me she'd be baking a cake today." He rolled his eyes and chuckled. "Guarantees I won't delay getting home this evening."

"Maybe I'll just take a peek at the chocolates. Glad to see you, Jim. I'll let you get back."

"They're a weakness for most of us, that's for sure. Come in anytime." He moved toward the meat counter and disappeared behind it.

I turned, but the fellow directly behind me didn't budge. He was a tall one, a wolfish schoolboy with carrot-red hair and freckles, my age perhaps, intent on pressing in on me. I was uncomfortable with his closeness and hoped Jim had seen the encroachment. It was obvious he had not.

The brush of his upper arm across the front of me was disgusting. I did not appreciate the suggestiveness of it. "You'll excuse me," I said with a disdainful look and moved quickly to my left.

His eyes were on me. I could feel them as I went to the front of the store, and I tried to concentrate on the case filled with a variety of milk chocolates. After one look, I cut my eyes to the side to notice his whereabouts.

Without a word to anyone, he left the store.

"Miss Baxter, do you know that person?"

The plump lady behind the counter nodded that she did. She shrugged. "Harmless, honey. Pay no attention to him. Made up your mind?"

"I'll take two of those," I said, pointing to the chocolate-dipped nut clusters. And three sticks of horehound. Thank you, Miss Baxter."

Through the store's large window I could see Father walking up the street. I ran out to meet him.

"Are you alright, Gracie? You look positively mortified."

"See that fella crossing over? Do you know him, Father?"

After taking a look in the direction of the stranger, he shook his head. "Don't believe so. Why do you ask?"

"Oh, no reason. He's just a curious one, I guess."

"Can we head back inside? I've got some business with Jim. Also, honey, I still need to stop in at the apothecary. In fact, if you like, you can go over to the ladies' shop instead."

"No. No, I'll stay with you for now."

We entered along with a young couple and their baby. I was content to keep an eye out the front window and picked through a selection of small hand tools for the garden but only for a pastime. I was ready to leave except for wanting to see Sister.

"See anything you need?" Father's voice from behind startled me. He was carrying a bag. "Next door, now. More liniment for Trojan Girl's leg, then we'll be on our way."

Outside, passersby acknowledged him. "Senator Maxwell, good to see you!" and "Senator, you're doing a great job for us!"

"Senator! Senator Maxwell, wait up there." A rustic-looking gentlemen with sandy-gray hair, waving a straw hat, rushed across the cobblestone street. He had a smile as warm as toast and a voice to match.

"Why, Geoffrey Hagan. You ol' son of a gun."

The two men stood by the curb and shook hands, looking as completely opposite as any two men could—Father in his tailored trousers and waist-coat and Mr. Hagan in overalls. His collarless shirt could have been one of Father's undershirts.

"Thought you'd like an update on my son," he said, and the corners of his eyes crinkled in delightful lines as he spoke. "I've got you to thank, Senator, for dangling Detroit like a caramel apple on a string in front of him."

Father smiled, obviously waiting to hear the outcome of his influence. "Ford Factory? That right? He sure took a liking to my Tin Lizzy alright. Remind me of his name."

The man held his hat by its brim, slowly rotating it in both hands. "Simon's his name. You had him a-goin'. Ford Factory to begin with. Policeman now. Captain," he said with a modest grin."

"Well, how about that for making good? I knew he wasn't a farmer. There was a city boy in that lad. From the first day I laid eyes on him." He turned to me. "This is my daughter, Geoffrey. Doubt if you two have met. Gracie, this is Mr. Hagan. He's got a place—what? Six miles or so north of here?"

"That's 'bout right. Hello, there, Gracie." The farmer looked straight at me, his eyes twinkling, nodded, then turned again to focus on Father. "Heard about the accident out at the old Peterson place. Felix Delaney was a good man from what I understand. Never had any dealing with him myself. He went and bought the farm from my wife after her husband was killed. Tornado of '20."

Father listened with one ear but acknowledged the glances from several men on the street with the other. Both of Father's eyes were on the passersby.

"Well, listen, I won't keep you from your business, Senator. Haven't seen you near the church since you went and got yourself elected," Mr. Hagan said with a winsome smile. "Don't make yourself too scarce, now, you hear? God's good."

Father flipped the butt of his cigarette to one side. "Yeah, I'll come around," he said in a brusque farewell between nods to passersby.

"Good day, Mr. Hagan," I said. "Very nice to meet you, sir."

He tipped his straw hat, already situated on his head, and gave me a wink.

I liked him. I couldn't help liking a person having eyes that crinkled in the corners with every smile.

"Mr. Hagan's the one who married Hannah Peterson, right? After Zack died on the property."

"Yessiree, Hannah Peterson. And Hagan's had his own tragedy. Lost his first wife not much before." Father seemed to want to reinforce the facts, so I listened intently. "Accidents are just part of living . . . right out of the blue at times. Disastrous barn fires. And a drought can destroy an entire crop. Guess we can lay that on God himself. But farm accidents in particular . . . They just happen all the time. Good man, Hagan. Got a slew of boys, I reckon. Can't imagine more than the one I've got. Trying to make a man of that one." He shook his head. "What say we head on over to your sister's?"

Father held the door of the Model T while I got situated on the seat, a little stirred by his varied comments on the subject of farm accidents. He walked briskly to the front end near the headlamps and cranked the automobile, waited for the familiar successful sound of its start, then hopped in, and we were off. Millicent's house was a short distance down Main Street to the south. He waved to drivers in oncoming automobiles and others in buggies as if we were parading on the Fourth of July.

"You seem a little subdued, honey. Everything alright?"

"Of course! And I have some horehound for Sister. I did eat two chocolates—before they melted."

"Chocolate? Maybe too much? That could certainly explain things."

Chapter 21

There was no need to knock at Millicent's house. "Sister! It is I!" Before I could say it again, I saw her through the glass door sections hurrying from the kitchen, wiping her hands on her apron. From the glow on her face, married life seemed to agree with her.

"Gracie! Come! Come and sit while I finish the last of the beans. Here, you can snap a few, if you would. Tell me about school. What's new in the world of books and dreams of teaching?"

"It's so soon." I sighed, not really wanting to talk about school. "Miss Avery—nothing new there. She's been my teacher forever. Everybody's teacher! But poor Mr. Delaney. How's his wife going to get along?"

"Oh, goodness, I don't know how. I'm more concerned about Father's going to handle the accident. Don't see how you can un-see something as awful as that must have been. You think a thing like that doesn't happen. It does. But the newspaper article . . . Honestly! Here," she said, "a few more beans. How's Mama? Jim and I plan to drive out tomorrow. I must see for myself. And I saw you with that handsome young man—at the funeral. Your secret's safe with me."

"Millicent! Stop! Please! Marcus? For Pete's sake. He's an old man . . . sort of. I'll bet he's eighteen, maybe even twenty. What would I have to do with him, anyway?"

Father came around the corner. I'd practically forgotten he was along.

"Come! Sit. I'll fix you some coffee. You look dashing, Father. Now, both of you. Tell me everything you know. I'm still shocked by the accident. Most folks are, and the newspaper said it all. Too much, didn't it? Honestly!"

But I wanted to turn the conversation back to what Millicent had asked me before. "Mama's getting better. Said so herself. But she's cold all the time. None of us can keep the fire hot enough to suit her. She promised to take a walk with me and Clarice when I return. A short one. She's weak. I think it's to be expected with the croup."

"Gracie," Father said, "it is not the croup. I don't think the doctor can pinpoint what's wrong."

I breathed heavily and sipped my coffee and tried to think I'd grown up enough to speak my mind. "I'm glad you're coming out, Sister."

"I plan to," Millicent said. "Tomorrow, Father. And bring chicken soup. And Mrs. Delaney . . . Any idea how she's doing?

"I 'spect Chester is overseeing things for the most part. I'll take a ride over later today. After lunch, perhaps."

"Everything developing as you'd hoped? I know this investment of time and money in horses is important to you."

"That's a fact. And Gracie shares my enthusiasm. I like that."

"Now, Father. You only hope I will share your enthusiasm." I looked from him to Millicent. "I don't know what Father's going to do without Mr. Delaney's help."

"Oh?" Millicent gave Father a quizzical look. "What does Mama think of all this?"

"She's a bit too ill to be involved. Even if she were well, she'd be pleased for me to find what gives me satisfaction. Horses are such superior creatures. In the night when I lie still, I can hear the sound of their hooves on the track, smell the dirt they kick up, feel the oneness with the race—the burst of pride as the animal passes a competitor. It's an unmatched moment, ladies. Unmatched."

He pulled back, took a sip of coffee. "I might have gone on too long. But mark my words. One day I'll have a champion, and you'll perhaps feel as I do."

"I think I've over-snapped the beans, Sister," I said with a laugh.

"Give them here, Gracie. I've made a hummingbird cake. Is it too early in the day for a slice?"

"A small one, maybe, and then we really should get going." Father squished his cigarette in the ashtray and took another swig of coffee. "You have the little Negro children waiting, Gracie. And I need to check in at the stable."

Chapter 22

F ather's Model T motored us back up South Main Street, around the courthouse and turned onto East Main for the start of the two-and-a-half-mile return trip home. The sun shone brightly in the sky. Not until late afternoon would it bring sweeping shadows of mammoth oak trees across the southern perimeter of Hillbound. Luminous white abstract shapes darted across my eyelids—closed against the sun—and the rest of the world was shut out.

"You're strangely quiet."

"Was my grandfather a good man?"

"'A good man'? In his way, of course. Slave trader, you know. He would beat them and break their spirits if he had to, but there were more where they came from. He'd be proud to know I've become something of a horseman, as he was in Virginia."

"Beat them? Why on earth? He must have been an awful person. Granny Maxwell wouldn't tell me much about him, except that he belonged to the devil. Is that so, Father?"

"What a thing to say! She was a little mixed up in her old age. Pay no attention to whatever she said. You were young anyway. It's hard to understand things when you're young.

"I was ten, Father. I remember her scary hands and scrunched-up face. Reminded me of a dried apple core. And she's buried out in the little plot at the back. I've seen her name on a block of concrete beneath where the tree lines grow thick and the undergrowth weaves spidery webs. I like going there. It's hard not to notice the tombstone that says MILDRED MOSELY MAXWELL. And the stones for the others who've perished for whatever reason at Hill-bound. Why wasn't she buried at the church, like Mr. Delaney?"

"Gracie, my goodness. I think I'm going to have to limit your choco-late intake. Humph! Your granny was a bulldog alright. Came here, settled in, and made a place for herself. Got herself known throughout the area for making Shaker-style crafts. Had the finest needlework around. When she died there were so many people who came by the house that you'd've thought she had a lot of friends."

"But she's buried in the backyard and not at Glen Haven, Father. Why?"

"So she could keep an eye on you."

He liked being clever, often arrogant. Mostly, he liked coming across witty, and being served coffee from a silver pot on a silver platter with china cups and sipping from a cranberry-glass tumbler that made his bev-erage sparkle. But I wanted something to be afraid of. I needed something bigger to learn during the countless hours when I sat on the verandah. Something more to pursue and consider. And I longed for something to love. Not something borrowed or something blue, but extraordinary. Father for sure wanted it to be horses.

Even though I didn't love remembering Granny Maxwell, I forced a smile for Father.

Her memory had a way of creeping in as an uninvited visitor—a super-stitious one at that, with a constant suspicious glare. She'd studied the heavens, stood and gazed at the stars, and at each new moon predicted what would befall. It was her way of inspiring terror, imprinting its mark on my ten-year-old brain.

Shortly before she died, she'd given me her description of Grandfather Maxwell "belonging to the devil" as a warning to be wary. I'd stopped let-ting it unnerve me until now, in my newly awakened interest in what had happened to Moe Lee's eye and what had made him limp before he arrived here from Virginia.

"Oh, well," I said aloud with a helpless shrug, not wanting to give the opportunity to get him veered off and into talking about the Derby, anyway.

"Mr. Delaney had a fine burial. I liked him. And Mister Sam is the nicest man I know."

"Gracie, you'll go with me to the Dade Park, won't you?" Father reached up and wiped his fingers across the automobile's dashboard, then blew off particles of dust. "Perhaps Sam would join us for the race," he said. "Just to see Trojan Girl win would be worth his time."

"What about Mama? Will there be lots of travel required with your new venture?"

"Gracie, it's as if you're turning a deaf ear to my wanting to take you to Dade Park," Father said, his voice resounding like notes on a piano. "What's wrong?"

I felt his hand on mine, unnatural, as if he wanted to try some rare tactic of manipulation to devote my interests to thoroughbred horses and racing. Father was accustomed to getting what he set out to get.

Nothing wrong with that, I thought. *I intend to do the same.* Only not how he was doing it: smoking his cigarette, smoothing his vest, polishing his shoe, flaunting his wealth, down-putting his underlings.

I moved my hand away. The power of his unspoken expectations over the Negro folks had formed a cloud over my heart. Had I mistaken Moe Lee's respect for unexpressed fear? I cringed at the thought that anyone could beat Moe Lee when he was a young person—or, even worse, as a boy—and blind him in one eye or do something to cause him to limp.

"What kind of person would do such a thing? To colored folks or white or anyone for that matter, Father?"

"What *are* you talking about, Gracie? Certainly not anything to do with my taking you to Dade Park!"

"No, not Dade Park, Father. I don't want to go. But thank you."

The notion that something, or someone, had broken Moe Lee was building a case in my mind. Unscrupulous dealings—especially where Negro folks were concerned—were the gist of what Father had said when he talked about his own father. I couldn't stop myself from being preoccupied by the subject.

The clomp of a horse team echoed from the other side of the road. As my home came into view, I looked up at the jib door that stood open to catch a breeze on the upper level. I was still thinking of Moe Lee as he carried his smiles across the acreage. A sense of joy filled me because I was teaching his children, oftentimes chasing the little ones into the thicket to hide when he started our way.

Moe Lee's concern can't keep me from loving to have the children near me, their eyes of wonderment looking into my face, searching it for meaning and light, I thought. *And perhaps, the light of knowledge will take them from their unexceptional existence.*

My two-story home rose against a backdrop of young sycamores, and hollyhocks grew higher than the white picket fence behind them. Its slender white planks dazzled in the sunshine. I squinted in self-defense. In our mere afternoon's absence, twisted watermelon vines seemed to have grown so quickly as to fill the space close by where Father steered the automobile up to the side of the house.

"Are you just going to leave Mama here when you travel?" I hadn't wanted to seem bad-mannered, but his look told me that I had.

Neither had I wanted horse racing to dominate all the happenings at Hillbound, nor for Father to be caught up in thoroughbreds and politics. The words had fallen from my lips with no recourse but to try and cover with a less harsh tone: "She needs you, Father. She's sick."

Father slid from the seat of the Model T and hopped out. "That's why we have Negroes, Gracie. I know she's sick. And Clarice is especially caring of Annabelle. Always has been," he said and opened my door. That is precisely why I had her move in here."

He hiked his foot on the Model T's running board and nonchalantly draped his arm overtop the shiny black door. He gazed at me as only he could and kept on talking. "Your mother is in no condition to hear of horseracing, let alone go with me to Dade Park, or Lexington for that matter. Gracie, I want you to go. You would surely feel the excitement. There's not a reason in the world for life not to go on. She probably won't recover, honey. Indeed, it looks pretty hopeless."

I stepped to the ground and stared off into the distance, batting back tears. "Where were you when the tornado struck? I can remember being terrified."

Shutting the door behind me, he faced the Delaneys' wheat field and pointed a long finger: "I watched as the wind hurled barn parts and debris all around us, Gracie. This property was practically untouched. A few tree limbs here and there, some strewn across the road and in the fields."

I could see the event in my mind's eye, deadly as it was. Father was toneless as he spoke. I could understand why. "Let's go on inside," he said, "shall we? After a bit, I'll ride on over to check on Francine."

"Sure." My mind was made up anyway to go in to be with Mama, go for a walk with her, then read to the children. I went up the front stairs and on into the morning room.

Mama was resting, if not asleep. Her eyes fluttered when I sat in the chair next to her, then closed again. I wanted to tell her about the trip into town and back, and my deepest thoughts about what could have happened in Moe Lee's past. I thought she would want to know about the nice fellow I'd met yesterday at the funeral. Then I decided there was nothing realistic to tell, even if she'd been awake enough to listen, or strong enough to go for a walk—wearing the brooch I'd given her.

After sitting for several minutes, I heard the automobile start up outside. I kissed her cheek, chose a book from the mantle to read to the children, and quietly left the room, heading to the front door. There was time to catch Father before he rolled onto Allensville Road, but I preferred to find the children out back if they were there. Father went alone to check on Mrs. Delaney. Her brother would still be there. Both Willoughbys.

Most likely, I told myself, *Marcus Willoughby would have no reason to want to see me, anyhow.*

⚡︎

Saturday's sun was setting on a glorious horizon beyond the meadow, the hours in it packed from beginning to almost their end without my having rounded up the children. Perhaps it had gotten to be too late in the afternoon, but they were nowhere to be found.

I made my way to the stable to look for Henry. Curry comb in hand and with a weather-beaten look on his face, my brother's inexplicable smile was ready and waiting, it seemed. He dodged Trojan Girl's tail and came out of the stall for a greeting, as glad to see me.

"You've been gone all day, haven't ya? Eaten?"

"Not yet. Clarice had chicken and dumplin's on the stove. Easy to smell them. Besides, it's her usual Saturday meal. Want some? You finished here?"

"I'm ready to call it quits for now. Let's eat. Father up at the house?"

I was sure Henry was going to be mad him having gone to the Delaneys' place. There was no choice but for him to know. I smiled and started out of the stable. Henry latched the stall door and came on behind me.

"So's Father at the house?"

"No, Henry, he's not. Probably be back after a while. Just wanted to check on Mrs. Delaney and the Willoughbys. I don't know how much longer Marcus and his dad are going to stick around."

"Oh, I see." Henry was walking ahead now. "Don't 'spect I have much say in the matter. He's gonna do what he's gonna do."

We had nearly reached the back stoop. Henry turned to me. His face was tired, like a wrung-out rag. "Look, Sis, I know how much you miss Millicent. Emma too. I'm not much for words, but I want ya to know: I love ya, and I'll be here for ya. No matter."

That was it. He went up the steps, took his beat-up old hat off, and hung it on the hook inside the kitchen door.

Clarice had two bowls sitting on the dry sink. "Y'all be wanting some dumplin's?"

I caught the back door and came on inside. The aroma was delicious. My mouth was watering before I'd taken two steps.

"Don't have to ask me twice," Henry said, and Clarice scooped up a ladleful for each of us. "Mother doing any better, Clarice?"

"No, sir. 'Fraid not. She sleeping now. Best she kin do, I guess."

Once Henry and I sat down at the dining table, I looked across at him. He started eating as if he hadn't had a bite in days, shoveling in mouthful after mouthful.

"You said some nice things. Thank you." I blew on a scorching spoonful of chicken and dumplings and held it, wondering how Henry could have put his in his mouth. "I know you're pushing hard to make Father pleased. I'm proud of you. I am. You're my brother . . . and we'll always be family."

"Yeah, Sis. Guess so. I'm glad you came down when you did. I was powerful hungry. Best be getting back." He gobbled down the last bites, pushed his chair back, and moved to leave.

"I love you, too, Henry. I do."

Even with his deep, sad eyes, his face lit up with a smile. I couldn't have been happier than I was in that moment. I finished up and stuck my head into the kitchen. "Wonderful dinner, Clarice."

"Your mama is in for the night, Miss Gracie. Early as it is, she's sleepin' good and sound. Maybe leave her be."

"Alright, then. See you in the morning."

I climbed the stairs, crossed the short distance to my room, and turned up the burner on the oil lamp on the drawer table by my bed. Some daylight still shone through the two windows. I could predict with certainty the blue of the softly shaded floral wallpaper was and always would be my favorite color.

My diary lay on table. I felt for its key beneath the drawer's paper liner, then sank myself into the softness of my feather mattress, unlocked my diary, and with so many things to say, started writing:

September 9, 1922

Where to begin? I am so confused with everything that is happening. Mr. Delaney—killed! It was so awful. His funeral yesterday was very sad. But his brother came, Mister Sam, and he's so nice. He feels almost like another big brother to me. Not to take Henry's place because Henry is dear—even though he can be, well, I don't know how to describe him. But Henry is not in a good spot. It's as if Father has outgrown Hillbound. His horse business is everything to him and he is keen on taking me to see Trojan Girl race at Dade Park. I really don't want to go.

And Henry is having to take care of more than he ever has. He is unhappy. I know it. I see it, and Father doesn't care. He's being too hard on Henry and sometimes mean. Kind of mean, anyway. It's upsetting me, and it's not right that he won't see Mama.

I've been thinking a lot about Moe Lee and how he lives and how we live compared to him. Father won't tell me about him. Not everything, anyway. I think Moe Lee had a hard life before he came here. But that, I'll never know.

I stopped writing and shuddered to think of the word *evil* or that it had a smidgen of a foothold inside our home because Granny Maxwell once lived here or because she should have been buried at Glen Haven Cemetery instead of our backyard. And Grandfather Maxwell—if he was a bad man of some sort. Mean to people. Then I went back to my writing:

The Willoughbys came to the funeral too. From Madison County. Marcus said it was 300 miles away. Too far! But since there are mostly no count boys at school, he— Marcus Willoughby—has caused a flutter somewhere in my mind, if not in my heart. I have had almost no time to think of him since meeting him yesterday. Even so, I am thinking of him now! Nothing can come of it. Of that, I'm certain. But he is ever so handsome—and kind.

I've never met the Petersons, but I don't know why anyone would want to stay on that scary place when so many

horrible things have happened—first Zack Peterson, now
Felix Delaney. Mrs. Delaney's doomed unless she sells the
place and goes back to Madison. Then, for sure, I'd never
see Marcus again!

Completely spent, I closed and latched the diary. My mind was made up: I would be going to the Dade Park Race Track when it opened. If Father could believe he had a winner, I would be there when it happened. *And*, I thought, we *should invite Mrs. Delaney.*

Chapter 23

O ctober arrived with crisp and sunny days. By week's end after the finish of the little house's construction, Luke and the tiny girl named Bertie that he had recently married came to live at Hillbound. An air of excitement surrounded the farm due to the anticipated grand opening of Dade Park racetrack, ninety or so miles straight north of Elkton. Neighbors from all around came to Hillbound to extend best wishes. Most of them were eager to see Trojan Girl on Father's track in her workout with the pint-sized jockey and trainer, and Luke was accommodating.

The beautiful bay with black tail and mane was regal and full of herself, a sight to behold. Trojan Girl seemed to be fancying the jockey and trainer who had come to Hillbound to make her a winner, and no such thing as a rash had been a problem since his arrival.

As race day approached, one had only to observe Trojan Girl in action to appreciate the peak condition that Luke had brought about in a matter of three weeks.

"She's ready for the run, Mister Maxwell." The filly side-stepped as Luke patted her hindquarters. "You're right about the breeders with cramped quarters for their horses—the quality of pasture and training facilities here at Hillbound have certainly helped put our girl in the right frame of mind. No doubt Cloverdale provided a perfect model, but you brought it about."

Luke stepped back, giving Trojan Girl her head, and off she galloped across the pasture, her muscular bay body taking great strides with apparent ease.

Father beamed. "Let her have her way out there for a while. She's got her vigor going, and the folks are loving the chance to watch. Wait'll we get another! Yessiree, might have us a stampede of visitors around the clock. Have t' charge admission." He tossed the last of his cigarette onto the track.

Luke picked it up. "I'm glad to be here, sir. Just want to say that. Hope we can pull off a win. She's demonstrating attitude. Hope she has the same on race day."

Henry stood by, as intrigued as anyone. "Guess I'm a born farmer," he said. "But a man like Father . . . he's good at everything he tries. Politics, horses, farming. You name it. You're like him. You're ambitious."

Moe Lee limped up, as curious as the rest of us. Henry gave him a hearty slap on the back.

"Morning, Moe Lee," I said as he edged in at the fence. What do you think of her?"

"That horse is something, alright." Moe Lee nodded and smiled. "Hidy-do, Miss Gracie," he said with a tip of his hat.

Henry continued. "No telling where all this might take Father. Guess you can get eaten up with the thrill of racehorses. Gets in your blood. Not a thing wrong with it, understand me. And if something suits, that's what matters in the end. But when all is said and done, I'll probably still be a farmer."

"You is a good one at that, Mister Henry," Moe Lee said "What if no one at Hillbound wanted to farm? That'd be a problem, alright."

"That's the way it should be, too, Henry," I said, "but I'm going to the racetrack."

Luke's coming to take over the responsibilities for Trojan Girl had lightened Henry's burden. With that and the respite from the harvested tobacco crops and the relief of having them laid up in the barn behind us, Henry was more at ease than I'd seen him lately. The track in front of us and the excitement of the upcoming race at Dade Park was enough to have us all enjoying high spirits.

"Clarice said maybe I should stay close to Mama, not go up to the track, but I think I will. It sure would be fun to see Trojan Girl race, wouldn't it?"

Henry wagged his head. He and Moe Lee exchanged amused glances. "I'd better mosey on, y'all," Henry said, a full grin on his face.

"Me too." Moe Lee tipped his hat and limped off.

I stood at the fence for a while, wanting to think that my going to the races would make Father proud. And happy. *Everyone wants to make sure Father's happy. Don't they?* I thought.

Chapter 24

Race day arrived, partly cloudy and seventy-one degrees. The unseasonably warm, late-November Saturday near Henderson, Kentucky, came and went without me. Mama was worse, and Clarice put her foot down about my leaving. Given her opinion, horses—thoroughbred or otherwise—were certainly not my concern with my mama so ill. With Thanksgiving less than two weeks away, it was some consolation to have something more to keep me looking forward.

Upon Father's return from Dade Park, the mood at Hillbound was less than gay. He had little to say to me about the particulars, only that Trojan Girl had not won the race. In the days leading up to Thanksgiving, Father was not around. Henry indicated simply that he was looking to deal with the sale of Trojan Girl and possibly the purchase of another thoroughbred. Not until several days following the race did facts leak that Trojan Girl had failed even to place at Dade Park. The loss more than explained the mere glimpses I had of Father's embittered attitude. It was a sorry replacement for his commanding personality.

Thanksgiving Eve posed lots of hope for an eventful day tomorrow. Millicent and Emma and their husbands and Father's only two grandchildren were expected, and Mama was showing a little sign of strength. The kitchen had Clarice and Odelia going in circles around each other.

I was purposefully absent when it came time to cook.

Father was rallying, it seemed, determined somehow to put a winner's spin on things—at least during the telephone conversation he was having in the hallway. Any conversation on the newly acquired telephone drew esteemed attention. Moreover, a conversation with Father multiplied my good excuses to abandon piano practice. I was poised to take my turn with him but kept my seat on the velvet stool.

In one swift move Father took the receiver from his ear and calmly dropped it in its cradle. He watched it swing there for a few seconds as if he were in need of a couple of seconds to fashion his announcement before leaving the front hallway. Confidently he strolled in, obviously pleased with his call, and moved across the drawing room in strides as straight as a walking stick.

"Well, well," he said with a flourish. "I've invited Francie to join us for Thanksgiving dinner. Plans have fallen through for the Willoughbys to spend it with her—as she had previously hoped—and I certainly think she should have a festive place to dine, don't you, honey?"

He lit up a cigarette and blew a smoke ring into the air. "I'm sure Chester will appreciate us looking out for his sister until his pottery business allows him to break away. Quite possibly that's going to be in a few weeks. Christmas would be the perfect time. Special times are hard ones to spend—"

"Alone?" Henry said and meandered into the drawing room with a disagreeable look. "Plans are just changing or falling through all around us, aren't they? So you're saying that Mrs. Delaney—and it's *Francie* now, is it? —is coming here? For Thanksgiving dinner? Why would you not consider us—our family—gathering, coming together for the first time in months? Mrs. Delaney is hardly part of the family."

"She's a neighbor," Father said. "That counts for something. Your mother would approve of us being neighborly." His tone was smooth, his eloquence rekindled.

"'Neighborly,' yes, Father. But—"

"Things have a way of working out. It's true, Chester and Marcus would have been good company for her at Thanksgiving, but things happen. There'll be other occasions when they can be with her. Francie said there was talk of them coming for Christmas. We should be good neighbors in the meantime."

Henry took a seat on the divan and bent forward, face down in his hands.

Father appeared to be sufficiently disgusted with Henry's intrusion. "You have business, don't you, Henry? I was going to ask Gracie to play a piano selection for me. You're welcome to stay if you've finished up with the chores. But if you're intent on arguing about what a good neighbor does for a lonely widow, then maybe you'd be better off elsewhere."

Henry sat back for a few seconds, stunned, I thought, as I was. Then he stood, his angular jaw hardened against the insult. With exaggerated movements he left the drawing room.

"You and Henry bicker over the silliest things," I said, cupping my hands over the piano keys. After two chords I stopped. "I hope Mama feels like eating Thanksgiving dinner with us at the table. I'll plan to help her get dressed if she does."

I twisted on the stool to see if he agreed. "Do you think Marcus and Mr. Willoughby will spend Christmas here? For sure?"

"Ah-ha!" Father's "ah-ha's" always had a jovial ring to them. This one was steeped in suspicion. "Marcus, is it? Nothing's been cast in stone, but Francie does need help when it comes to family matters. Sam's outta the picture with all his obligations at Cloverdale. That leaves Chester . . . and Marcus . . . to help her make adjustments. Losing Felix and all . . . Been awfully, awfully, hard on her."

Chapter 25

—◦◦◦◦◦—

T hanksgiving morning passed in a flurry with Clarice and Odelia preparing food fit for a family of eight adults plus Emma and Arnold's
two young ones. And our guest. Mrs. Delaney's arrival had put an
unusual tension in the air at Hillbound.

Mama had suffered more in the last several hours than any other recent
ones. The small amount of gained strength she'd shown had disappeared. I
could hear her in the night, and when daylight broke through the windows
in my second-story bedroom, I had heard again the agony and suffering
she endured.

"Mother's more ill than anyone told me," Emma said after coming
from the morning room. "I'm not sure she can make it to the table. Says
she wants to try, though. I wish Father hadn't ask Mrs. Delaney, honestly.
It's just awkward under the circumstances."

"Yessum. She's done gone and took a turn overnight. I does what I can."
Clarice plopped a feather pillow on the chair closest to the dining room
door. "She can sits right here," she declared as Millicent came through
the back door laden with a caramel cake and Jim followed with two large
Mason jars filled with boiled custard.

The house was filled with the aroma of roasting turkey, and it wasn't
long before mounds of food covered the sideboard. Then came the knock
on the front door. The shift in gaiety was noticeable. The preschoolers were
hushed by Arnold with an index finger pressed to his lips, which prompted
Clarice to hurry them off to the kitchen.

Mrs. Delaney was ushered inside. Father was polite, in his usual manner, and helped her remove her wrap, revealing how beautifully dressed she was in a form-fitting blue dress. A long strand of pearls casually draped down the front of it.

Father took her jar of peaches and handed them off to Henry, and there was no mistaking Henry's sulk for a smile. Father had managed to bring out the worst in him. The odd tension between them was noticeable.

Even so, everyone else welcomed Mrs. Delaney with a dose of Hillbound's graciousness, and after several mad dashes from the kitchen, all lay in readiness for the feast to begin—except that Mama needed to be helped to the table. She was awake, but I was concerned, for as much as she wanted to be present, Clarice wasn't in favor of it.

Father leaned on the table, elbows positioned on either side of his plate. "Bet y'all wanna hear all about the recent episode with Trojan Girl at Dade Park."

Odelia brought in the platter with a bronzed turkey solidly balanced thereon. Clarice and I gave each other a look that both of us knew meant it was time for Mama. "Sit, Miss Gracie. 'Delia and I kin get her."

"Wait for Mother, and we'll say a blessing," Henry said as a surprise for us all.

"If you say so, Henry. And you can do the honors once Annabelle gets in here."

The children could be heard jabbering over their food in the kitchen. Emma passed the sweet tea. Mrs. Delaney just smiled. Everyone else looked like they were waiting for a chair leg to break.

"Jim, I know you're more interested in groceries and the like, but you just might've been amazed to see that crowd at Dade Park. Why, it exceeded four thousand spectators. They jammed into the grandstand to view that very first race. A glo-*rey*-ous day it was too."

We could hear Mama shuffling as she came down the hallway, making her way to the dining room in unsteady steps with the help of Clarice and Odelia.

Henry rushed to help.

"The fans were out in great numbers," Mrs. Delaney said, reinforcing Father's enthusiasm for the race that had recently taken place.

Mama entered weak and pale. Her hair had grayed almost overnight, it seemed. Deep lines had etched themselves into her face. She opened her mouth but slowly closed it. Clarice and Odelia helped her to her chair.

Father glanced at her and picked up his fork. I wondered if Mama saw his repulsed look.

"I'll pray," Arnold said, and Henry looked relieved as Emma's husband bowed his head.

With the amen spoken, Father took a bite. "The starting gate was pulled by dang mules, if y'all can believe it! And there I was parading Trojan Girl to the post for the first race. It was unbelievable."

Arnold looked impressed. Henry's face was distorted. He had not taken the first bite, waiting to speak, but Father continued: "Purses for the entire opening meet shaded sixty-two thousand dollars!"

Collard greens were passed. Biscuits followed. Jim looked concerned, chewing slowly on a bite of turkey.

Mama's eyes no longer sparkled in shades of sky blue but sat instead in dark, hollowed caves. Circles hung like aprons beneath them. I was afraid to hand her even the butter dish for fear she couldn't hold it. "Want me to butter your biscuit, Mama?"

She nodded yes.

"Mrs. Delaney," Millicent said, "have some stewed apples. Mother canned them back last fall when she was feeling—

Mama slid from her chair, crumpled in a heap on the floor. I jumped to my feet, afraid she'd passed out, and Emma rushed to help.

"Stay there, everybody. We need a doctor," Emma said with urgency.

Father kept his seat. "On Thanksgiving? You know what the doctor said."

Arnold pushed his chair back from the table, ready to help. Clarice scurried over to Mama and fell on her knees beside her.

"You need to call the doctor. Or I will, Father," Henry said. "We can't let Mother go on like this."

"Perhaps I should go," Mrs. Delaney said.

"That isn't necessary. Everyone just simmer down. Annabelle has had spells like this. Clarice knows precisely what to do. Go ahead, Clarice. Get her to bed." He shot Henry a warning look.

I followed the three who were helping her and carried Mama's pillow as Father started in again. "I, in the first meet, was—"

"Robert was one of several notable horsemen who surfaced. He's too modest to tell you. I so wished Felix could have been part—"

It was easy to hear Mrs. Delaney filling in the details of all the excitement. When I returned to the table, Father had taken over the telling of the horse race.

"Yep!" he said. "We were right there for the momentous occasion. Right there as the gates opened for the first thoroughbred meet. Barrett Dade—the owner, of course—waved to the crowd from the steps of the tower—"

"Arnold, tell us, since Father may not want to rehash the fact that our filly not only did not win, she did not even place, how are things going out at your way?" Henry was foaming at the mouth.

Father ignored him. "Except for the fact that I'm gonna turn her into a broodmare . . . I'd sell her. Might sell her anyway. Start over with our new gal. Yep. Free Rein is bound to do better. And if she can't, then another one will. I'll bet on that. She'll outperform 'em all come May. The Oaks is gonna see what we're made of here in Todd County. Yessiree! Wait'll they see what I come back with next year. Free Rein's Derby material. Judge could've been a little off where Trojan Girl was concerned anyway, if you know what I mean. Odds were calculated by hand."

"You picked up a healthy sum, Robert," Mrs. Delaney said. "So, no complaining. Especially on Thanksgiving!"

Henry looked like he was going to come across the table, and I thought of Mama having to lie in a makeshift bed in the darkened morning room. I got up to go check on her. "Would you excuse me?"

Mrs. Delaney glanced at Father. "Marcus is coming for Christmas. Chester, too, of course."

Positively nothing else had felt thankworthy during the whole meal. Henry tossed his napkin aside and left the table.

Chapter 26

O utside, a mid-December wind howled, but still it could not drown out the cries for help coming from the morning room. The doctor had left, offering no hope for Mama. He'd come and gone several times since Thanksgiving. And then the endless nights had begun.

Clarice bathed her, put cool compresses under her armpits, and suctioned her nose and mouth when her lungs began filling with thick red fluid. Sometimes she seemed to know us, and sometimes she didn't. We took turns holding her hand: Emma, Millicent, Henry. When it came my turn, she held mine tight and told me she'd come help me cut hollyhocks when she could. Millicent gazed at me through tears. We both knew she wasn't talking about getting better.

Free Rein had come to Hillbound. A horse. Father was so absorbed that it didn't seem to matter how his attraction defiled his heart and relationships.

Slowly Mama's memory and reasoning skills dissolved. She couldn't communicate much at all—a few words, maybe, or a gesture or two. One day she screamed for her mother and fell out of bed. After that she went downhill very fast. She began vomiting, a lot, and couldn't eat. Not even the softest of food. She fought the air, swung her arms, and made noises, battling with everything she had left.

I looked at her, helpless, and had to leave the room again to cry.

Finally, Father came in, walking soullessly into the room with me, bypassing Henry's blank stare and his cursory comment about the arrival of Free Rein at the stable. Mama seemed to somehow sense his presence.

A hush fell over the room that mid-December morning. Her breathing changed—quieter now, gaspy, like a fish out of water. Her lips turned bluish-gray, the same shade that pressed its ugliness against every windowpane in the house.

The hours passed, and the clock's hands moved to one o'clock. Mama's eyes had been closed for a time, and yet now she opened them and looked up, beyond any one of us standing by her side. Henry was near me. Millicent. Emma. Father stood off by the fireplace, the flicker of its flames coloring his face.

Clarice put a log on, stoked the embers, and left the room.

Mama's breaths got farther apart until eventually there was one breath every few minutes. And then we realized there were going to be no more.

I felt a grip on my throat and a tightness in my lungs, a racing in my head. My hands were covered with clamminess, and in a single moment everything that was Mama became a heap of nothingness. Gone.

I dropped to the rug, unable to stand, unable to speak. Unable to stop the sobbing, I scratched at the hardwood floor, blanketed with a patterned wool rug. The floral walls in celadon and pink drooped around me, hushed and silent.

On hands and knees, I crept to Mama's side. So peaceful now.

Sister crumpled beside me on the floor. Then Emma.

And Father came to the bedside. Stoic. Strong. Without a whimper he lifted her hand and took the ruby and pearl ring from her finger.

Henry edged in closer, soothed back the gray wisps of her hair that had fallen across her forehead. Tenderly he kissed the place where her curls had been.

Mama lay untroubled on the borrowed bed that belonged upstairs in Sister's room, and my heart and I were alone to walk my Mama home. Grief entangled me like the brambles in the backyard cemetery, and when my eyes closed on a day that ended Mama's cries forever, the farm fell quiet.

—◦◦◦◦◦◦—

I sat up with a start, my heart pounding. Quickened by the unknown, I listened from my bed for the song of a bird or lowing cattle that should have lifted my crushed spirit. But my room was silent. The windows were closed shut against December's frosty morning, the day after Mama died.

I wrapped my robe around me and went to a window, watching from the second floor through tears as the horse-drawn hearse slowly pulled away from the picket fence and rolled north past the frozen, flowerless landscape along Allensville Road.

My legs seemed to go numb as I waited for the carriage to go out of sight beyond the barren trees. I moved away from the window, feeling like the numbness was more than in my legs. The room was cold. Last night's fire had all but died down in my fireplace. I laid a log on the embers and stoked it with the encouragement it needed to burn, then sat down on the hearth and warmed my hands close to the awakening flames. The house was morbidly quiet. I hadn't heard a door slam.

The picture of Mama tenderly holding me as a baby close to her breast sat next to my diary on my bedside table. Young Henry, Millicent, and Emma stood on either side of Mama's knees. Father stood in the background in the photograph. I wanted to scream at him, accuse him of all manner of unkind things, and press him to tell my why. *Why* he'd deserted Mama.

Is that what illness does?

I pushed myself off the hearth and carried the image back and sat down again, touching Mama's beautiful face beneath the glass. She had begged me to leave her, not wanting me to see what was happening with her. And now I could not *unsee* her agony or Father's callous disregard.

Grief taunted me, like a low-winded voice—Granny Maxwell's, perhaps—warning me of impending doom, and none of my trifle petty complaints about hating to cook or piano lessons were anywhere close to reasonable now. How could I have ever considered leaving Mama to go to a silly horse race, or not know at Thanksgiving the end was so near? Why had I not understood that her telling me she would "come to help me cut hollyhocks when she could" might be the last words Mama would ever speak?

It must have been awhile that I sat holding the frame. I'd neglected the fire. The room had chilled. I'd just put on another log when there was knock on my door.

"Sis. Sis! Let me in."

Henry was waiting on the other side when I opened it. His expression was pathetic, his thick brown hair tossed. I was sure I looked much the same.

"They've taken Mama to the funeral parlor." He caught himself, swallowed hard.

"I know. I saw. Did Father go?"

"No, he didn't go. No need, I suppose. He's in his office. Haven't seen him since the Latham's came for her. Why don't you go and get dressed? Come on down. I'll fix us some coffee."

"I don't drink coffee, Henry, but I'll get dressed and meet you."

He shrugged off his absentmindedness and turned to go.

Before shutting the door, I suddenly reached out, needing him more than I ever had, and he put his arms around me. "Henry, will we get through this funeral? And what about Christmas coming . . . without Mama?"

"We will, Sis. I'll be here for ya," he said with enough conviction to give me hope.

Dressed and pulled together—for the moment, anyway—I went down the stairs as Moe Lee came through the hallway with a bundle of logs in his arms. He nodded at me before he ducked into the morning room. At the bottom step I could see Clarice folding the bedding in the morning room.

Someone had taken the mattress from the bed. It now leaned against the far wall, and the place where Mama had lived since last spring was gone.

Chapter 27

I pulled my layers of clothing around me as Father brought the auto-mobile to a stop at the side of Mt. Zion Baptist Church. It was just the two of us in the Model T. Henry had refused to join us for the Sunday Christmas Eve service. I suspected it was due to the plan to meet Mrs. Del-aney and the Willoughbys here. The mention of it had brought about yet another squabble between Father and Henry.

Father opened the Model T's door for me. Somewhat distracted as he was by the comings and goings of his constituents, he offered to give me a hand.

I needed no such thing. I was, however, interested to see if Marcus Willoughby had arrived.

In the commotion, no one seemed to have heard me quietly inquire as to his whereabouts. It was probably just as well since he'd most likely have forgotten about having ever met me in September. Even so, I remained slightly infatuated with him or the memory of his fetching appearance. Most of me was just plain lonely.

Surefooted, I walked out across the frozen ground toward the church. I tried not to let it register too heavily that it was Christmas Eve, because inside I was broken off like a limb from a dead tree. Snapped, and the gaiety seemed to be a ridiculous effort to celebrate a whole lot of nothing.

I hadn't set foot in this place since Mother's funeral. Even though it had been only two weeks ago, it had been a lifetime. I wouldn't have been here now had it not been Christmas Eve. As much as I appreciated the beauty of the white steeple that pointed right up though the barren trees, I still might never come again. The building was sure to be drafty and cold.

I walked into the church, shivering, and looked closely at the pew where I'd steadied myself to honor Mama. It had been cold then too. The steeple had pierced the same blue sky. I cringed at the awful sight where Mama's coffin had sat for endless minutes while the preacher talked.

But because of Christmas Eve, out-of-hand children and the elderly with colorless features and Bibles in their hands filed inside, crowding the aisles, talking before the Sunday service. I smiled at them, trying not to think of Mama in a box with dirt piled high. We hadn't been back to Glen Haven Cemetery since the day she was buried. Still, I could picture the cold gray tombstones and flowers in bunches, frozen. Certainly by now the winds would have carried them away.

Father had still not come inside when I caught a glimpse of the automobile carrying Mrs. Delaney, Chester Willoughby, and Marcus.

Marcus Willoughby.

He didn't waste time getting out of the automobile and didn't wait for Mrs. Delaney, leaving the task to Chester, who was assisting her. No longer wearing the black dress or a veil over her face, Mrs. Delaney seemed to have resumed a quite lovely style of dress. An animal fur of some sort snugged up to her neck and down her backside, and parts of its relative had been made into a chic little hat.

Father made haste to greet them as they entered the church, and I continued to observe the arrival of miscellaneous folks. As interesting as they were, when it came to friends, fifteen-year-olds were on the stick's short end. Jean Morgan was nowhere to be seen.

Marcus hurried on ahead of his family, came inside Mt. Zion, and eased past some slow-walking churchgoers. It was then that I realized he was making a beeline toward the window where I stood.

A heavyset elderly lady with a cane hobbled past me, and I backed up as close to the window as I could. As I did so, the potted plant sitting on its ledge fell with a decisive smack to the floor, and all heads turned. Marcus was there in an instant. "I'll get it. You just stand there and look like I'm to blame." He gave me a mischievous grin and stooped to pick up the pieces.

I had not felt lighthearted in—I couldn't remember when. Nor could I remember whether or not it had caused a sensation as warm as this. Seeing Marcus squatted, looking up at me, I had to tell my heart not to pound out of my chest. "Jesus wept," I said, making this moment the first time I'd come close to a smile since Mama died. "That's too bad. The pot is worthless now, I guess."

With his hand he swept the pile of dirt off to the side and stood up to place the broken pieces on the window ledge. Having taken care of the accident and whisked his hands, he was all smiles. "A potter wouldn't see it that way," he said and gingerly laid the last piece on top of the other pieces.

"See what, what way?" More questions than I was prepared to ask out loud—especially to a mere budding acquaintance—crossed my mind with the assurance I'd better hold back on my usual inquisitiveness. I could mask my attraction to his bounteousness with a very deep breath, but in truth, I was laden with guilt at how much his presence meant.

I was left no choice but to be enchanted by his gentlemanly quality. It had surpassed, during our very brief reunion, every recollection of him that I'd hung onto. He was older. Of that I was sure since not a fellow at the school, in or out of harvest time, could have matched his maturity.

"What I mean is this: don't you worry about the broken pieces. A potter is intent on revealing a vessel's purpose . . . because it's his creation, it's his say-so. Especially if it is cracked."

"Well, that sounds practical," I said with a grin, "but I think the pot's more than cracked."

"You're right. Gosh, it's good to see you again, Gracie. And nice to be here with family for Christmas. I know my dad is glad to see Aunt Francine," he said at the same moment Jean Morgan brushed by us with a silly smirk that reflected her insider-girlfriend's knowledge of my crush on Marcus and a silly tenth-grader wave.

But my eyes never left Marcus's attentive gaze despite my knowing Jean was continuing to wave as she and her parents took a seat. Marcus had me convinced of his pleasure in being in Todd County for Christmas, and I was nodding in affirmation.

"Listen, Gracie," he said, lowering his voice, making me feel what he had to say deserved a resonant tone of its own. "I'm so sorry about your mother's passing. This has to be a really tough time for you." He seemed to look straight through me as if he knew my heart.

Without thinking, I turned away, fighting back tears, knowing I could say nothing without consequences. I struggled to keep my composure, swallowing hard. A smile was impossible.

I felt conspicuous, and Mrs. Delaney was motioning for Marcus to sit down, and if Marcus and I weren't the last ones standing, we were close to it.

"You might be surprised," he said with a happy uptick and sufficient calmness to bridge an awkward lull in the conversation we'd begun, "but I should know about broken pots. I've seen examples time and time again with my father—when he fixed what looked unfixable. It's the marvel that transpires between the potter and the clay. But for now," he said, guiding us away from the window, "we'd better sit down. Here, Gracie, next to me."

I squeezed in next to a man who gladly scooted down to make room. "I hope you didn't think I was making light of your dad's business," I whispered to Marcus.

"Not at all," he whispered back. "Just wanted you to know a potter can turn brokenness into a masterpiece. It's what makes his stoneware worthy—valuable. That's an amazing connection between the creator and his creation."

The piano chords sounded the beginning of an unfamiliar hymn—most of them were. My tears were held at bay, and I smiled an appropriate smile for the people who were looking our way.

Jean was seated with her parents on the pew in front of us. "Hello, Gracie. Merry Christmas," she said, turning almost completely around to speak.

"Merry, Merry Christmas, Jean!" I said with a big smile, unable to introduce Marcus this close to time for the service to begin. Everyone stood as the lady at the piano began playing a song, one I actually recognized. I mouthed the words to "Hark! The Herald Angels Sing," knowing I should not make myself heard.

With the song's end and the rustling sound of people seating themselves ceased, the preacher began to speak. More than once I felt the imminent intention of Jean to turn and have another look at Marcus, perhaps put together for herself questions that would need to be asked on an upcoming school day. But she remained face forward for the duration of the sermon.

Mrs. Delaney had barely let the service come to an end when she started a conversation with Father, chattering first with him, then pulling in her brother, not looking to include or interact with strangers. Dutifully, she engaged me and Marcus, keeping us from peeling off to continue the topic he and I had started by the window.

I wanted to tell Marcus privately it was his words that had held my attention for the last hour, not the preacher's, but the small crowd had its own way of guiding the direction we went, and no such moment presented itself.

Mr. Willoughby was talking to Father as we left the church. Mrs. Delaney was adding in her two cents. "I'm trying to get her to sell you the farm, Robert," he said. "Come on back to Madison County. But she's insistent on staying. She'd surely be welcome at our home, right Marcus?"

He stood next to me, providing an added layer of warmth. If, in the jostle of people, his head gave an affirmative nod, I missed it.

"I've so many decisions to make," Miss Francine said. "It's been such a help to have you here. Proves a brother is a good person to have around." She flung her fur extension across her shoulder with a swift flick of her hand. Marcus ducked to avoid the oncoming pelt.

It was colder as we walked to our automobiles than when we'd gone inside an hour earlier. We all pulled our outerwear closer and tighter around us against the misty, biting breeze.

"Give it time, Chester. She's dealing with a lot," Father said. "We both are, considering our losses. Christmas and all . . . makes them seem that much worse. Best I can do is hope y'all will have yourselves a merry one."

"And the same to you. And regards to Henry for a Merry Christmas. We'll be startin' on back to Madison County come Wednesday. I'll ring you up. Perhaps we'll have an opportunity to see you before then. You and Gracie. Henry too."

Goodbyes said, our Model T rolled down the slope of a hill, and except for the crunch of the tires on the frozen dirt, the ride home started out quiet. But I had to know. "Is Mrs. Delaney going to sell the old Peterson place, Father?"

"Don't know, but Francine sure seems to think Marcus has taken a liking to you, Gracie."

"Based on what, for Pete's sake?" I quickly decided I didn't need to hear Miss Francine's take on the subject. "Let's just not talk about Marcus."

"Now, now. Evasiveness doesn't become you, Gracie."

"Alright. He's extremely kind, but he won't be back. He lives very far away. He's going off to Asbury College next year. He plans to be a preacher. He's probably nineteen—too old. So he's not exactly my type. And I want to go to college."

"Whoa! You know your type, do you? I might've heard that before." Father took his eyes off the road, looked over at me with a quizzical head tilt. "And college? Mighty ambitious. You'd be the first. Although . . . Henry talked about it, but he's sure as heck not cut out for it."

I stared through the windscreen where a light snow was starting to stick, not liking the remark. "Why are you so down on Henry?"

Father turned on the wiper blade and repositioned himself on the automobile seat. "One day you'll understand—"

"And I've heard that before, Father. Understand what? That you like Mrs. Delaney?"

His head whipped around. "Where'd that come from? She's a neighbor who needs a friend. Of course we like our friends."

I sat for a moment, trying not to be a pill. "Has she cast a spell on you? That's what Granny Maxwell would say."

Father took a breath deep enough to swell his chest. His nostrils flared. "Stop, Gracie. My mother mighta been a mite superstitious, but not deranged. My goodness! I wouldn't entertain such views if I were you." He turned the automobile onto Allensville Road. Hillbound was spread before us like the frozen wintry scene in a snow globe. He relaxed his hands on the steering wheel.

From deep inside, I wanted to fight him and keep him from getting away with whatever it was that I was supposed to understand.

"Mama *needed* you." There, I'd said it, and the wait for the sky to fall came and went. I pulled a glove off and with my bare knuckle wiped away the tear that had started down my cheek.

"Here," he said and reached into the breast pocket of his overcoat. "Not trying to make a big thing of Christmas, but I want you to have this."

The automobile swerved as he held out Mama's ring. The ruby sparkled in the center of the pearl petals that encircled it. Ceremoniously, he laid it in my lap as if it were a peace offering, then stopped the Model T in the usual manner up next to the house and paused to watch me push the ring onto my finger.

On that day—when? When I'm old and gray, I thought, *then and only then, I'm supposed to understand and accept that Father was attracted to Mrs. Delaney before Mama had been gone less than two weeks.* Grieving felt like a clay pot hitting the floor and shattering. "Sometimes I think I can't live without her," I said.

He shut the automobile engine down and hastily pushed the door open. "You'll manage, honey," he said. "Got your whole life ahead of you."

He sounded indifferent.

I didn't wait for him to come to open my door. Token gestures of courtesy felt inadequate to cover dirty little violations. As much as I wanted to motion for to him to leave me sitting in the Model T with snow accumulating on the windscreen, my feet touched the ground. I needed my father as deeply as my mother had needed the husband who'd given her a ruby ring to signify his promise.

Father stood erect, holding open the door. His eyes were fixed on a point in the distance.

Perhaps it was the cold that caused the peevish ritual I saw behind his smile, but I placed my trust in him to steady my steps as a child learning to walk. I saw in him the man whose outreach offered only a fleeting significance. I wanted a strong arm with a gentle hand, a father, not a dutiful offering on a slippery piece of Hillbound that was sure, in time, to give way beneath me.

———◦◦◦∫∫◦◦◦———

The telephone in the hallway rang on Christmas morning. With Clarice's continual presence no longer necessary, it was Odelia who had the receiver to her ear before I reached the last step down to the rug in the front hallway. Thanks to Henry, a fresh cedar tree graced the spot in the morning room where Mama's makeshift bed had been.

"Miss Gracie," Odelia said, "this be for you." She held out the receiver as if it were an unsavory object that I should take from between her long fingers as soon as possible.

"Who is it?" I asked Odelia, taking it from her hand, but she shrugged and was retreating to the kitchen without a sound before I'd said hello into the mouthpiece. "Yes? Gracie Maxwell here."

I immediately recognized the deep, throaty voice once the operator made the connection.

"Marcus?" I hedged. "Merry Christmas!"

"I wanted to say a Merry Christmas to you, too, Gracie. We had so little time to talk yesterday at the church. My dad and I are going back to Madison County day after tomorrow."

I heard the hesitation. Unsure what to say, I butted in with a nervous little laugh. "That's soon. Thanks for picking up the pieces . . . at the church. I made a mess, didn't I?" Immediately, I wished I'd said something more mature, or anything more interesting than a sentence about a broken flowerpot.

He was already coming to my rescue, for I heard Christmas music in the background. It had gotten louder as I talked. "Can you hear it? 'Silent Night'? Listen," he said.

The melody came through on the telephone, falling on my ear with the essence of magical moments, powerful and tender. "Yes, of course,"

I said, glancing across to the morning room and the cedar tree, and I stopped breathing long enough to listen to the peaceful sound of Christmas filling my soul. When the song was finished I could hear Marcus smiling. "Like it?"

"Of course! I heard it all, Marcus," I said, shooing Henry away as he came down the staircase, acting out his intention to come eavesdrop. He shook his head and moseyed on into the drawing room. "I loved it. How beautiful!"

"'I loved it,'" mimicked Henry on the other side of the doorway.

I gave him a serious frown and turned my back. "Thank you. I don't have anything in return, but I hope you have a lovely day today."

"It was my gift. I have Aunt Francine to thank for the use of her gramophone. Beautiful, yes. I'm glad you liked it. Are you having family?"

"Your aunt has all the latest, doesn't she. And stylish. I love that!" I squirmed at being so silly. "We're going out to my sister Emma's later on. Gonna be different without my mother," I said, fiddling with the telephone cord to ease my jitters. "She'll have a houseful. Emma, I mean."

"The first Christmas without our mother . . . I remember how difficult. Listen, Gracie, I don't have an idea when my dad and I will be back this way. Even if Dad comes, I'm not sure how to get here if my work . . . How about I write you sometime?"

"Would you? I'd like that," I said. "Merry Christmas, again, Marcus."

With our addresses exchanged and our greetings ended, I hung up the receiver and went to the Christmas tree in the morning room. The curtains were pulled back from the windows, and daylight streamed across the room. No shadows, no lingering voices—save the one of sweet laughter—and the prickly sensation in touching the luscious green cedar boughs and smelling the fragrance of life in them was the gift left under the tree from Mama to me.

Chapter 28

An awful winter had given way to another lovely May bursting with redbuds in bloom and flowering pear trees down in the meadow, and Hillbound was alive with the enchantment of pre-race day hopes. Father's enthusiasm for a winner at the Oaks and the potential for dealing with Mister Sam for a thoroughbred colt had kept him in a tailspin for weeks.

Bag packed and dressed to the nines, he and Luke had taken off days earlier in the automobile to meet the train carrying Free Rein to Louisville. Here at home, the first signs of springtime were making gentle attempts to replace the barren earth, bringing with them the fresh smell of new grass and the churn of the plows in the fields. The rich aroma of freshly turned soil filled the air.

God seemed relevant somehow in the beauty that presented itself in every direction, making it feel like a most beautiful anointing. Quite possibly it was God's offering of grace for my wounds—still open five months after Mama had died.

It was good to envision her pleasure in digging the soil around where the hollyhocks grew, yet to rise again as they would in midsummer. Moe Lee had cut off their stalks at their bases after last year's flowers faded, so I could expect them to return in their majesty, and I'd hear in my heart Mama's last words, telling me she would come cut them with me. Now, with lessons to do and piano to practice, I headed around the side of the house, intending to go inside.

Bertie was sweeping the verandah. She had made herself useful, and

Hillbound was all the better for her having come to live in the little house on the narrow edge of the property, out by the thoroughbred track.

"Good morning, Bertie. Guess you'll be happy for Luke's return."

"Yes, ma'am. Day after tomorrow." She sounded convincing, but Luke's extended time away had her looking in need of a friend.

"He a good trainer. And jockey. Father says so. Hope he made a winner of Free Rein." She smiled and kept on sweeping. I went inside, bypassed the drawing room not once glancing at the piano, and tiptoed into the morning room as if Mama were still sleeping.

Sundays were lazy that way. School was going well—one week into May and soon to be over—and lessons could wait. Piano could too. The afternoon was young.

"Hi, Sis." Henry's low-throated voice gave me a start.

"What are you doing?" It was plain to see he was doing nothing. I sat down beside him and waited, knowing he had to be thinking of something.

"Hoping Father has a win, or he'll be hard to live with. Got us all in an uproar over that and some new horse. Don't know where it's gonna end. Don't know much of anything except he's being twisted around Miss Francine's little finger. Know what I mean, Sis? She doesn't belong here, but she's here. 'Bout every time I turn around, he's got her coming for dinner."

"She's got no one else, I guess. What else should he do? Besides, I like seeing what she has on. It's always so fashionable. I want—"

"For Pete's sake. Stop! What if they get married? What then? Will pretty dresses make her take Mother's place?" He got up and walked to the cold, black fireplace, his head bent low. "I'm sorry. Honest I am," he said. "It's just that she stayed right there, too sick to lift her head, and Father . . . Father . . ."

"Father couldn't stand to be in here to see her suffer. So, he stayed away. That's what I'm trying to believe. I wanted him here, too, but . . . Henry, this will always be Hillbound, and Mama will always be here."

"You've got your letters from what's his name—"

"Marcus. That's his—"

"Well, fine. You have him and his letters to make you see everything through rose-colored glasses, don't you? And what about Jean? Friends . . .

and freedom to do as you please, Sis. I might've gone off to college, but I'm here. That's all. And Father takes off." Henry leaned against the mantle, tossing his hair, seething in a quiet way.

I looked at the flower ring on my finger, seeing somehow and hearing the truth of what he said." You could go, couldn't you? To college?" I asked, but inside I knew full well the answer.

"Heck, no! You think he would ever let that happen?"

"He loved Mama, didn't he? Mrs. Delaney is just a friend. She's a horsewoman. They're both crazy over horses. I know that, but it's not something that can change what Hillbound is. It's our home, and nothing can change that."

"She's not good, Gracie. She's not. She's not good," he repeated over the *rat-tat-tat* of an oncoming automobile.

The engine noise increased as it pulled to the spot next to the house, then died. Henry shot me a puzzled look, and I returned one of my own. By the time we got to our feet, crossed the room, and walked to the front door, Father had pushed in, all smiles. He dropped his bag at the base of the staircase and left the door standing ajar. "Afternoon," he said, a tilt to his head. "Y'all doing alright?"

Father was poised, perfectly polished in every way, but something was up. I could feel myself nodding affirmatively, but I felt more than a head bob, and he was neither listening nor looking for my answer or Henry's. Furthermore, he did not seem to care, as far as I could tell, that we were about to be caught completely unaware: Mrs. Delaney, gripping a small bag, walked up the steps and across the threshold of our home. Father rushed to catch the door for her. "Here, honey," he said, "let me help you with that."

He relieved Mrs. Delaney of her petite parcel, and she sashayed across the hallway with a smile and look. "Henry, can you give a hand with her others? They're out there in the T," Father said with a back-handed motion to the outside.

It was not what he said, rather how he said it—a designated tone, an in-control and pleased-to-be-there tone. I supposed the worst and was sure Henry had reached the same conclusion. Having taken a step backward as if he'd been kicked, he slipped by me in deference and moved quickly to the verandah, reduced to an errand runner. I saw him cheated out of the privilege to, of his own volition, be a gentleman, his dignity snatched by Father's careless lack of consideration.

Mrs. Delaney was smiling—undeniably fetching—and her features were delicately feminine, her sleek, saucy dress streamlined with a flair that I loved. Father looked at her as if she were the top prize at the county fair.

"Francine and I've tied the knot," he said, "and we're mighty pleased to tell you, Gracie, how happy we are. You're the first to know. Yessiree—no more Mrs. Delaney! This is your new mother." He moved to her side and slid his arm around her waist. They gazed into each other's eyes until I thought they'd seen enough, but it was the kiss that he delivered to her cheek near the ear underneath her low-slung hat that got me. It nearly toppled the hat, and they both laughed giddily over nothing.

Henry, having brought Miss Francine's assemblage of bags up the verandah steps, came inside and set them down with a sigh. I was glad he'd missed the affection.

"You might not've heard, Henry. Francine and I have tied the knot."

Father had not yet ceased to gaze at Miss Francine. Hearing his announcement didn't sound any better the second time around. Henry looked to me for the truth.

"Go on and take those up to the bedroom, Henry," Father said, and Henry started up with them, his head down, his shoulders drooped.

"Please, call me Miss Francine. I'd just love it if you would do that," she said with a polite smile. "We're going to be one happy fam—"

"You went to Cloverdale to get married?" Henry looked from the second step in disbelief, first at Father, then me. And finally at Miss Francine.

Father lit a cigarette and paused long enough to inhale deeply and blow out a stream of smoke. He gave a dismissive wave. "Go on, Henry," he said with his cigarette bobbing between his lips and turned toward me. "Not likely that I needed to make a trip back there since the horse deal was done. I can bring the colt here in a month or so. No rush. The Derby—ah, Churchill Downs—just got us in an exalted state." Father wagged his head with a sense of pride and leaned in to Miss Francine." Didn't it, honey? And possible ownership of the new colt. Yessiree, Bona Fide. He's a winner if I've ever seen one, and of course Francie and I've decided to partner. Makes perfect sense. Merge the two farms. She has great fondness of racehorses. Anything with hair on and four legs."

At the moment I couldn't have cared less about horse talk or describe one beyond its having a tail at one end and ears at the other. I had not missed that in a matter of minutes our neighbor had gone from "Mrs. Delaney" to "Miss Francine" for me and Henry and from "Francine" to "Francie" for Father. But *nothing* would ever elevate her to "Mother" in this house.

Odelia came out of the kitchen and through the hallway bearing a tray of hot tea and shortbread and went into the drawing room.

"Perfect," Father said. "Shall we?"

Henry joined us as we seated ourselves, and Odelia began to pour tea. She handed a cup to Miss Francine, ensuring Father's unspoken expectation for service was fulfilled.

"This is the new Lady of Hillbound, Clarice. You'll refer to her as 'Mrs. Maxwell.'" he said and loosened his tie.

There was no need for Father to look my way or regard my feelings. Henry sat quietly on the green brocade wing chair next to the empty fireplace and twiddled his thumbs.

"Yessir, Mista Maxwell. Yessir," Odelia said and continued pouring tea into other cups.

"I might, however, have been better off boarding Free Rein at Cloverdale. She didn't manage to place, but there's always the chance to run Bona Fide next year. And a whole lot in between! No sense second-guessing myself. Thoroughbred racing's a gamble." Henry didn't like anything being said. He was getting madder by the minute. I think we all knew it.

"Good thing I parked the ol' tin lizzie at the train station. Gave us the flexibility to come and go as need be. Independence . . . a good thing," Father said.

"Yes," Henry said, "nice to be able to do as you please."

"Luke's gonna take a few days with him at Cloverdale then come on back. Start in with training once we set a date to bring Bona Fide to Hill-bound." Father took a sip of tea and stood. "No reason we can't go on and settle in here, honey, and make a trip over to your place tomorrow morning. One step at a time. We'll get Moe Lee to move what you'll need, but for now, you might want to go upstairs and have a look around. I'll be up shortly. Need to speak to Moe Lee about our plans."

Miss Francine scooted to the edge of the divan and set her cup on the marble top of the nearby oval table. "Gracie, you're being very quiet. Well, now, you'll want to know that my brother will surely be coming this summer, bringing Marcus before he goes off to be a preacher. Isn't that exciting! I'm sure we're going to adjust very nicely as a family. We all have grieving in common."

Henry's lips curled in disgust. "Perhaps we can all go to the races . . . take our minds off it."

Henry's insolence did not go unnoticed by Father. They grimaced identical angular jaws. Miss Francine swished past, went to the staircase, and turned. "You'll be up soon, love?"

"Sure, sure, Francie. Make yourself at home."

Once she'd disappeared past the upper landing, Father turned to Henry. "I expect you to show respect." He could have been a hissing snake. "If that's too much to ask, you can leave."

"It's only my *mother* that I've lost, is that what you're saying?"

"I don't mean to be insensitive. It's just Francie has certainly picked up your displeasure, Henry. I'm your father. I have a right to call you down as needed."

"I can't imagine why she would think I'm *displeased*." Henry gave Father a once over as if Father were the last fish in the market. "What did Sam Delaney have to say about all this?"

"How would Sam know? We had no reason to return to Cloverdale, let alone a reason to tell Francie's brother-in-law, for Pete's sake, of our business." Father stiffened his back and squared his shoulders. "Felix is out of the picture. We do not need Sam. End of conversation about him. Understood?"

"That woman's young enough to be your daughter. Almost, anyway.
"Henry was incensed, no doubt about it.

The door to Mama's bedroom upstairs closed with a smack, like the sound of a clay pot that might have smashed to the floor.

Chapter 29

Marcus and I sprawled upright against a tree, talking—distant enough from the house to speak our minds. We could talk for hours, hidden behind enormous clumps of burley tobacco with the early-August afternoon sunshine peeking thought leafy separations.

I'd had my fill of grist mills and cornmeal and waterwheels and horse ills—not to mention the lonely look that Henry seemed bent on serving me with every turn of his head. He was a waterless pit, and Miss Francine was fine with it. Fine with her if he was parched, fine if he languished. She was backing him down. Even if it wasn't visible, he trembled in her presence. Standing up to Miss Francine appeared to be impossible for Henry.

"You know," Marcus said from out of the blue, "it's obvious: Lucy's been perfect for my dad. She's a wonderful person. And he needed a wife, a friend. Losing my mother was hard. You know better than I do. Maybe it's because girls need their mothers in different ways than us guys. Guess that's it, but my mother meant the world to me. For sure."

"It's different for Father. He had a friend." I felt her ring without looking at it. "My mama. But it's as if he requires something else. Trophies and pats on the back. You can still be a friend when you're sick, can't you?"

I could hardly ask him to understand my ramblings, let alone answer them, but that hadn't kept him from trying. From across the miles, his letters had been delivered to the mailbox by the picket fence as if to cover the fragile state of my well-being. "You wrote to me at all the right times, Marcus. I don't know how I would've survived since last December," I said. "You're a good encourager. Really, you are. My friend Jean's been a sweetheart too. She can be silly at times, but I like to laugh, so that works out fine. Encouraged and laughing."

There was nothing said in the gap of time that followed. Outdoors sounds of fields being harvested were always gratifying. The loud hum of the machines was mesmerizing, and neither Marcus nor I rushed to clutter the lull.

"You're holding your own with my Aunt Francine?" He grinned at me, but there was a serious pitch to his question. "Aren't you?"

"She's certainly not providing any laughter, if that's what you mean. I do like how fashionable she is, but that's kind of shallow sounding isn't it? Especially when I see plenty of folks who don't have a lot. They're the ones I really care about. But I like pretty things too." I glanced at him plucking blades of grass, twisting them.

I desperately wanted to be as carefree as he and let go of the past, let Father move into a future that didn't include a shred of what he must have once shared with Annabelle Grace Morris Maxwell, if that's what he had to do. But to allow Miss Francine to fill the void in our home where Mama had lived and loved me—and Emma and Millicent and Henry—through the years and held us close during the frightful nights and rocked us when we cried and loved Father even when he didn't want to be bothered with her pain or her plight . . . That was asking too much.

I couldn't imagine telling Marcus of his aunt's underhanded dealings with the black folks or the duplicitous countenance that presented one side of herself for Father and quite another for me. Or most especially for Henry.

Neither could I envision myself divulging to Marcus or Jean or *anyone* the extent to which Miss Francine took pleasure in squashing every hope and denying every dream of Henry's and mine as if they were ships to sink or birds to shoot from the sky.

Henry and I had no place to savor the essence of our mother that had filled our home.

Neither could I interpret beauty as an outcome of the changes Miss Francine had made. Every nook and cranny were instead overly lavished with luxury and shallow pursuits.

Nor could I fully come to terms with the newly constructed edifices that overtook tobacco land at Hillbound to exalt equestrianism over loyalty and devotion to family—never mind how elegant the thoroughbred—and betting on and brandishing the potential to bring home a trophy to sit on the sideboard and tarnish.

The thought of what Miss Francine might cook up for Henry or me if she wanted us to be forever gone from Hillbound caused me to cringe.

I ran my thumb over the face of the ruby ring, grateful not all truths were any less defensible while they remained unspoken. And grateful, too, that no one but I noticed Father looking to defend Miss Francine on rude remarks that could shake the very floor beneath Henry. Or the bullying that could send me tearing up the stairs to my room rather than tolerate her tirade or tip over the pedestal where her fresh-faced advantage lived to lure Father's affection from the one women he'd vowed to love forever.

"I really do love pretty things," I said. "But I also yearn to help people who have almost nothing. Wonder what God says about that?" I gave a cursory swat to the curls that insisted on being a nuisance. "Do you think Miss Francine believes the way you do? I mean about God and all?"

Marcus was listening. He smiled. But there were blades of grass sticking out between his teeth. I laughed out loud, concluding that I had experienced the extent of his sympathetic ear.

"See! I can make you laugh oh so easily." He chuckled and pulled them out. "I'm not making light of you, Gracie. Just couldn't resist the grass thing. You have a heart for teaching. It's written all through your letters. You spent all summer working with those children at Hillbound. I'm proud of you. Honest." He flipped the limp grass pieces as far as they would go. "I'd never go so far as to say what Aunt Francine believes, though. She's something else, alright. And I'm not seeing that she has much room in her life for anything but horseracing and betting. And your father, of course. They're both pretty well wrapped up in all that. Very different from what most people around here seem to be about. Yep!" he said. "Salt-of-the-earth folks, at least from what I've seen. Lucy's like that—genuine, warm. Good qualities, they are."

Having openly expressed himself, he was quiet, perhaps coming up with additional tidbits of wisdom. I liked the way he had written a bundle of them in his letters since Christmas. His insightful words were more than appealing.

Then there was the fact that he carried off, very well, his suave look, reminding me of Father.

But it was Marcus's sincerity that radiated. If he had handed me the moon, I couldn't have been more warmed. Even so, I held back, wondering if it was my view of integrity that created a dividing line in my logic. I balked at the confusing rub of discontent that had me judging Father with nothing more than a single measuring stick for the way he had treated Mama. I suspected my estimation of admirable qualities should not be weighted in ounces of sincerity, but with so few boys and only one Father to compare, it was.

"Lucy adores you, Gracie. She's taken a real liking to your . . . what, your spontaneity? . . . during the week we've been here." Marcus grinned. "It's easy to do, you know. And now that Aunt Francine's house has sold, I'm not sure what's going bring me and my dad back here."

He couldn't have missed hearing the thud that hit the floor of my heart. Everything in my consciousness was a reminder that he would soon return to Madison County to resume working and soon after go off to Asbury College. None of me wanted to accept it.

"You and your dad have been a big help, I'm sure. A lot of details. Good thing the house was off to itself, more or less, since Father didn't want it," I said. My knowing smile began a leisurely creep across my face. "He sure did want the forty acres attached to it, though, so of course there were various things to be tended to. Merging the land parcels . . . Oh, I don't know about things like that, Marcus. Tell me some more about your plans for Asbury." I pursed my lips. "And will you still write me?"

"Um. Well, I am starting a year late. Guess no one's paying attention to that but me. Even so, I'm gonna double up on classes as best as I can to get finished. I've saved the money to put myself through for two years. Working summers should take care of the rest. It's a good theology school."

"That's impressive. So you're gonna be too busy to write. Humph!" I laughed and began to study his profile: the point of his nose, the length of his eyelashes, the intricacies of his ear. "It's what I heard, anyway. Too busy to write."

"Are you painting me?"

"If I were a painter, I would. But I'm not." My assuring him seemed an altogether necessary thing to do. "I am making a replica of you in my mind, though, for when you're gone and I'm sitting here alone. A plaster of you in case you don't write to me. How does it feel to be a head formed in clay? Makes you a clay head, like one of the pots your father makes . . . only with a nose and ears."

He laughed out loud, and my imaginary cast was broken. "Maybe you've gotten your silliness from your friend Jean, but I do like you. And I hope I've become a true friend. More than a friend."

"You're serious?" I said. "You're a neat, long-distance friend, and I'm glad you're here this close to my birthday. Especially to have a piece of Odelia's delicious chocolate cake. My most favorite cake ever!"

"You're a master at changing the subject, Gracie. Do you know what I think?" He rested his head back against the tree trunk and waited. I didn't dare present an answer for what he might be thinking. "I think you're trying to cover your brokenness with silliness. Brokenness isn't the end, believe me. Sometimes it's the beginning."

I looked away, feeling the burn in my eyes.

"That clay pot?" he said. "It's only because that pot fell and broke at church when I hardly knew you—that predicament has given us a chance to discuss brokenness in our letters during these several months. Even now. And that's life. It often takes brokenness to search for wholeness."

"You'll make a good preacher."

"There you go again, changing the subject. It's okay. We should proba-bly head back. Aunt Francine'll be sending out a posse."

Dreading to think of him leaving in the morning, I sighed and rolled over into the grass. Marcus laughed and did the same. I was sure he was about to kiss me, so I rolled farther from him. We both looked up, instead, at an inky black sky that had formed in the west.

"What will I do, Marcus, when you leave?" I asked, feeling safe, liking that he couldn't reach me. "I can't bear to think of the time ahead, forever with Miss Francine in Mama's house. I don't intend to be rude about your aunt—"

"You'll finish high school, Gracie, and then you'll go to college, just like you've been telling me all along," he said. And then he was closer. "Can I kiss you?"

I scrambled to my feet and flitted away like an elusive butterfly. At a safe distance I stopped, panting, and shouted, "Why would you want to?"

"Because tomorrow you'll be sixteen!" And he came after me, mimicked a madman with the great crinkled face of a devious soul, and we laughed before I tore off again.

Carefully, cautiously, I sneaked to the back of the tree trunk, and I stood there, trying not to make a sound. He had hidden himself from view, but I knew he was close. I could hear him breathing.

Without a warning he grabbed my hand. "Better go. The sky's started to look a little threatening," he said, and we began walking, dodging the robust clumps of tobacco that covered the land in our path. "Gracie, one thing before I go. Not making excuses for her, but Aunt Francine gets what she wants. She was once pretty darned determined to have Sam. Had her cap set for him."

"Mister Sam?" I was stunned.

"Yes, and while I don't know much about it, I do know she tried to ruin him. Happened around the time he left Madison County and went to Lexington. Of course, that's all worked for the best . . . with Cloverdale, and all."

"But he's such a fine man. How could she do something to hurt him?"

"Honest, I know what you've been going through. Just be aware, for your own sake. That's all. No other woman could—or should—try to take your own mother's place. Lucy's certainly not trying. She's never tried to push her way in. I wish that were true for you, Gracie."

As we approached the house, he stopped. Before I could resist, he'd kissed me. Straight on—intentional. In detail and prolonged.

He backed away, then, looking rather proud of himself. "Maybe you could come to Madison County sometime."

"Um. Who knows?" I said, glancing up at the clouds that had rolled in, beginning to fill the sky.

We had a remaining few steps and so reached the verandah with only the crackling sound of twiglets beneath our feet. "Lucy's already said she'd love to have you. And I would."

"That's such a lovely invitation, Marcus!" Miss Francine appeared out of nowhere.

I shouldn't have been taken aback but I was. Marcus was unreadable. Far away, the sound of thunder.

"Gracie, love, you must say yes. It would no doubt be a wonderful visit!" She tapped ashes from her cigarette over the railing. "And Lord knows you don't get invitations like that very often, now do you?"

She turned and began making her way across the verandah—a slight wave of her hand, a huffy *ta-ta*—as if she had managed a tidy little strike to her opponent." Y'all, do come inside. It's gonna rain," she said over her shoulder. "And Gracie, we'll be sure your father hears that you've been invited to my brother's."

"Francie, honey, go easy on them," Father said from behind the door that stood ajar. "Come on inside."

Chapter 30

With supper over, and Marcus gone, I finished up a second piece of the chocolate cake Odelia had baked for my birthday. The feeling of his kiss lingered, sweeter still than the frosting on the cake. "That was *de*-licious! Odelia, you'll have to teach me to make it."

"Humph! Thought you didn't want nothing to do with de kitchen, Miss Gracie. You change yore mind?" She removed my plate, laughing as she did, uproariously, with her mouth wide open.

"You have all kinds of things to celebrate on your sixteenth birthday, don't you?" Miss Francine's voice had a way of ruining everything sweet. "Run along, Odelia. Be back at six in the morning and bring my breakfast up at eight. Not ten after." She motioned for Odelia to move. "Eight, with tea. And honey."

I blinked several times at Miss Francine to acknowledge I'd heard her—not wanting to rile her for any lack or responsiveness on my part—while I washed down the last of the richness in my mouth, wishing I'd saved the dark gooeyness across my teeth for the halfhearted smile I presented.

"Yessum, Missus Maxwell. I-I be here at six. Be remindin' myself of it too."

I couldn't bear to look at Odelia, reduced to a stammering, stuttering woman who would've baked two birthday cakes if she'd thought I wanted two. Her teasing had pointed to how obstinate I'd been, not wanting to help with the cooking and sharing some kitchen duties when Mama got sick. A tinge of remorse remained in my mind: *I would have done it all with joy to have Mama back again.*

I would have felt extra shame had it not been for my splendid day with Marcus.

"Odelia! A napkin . . . on the floor. And hurry on, Odelia." Miss Francine's peculiar motion of dismissal sent Odelia scurrying. "Now, Gracie, as I was saying, lots to celebrate here. Come along, follow me to the drawing room," she said, appearing quite satisfied with herself.

I was on my feet in a jiffy, wondering if the piano could possibly have, as a birthday surprise, been removed without my knowing, halfway hoping that it had.

Father stood as we entered. The piano had not budged. Henry, in fact, sat on the velvet stool, his arm draped on the music ledge near the metronome. He stared at his feet, and Francine sidled up to Father. She slid her hand into his. "Your father and I have news, Gracie."

She took a breath, deep enough to puff her like a frog. Outside, the rumble of thunder not that far off distracted me for an instant and I continued to stand, feeling much too much excitement to sit. Henry shuffled his feet and looked at me as if he might already know the news. Something about his eyes stopped my heart. Lightning flashed.

"We're giving you the opportunity to attend a girls school, Gracie. This means you'll get to spend your junior and senior years elsewhere. Crescent Springs, not that far north of here. Lovely girls school. Right, love?" Miss Francine glanced at Father, her chin upward in a victorious little lift.

No smiles backed the news of the wonderful opportunity. It reeked of a death sentence. I knew it instantly. And Father knew it. Henry knew it too. I felt the life run out of me—from the tip of my head to the end of my toes.

"Father?" If only to satisfy my rage, I turned to him in disbelief. The source of her news was unmistakable. "You agreed to this? Honestly? *Did* you? How could you?"

With every fiber of my being, I pleaded, feeling the cake curdle in my throat. My face burned as if I'd been struck with a hot poker. Anger, in a category I never knew could exist, boiled in my breast. The room paled, oddly, as if the windows had been closed on this August evening to ensure it would be rendered stale, on the brink of suffocating everyone present.

And Father: not a word. Just the amazing arrogant tilt to his head that had only this morning looked so senatorial.

I swallowed, still able to taste the buttery slime that had been icing on my birthday cake. Rendered completely motionless, I looked straight into Miss Francine's eyes as rain pelted the metal roof of the verandah. "This is *your* plan to be rid of me, isn't it?" My heart beat as if its pounding might break my ribs. "You look so pretty, Miss Francine. So very pretty. Did Mister Sam not think so?"

She sidestepped me, went to the divan and cozied up next to Father. "It will be an unparalleled year, one to give you maturity, my dear."

"'My dear'? 'My dear,' *my foot!*" I screamed.

She covered her ears. Father put his arm around her.

"This is my home. I can't possibly go away!" I walked to the divan and leaned in. "For *two* years? Father?"

I watched him rest his hand on her lap, coming to her defense, and I was certain he'd been coerced. "It's only the school year. Um, two, I guess," he said, squirming. "You'll be benefitted from now on, honey."

Henry rose to his feet and helplessly stood in the background. Then I could see him out of the corner of my eye, moving to my side.

"What father banishes his child from home? Mama . . . *Mama* must be crying from heaven, Father," I said, flinging open for him a window into my soul, but Miss Francine's head lay on his shoulder as if she were sewn to his coat lapel. Tight threads of coercion united them, and Father remained wordless.

"This is your doing," I said, simmering down beneath the touch of Henry's hand on my waist. Still, I glared at Miss Francine, better able to think with the support he was giving. "You're a curse on this home, Miss Francine. I didn't want to believe it, but that's what you are. I was warned."

Father stood, a rigid replica of the one I'd known, and not so very long ago. "That's enough, Gracie. You'd better let it go."

"'*Warned*'?" Miss Francine hissed. "A warning? By whom!" She was off the divan, her delicate little features drawn up in a snarl, her hands on her hips. "You'll regret those words, Miss Maxwell!"

"Francine, please. She's just upset." Father's poise seemed to have been lost in the quandary.

Henry gave me a gentle nudge, a suggestion for me, if I wasn't mistaken, and I pulled away, fled from the room. I ran up the stairs to my room and slammed the door.

Within minutes, I heard a faint knock. "Let me in, Gracie," Henry said from the other side. "Open the door."

I couldn't. I could not! Henry was as powerless as I was to stop the cruel push to make me leave my home. Going to high school in some obscure place was unthinkable.

Nothing can or ever will be the same, I told myself, and what had begun as a perfectly wonderful day ended. I had no idea how to get through the night ahead.

Chapter 31

───⟨⟨⟨⟩⟩⟩───

S lipping on the dewy-wet leaves under my feet, I stepped gingerly across the road in front of my house, savoring the picturesque magnificence of the old barn. Its one low-sloping side nestled in silence against morning's first glimmer of the rising sun, and tobacco hung from its cross rails.

My final day at Hillbound had begun with an early-morning chill. Autumn, ablaze in bronze and yellow hues, tried to warm my soul. I pulled my sweater closer and buttoned it up, hoping the countrified beauty that surrounded me would etch itself in my mind. I told the barn goodbye in the only way I knew how to tell a barn goodbye.

Train tracks wound unendingly across the property, suggesting they would soon take me away and not return me again before Christmas.

Not far off, beyond the fields and the grist mill, stood my school. The thought of Miss Avery and the absentee boys working in the fields and Jean Morgan in the remote one-room building made me smile, if only for a moment to believe she would find a new friend. I tried to picture doing the same in the make-up of girls I'd yet to meet up north at Crescent Springs.

I walked alongside the yellowing tobacco mounds, clutching a small flannel bag, breathing deeply the pleasant earthy aroma, remembering Father's comment that this land wouldn't have been worth a nickel had tobacco not been grown here. Walking faster, I made my way back across Allensville Road where thoroughbred horses and exercise tracks and jockey and trainer had eked out their positions and changed the landscape.

I moseyed out to the sprawling oak tree at the top of the meadow, cherishing as I went the memory of the black children I'd taught to read, their smiles erupting triumphantly with any measure of accomplishment they'd made.

Father's farm was going to be run the way it always had been, because he, Senator Robert Rutherford Maxwell had the last say in most every situation, I reminded myself. *Until this past May*. I was sure on the day that he'd brought her to live at Hillbound, Miss Francine had taken charge. It was more than the merger of a solitary land parcel with Father's that rippled the water at the Maxwell homestead. I shuddered to think of the plans the Lady of Hillbound must have begun devising on the sunny afternoon she set foot across the threshold of Mama's house.

In the few quiet minutes before the arrival of the hired hands and the commencement of a morning in full swing, I reached the clump of pine trees that had sprung up in pitiful grandeur where burley tobacco had isolated them into a most mysterious family and began walking like I owned the place. As the underbrush thickened, I crept like an inchworm—vertical but hunkered and creeping—through the solemn disarray of tombstones in the cemetery in the outback, pondering whether or not I should be praying as I went for the souls of the dearly departed who slept beneath me.

I clung to the flannel bag that I had carried, sat down next to the concrete slab I finally found, and considered for a moment my position next to *MILDRED MOSLEY MAXWELL*. With mushrooming resolve, I leaned against my old granny's marker and, after having detected nothing but the musty, moldy smell of the thicket—nothing in the way of a superstitious nudging— loosened the drawstring, pulled out my pen, turned the tiny brass latch on my diary, and began to write in the peacefulness of the stifled opinions of others.

August 31, 1923

This is my goodbye to feathery trees and lifeless rocks and animals with agendas and land with no end.

Pausing, I stood and shook damp pine needles from my skirt, then sidestepped the concrete slabs and hunted down a broken-off limb of tree. Small as it was, I took it back to my spot. *Why, but to be undisturbed in my secret sanctuary, would I do such a thing?* I asked myself and cautiously sat down on its prickly surface.

> *Miss Francine has changed everything in my world. I long to stay here on the farm, but she has changed Father into someone I don't even know anymore. Maybe someone I don't even want to know anymore! She is behind the decision to send me away and I will die there, in the wilderness of Crescent Springs, far from home. How could Father think that such a decision would ever, ever make me happy?*

> *And now l hate, and I didn't know that I could hate the way I do. The nights that I wake up because I can still hear Mama cry out in pain, I hate Father for not loving her, for turning his back on her.*

> *Father is pretending. How can he possibly say that I will be happy at Crescent Springs? He is wrong, wrong, wrong! And he had brought a monster into Mama's house! How could I ever have known Miss Francine would turn out to be so mean? Did he?*

> *When I awaken in the night and Mama is calling, I hate him the most for leaving her alone. I know what it feels like now, to be disregarded by someone I loved with all my heart.*

> *Miss Francine is greedy and mean. I feel her plucking like a chicken, pick-pick-picking after whatever she can*

*get. And he smiles, and she goes on picking, gobbling up
what she can.*

*And Henry has her marks all over him. Pick marks cover
his countenance. Pick marks have caused him to bleed.*

I stopped writing and thumbed to the next page. Tears dripped onto the clean surface. I caught my breath in irregular gasps, unable for a moment to calm my blubbering, then wiped my face with the back of my hand. Again, I took a deep breath, slowly controlled, with Marcus's words somehow sinking into my soul.

I flipped back to the pages I'd written in days past. Starting with the day of my birthday, I reread the account of the evening before when Miss Francine had spelled out the news of my being sent away. Page after page was dried and crinkled from tears that had fallen while I wrote how alone, how deserted I felt. Cheated as Henry had been cheated of his dignity. Banished from all that I had come to love at Hillbound. Separated from him. Separated from my sisters.

Anger scorched the pages where I'd mocked Marcus's words of his God who reshapes what is broken. Mad because Marcus had gone back to Madison County. Burned for having let myself fall head-over-heels for him.

I straightened my back against Granny Maxwell's slab and ripped out the pages. With another deep breath, my head seemed to clear. I wiped tears from the new page and began to think afresh, twirling the pen between my thumb and index finger, relying on a bird's song to lift my spirit.

*I have to survive leaving my home and all that I've come
to know on the farm. For my own sake and for Henry's.
Together we can hold onto Hillbound, no matter what.*

*If what Marcus says is true, then I am greater than any
or all of my failures. If God is the—my—Potter, then He*

is able to mold and remold me as I submit to His wisdom and skill. If God, as the Master Artist, is able to take the dark thread of my life, my wounds, my scars, and the mess that's been made and blend them into a beautiful vessel, then I, a common earthenware jug, can contain the price-less treasure of His plan for my life.

I closed the latch and put my diary and pen back into the flannel bag. The pen clinked quietly against the ink bottle inside. With new resolve, I arose and began running between cut rows of tobacco and out into the wide-open space of the meadow, envisioning the dwarf iris and wild columbine blooms. Wanting to accept with a new attitude that I would not smell grandiflora that would have me covered in fragrance were I to be here next spring, I made a dash for the house and hurried up the steps to the kitchen and went inside.

Father was grouchy looking. It was clear the minute I got past the back door that he and Miss Francine had a quarrel in progress.

She turned to me, cigarette in midair. "Crescent Springs has rules and policies. We all know you'll be enjoying quality instruction without interruptions of any kind. They've made it abundantly clear that you're to have no visitors—"

"Pay no attention, Gracie." Father traipsed to the other side of the kitchen, set his ashtray on the windowsill, and stared out to some unknown point beyond the window.

She kept her glare, first at him then turned it on me. "As I was about to say, you *are* going to get to see Marcus at Christmas. So, it will be next spring when we'll have you back here."

Next spring? Her news came out of nowhere, as if it were a worm slithering out the cold, dark earth. She cut her eyes at Father, and I had to tell my heart to be still. She was bent on telling me about the girls school. And more. If I could have scratched her eyeballs I might have. I reminded myself instead, of my very recent commitment to allow God to remold me. It didn't feel possible.

"Lucy has been an absolute jewel, insistent that you come spend it with her and Chester. Much closer to Madison than coming all the way back here, right, love," Miss Francine said in her sing-song voice. "She and my brother have a little place. Adequate, I guess. Don't know where they would put us, but we'll discuss Christmas another time."

"Sister's—"

"Gracie! Listen to me. Lucy is welcoming you with open arms. And of course, Marcus is going to be elated. After his week here, everyone knows what a play he's made for you."

I lost my balance slightly and stumbled against the side of the potbelly stove. The flannel bag fell from my hand. Father hustled over to retrieve it.

Miss Francine chuckled. "In addition to other things a lady should know, perhaps they'll also teach you at Crescent Springs to walk like one."

Father looked into my eyes and then moved away. "Honey, who knows where Francie and I will be? Our lives truly are . . . so up in the air these days. We'll have to wait and see. Now then," he said, getting down to business. "Your trip, Gracie, will be an unscheduled stop along the Cincinnati Southern Line. The train runs from Ludlow to Somerset.

"In Kentucky?"

"Yes, Gracie, where else? Northern Kentucky. It's considered part of the country south and west of Cincinnati, Ohio. I've requested a special stop in order for you to be off-boarded along the route." Father's lips were tight, his jaw set, but he spoke with less angst than when I'd entered the kitchen. "It's grown out of a nice farming community much like Todd County. Buttermilk Pike is your stop. It was once a one lane dirt road."

He stopped speaking long enough to check if I was amused. I tried my best to look interested, but I had nothing thinkable to say. I felt a wisp of my curly black hair fall across my forehead. Before I could brush it back, he did.

"I'm sorry, Gracie"

Not now, not ever, would I believe him.

I caught sight of Henry coming up from the stable. "It's growing late, Father," I said. "I'll go finish packing. Y'all excuse me, please. And would you ask Henry to come upstairs?"

It was Moe Lee who took me in the carriage to Guthrie and put me on the train to a world unknown.

"Miss Gracie, God's gonna see to yore life. I knows it." But Moe Lee's shoulders were bent forward and his plaid shirt crinkled under his overalls.

Neither of us knew how to say goodbye.

"Miss Gracie, you made school chill-ren outta my young'uns. I is grateful fo' it."

One-eyed Moe Lee looked at me. It seemed that his arms started to reach out, then fell back at his side, squelching the hug he was not allowed to give.

From the distance came the mournful wail of a train whistle, and I waited, trying not to feel broken like a pot on the windowsill.

Chapter 32

———✦———

S hortly before noon on the twenty-second of December, the train rumbled into the Waco station in Madison County, its brakes hissing. The Saturday had turned into a blustery one. I held tightly to my hat with one hand, my bag with the other, rushing to meet Chester and Lucy's embrace.

Letters from home, both brief ones from Father, had pointed to the world of horse racing, its duties, its required travel, its all-consuming glories—making it clear my absence was indeed the best possible decision for all concerned. The last one spoke of our upcoming Christmas reunion at the Willoughbys'. Father indicated in a few words how it would top every expectation for abounding joy. According to Miss Francine, it was going to be quite cramped in her brother's small place there in Madison County. As intriguing as my going to Marcus's had once sounded, nothing could compare with my longing to go home to Todd County.

It was Lucy who rushed to greet me, all smiles and thrilled. Coming up behind her was a subdued Chester, bearing the news that there'd been a change. Father, Miss Francine, and Henry would not, after all, be joining us. Plans had taken them elsewhere, and Henry was not going anywhere.

"But," Chester said, attempting to sound upbeat, "you do have a telephone conversation with Henry to look forward to on Christmas Eve."

We hurried through the station and over to the waiting automobile, making the most of time. Marcus was fifty-three miles away in Wilmore. Chester needed to get on the road and drive there to get him.

Although the two letters I'd gotten from Marcus had been cordial, I'd left them propped on my bureau, looking like forlorn figures at a bus stop, back at Crescent Springs Girls School. Unsure he held—if he ever had—the feelings of love that I had, I'd ceased to send my own letters on a regular basis to him, and certainly not at the same rapid pace. My having written numerous letters to him at the beginning of the school term now loomed as an awkward fact.

I wondered, too, in hindsight, if Crescent Springs would have been the better choice of a place to be, even at Christmastime, with the girlfriend I'd made. Freida Ledbetter had begged me to stay with her and Ramona Jenkins, both of whom had gotten themselves in a family way.

Their predicament, I discovered soon after I was oriented at school, was not uncommon for enrollees. Unfortunate as it was, they were not going home for a while, and it wasn't clear to me which of us was the worse off. They were as disheartened as I over missing Christmas at home, and try as I might, I was struggling to see God taking anything in my five-month experience away from home and blending it into a beautiful vessel, especially when my hopes of Millicent and Emma and what-ifs for my holiday plans had fallen face down.

Lucy filled that gap. Easily, I felt the warmth of her hospitality before we ever left the station. "We're *delighted*, Gracie, and hope you'll make our home yours! What a special season! And all the more because you're here," she said as we motored toward their place. "Right, Chester? I don't know when I've looked forward to anything so much."

Lucy was a head taller than Mr. Willoughby, a stout woman and younger. Their age difference had me thinking back on Henry's comment about Miss Francine being young enough to be my sister. I had not paid much attention to such things until Father married Miss Francine.

Lucy smiled at me, continually turning her head to glance back at me from the front seat of the automobile. "I don't understand why such a last-minute development has happened," she said, "but we're going to make this the best Christmas ever!"

Chester let us out at the door to their modest bungalow. His eyes followed us to the door until he waved and drove away.

"Don't you worry. He'll bring Marcus back here, we'll have dinner together, and you'll see," she said.

There wasn't a doubt in my mind that she felt my disappointment, perhaps seeing my efforts to come to terms with a Christmas without family—*life* without family.

"I've not ever seen where pottery is made," I said with my interest up.

"Not surprised! Well, this is it for sure. Waco area's known for its gray and white clay deposits," Lucy said. "And they're certainly a significant natural resource—provide ample livelihood for stoneware potters like Chester. Of course, he'd hoped Marcus would carry on the business his grandfather started. Who knows, maybe he will come back to it one day. For now, looks like he's intent on being a preacher. Loves the Asbury campus."

Her personality amused me, the way she ran everything she said into one bubbly outpouring. We had barely gotten inside when she reached over and picked up an earthenware vase from the table in the front room. "The pottery's notably plain in decoration like this. It's one of Eb Stone's. Artful. Not as dull as the type Chester produces, not as functional either, but I like the patina. Pretty, isn't it?"

She handed it to me, her eye darting from me to the beautiful piece. "See there . . . the imprint of the potter? His style makes it lovely, his imprint makes it distinctive. Owned it before I married Chester or I'd never have bought it. Chester might not've married me if he'd known I had a competitor's piece in my possession."

Another of her hearty laughs recalled for me her warmth and the jolly, genuine woman who'd opened wide her arms for an embrace the first time she'd met me.

"Goodness sakes! Let me take your coat. Come on in. We don't live high, but I think you'll be comfy. I can show you the pottery workings, but that should wait till tomorrow. Put your things in there," she said and pointed to a doorway where a light shone from within. "And we'll eat a cookie or two, sit a spell before I get you to help me with dinner. But I'll bet you're hungry, so here, let me fix you some chicken soup—left over from last night. It is *de*-licious!"

It sounded delicious. I was hungry as a horse.

The afternoon eased past with my tales of Crescent Springs, flowing in direct response to Lucy's continuous questions. She pumped me as if I were the water source at the back of the house, and our laughter filled the quaintness of her living room. Logs crackled in the fireplace, and I hadn't felt more at home in months. She wasn't Mama, but she was all I had.

"The men are going to be coming in here before long. What say we rustle up some fried chicken and mashed potatoes? Put another log on, and I'll get you to peel the Idahos."

Uh-oh came to mind, as did *Oh, no*, but I dropped a sycamore log on the fire and followed Lucy to the kitchen. "I'm not much when it comes to cooking, but I sure want to help. I can learn."

She cut her eyes at me. "Then you won't be wringing the chicken's neck, that what you're saying?" And she roared with a laugh that made me wish I'd asked earlier the direction to the outhouse.

"Yonder," she said, stretching her large bosom over the sideboard to point through the window to the small building beyond. "Don't try to escape. You'll learn to peel potatoes or you'll not eat." She was still laughing as I hurried out the back door.

On my return I saw Marcus getting out of his father's automobile. No sooner had I gotten inside the house when he came bounding through the front door. Not since our final moments together in August at Hillbound had I seen him, but there had been few days that I had not had him on my mind.

—◦◦◦◦◦—

I didn't know how to pinpoint the distance that Marcus seemed to have put between us, but it was as noticeable as the crust on apple pie. Following a lively conversation at the dinner table, Lucy and I washed and put away the dishes, then adjourned to the living room to join the men. Talk of girls and classes at Crescent combined with schedules and ambitions at Asbury left Marcus and me hammered by his stepmother's questions.

Plenty enough to last for days, but Marcus suggested some fresh air before calling it a night.

At first, we walked at a brisk pace without talking, our breath forming frosty clouds in the moonlight. Beneath the arc of a streetlamp he stopped. Light glistened off the frozen vapors on his beard. "I'm really glad you came."

"You look older. With all that, I mean," I said and rubbed my chin.

"I see that the girls school hasn't taught you to stay on the subject." He sounded serious, so I shaped up. "You're a special person, Gracie. And I'll say it again: I'm really glad you came. We can count on some good talks."

"Oh. Um, okay. In a way, Marcus, it doesn't seem like you mean it . . . that you're glad I'm here. Tell me if I'm wrong, but something's changed. Your letters . . . um . . . they're different. I feel odd being here. Odd and out of place."

"I won't deny it, Gracie. I've not been as good about writing. Thing is I'm very involved with my education and the ministry. That's one thing. I even get to help with the service tomorrow night." He hesitated.

Intuitively, I knew beyond the one thing another one was coming. It was more than the cold of a December night. My cheeks felt the bite. My lips would not stop quivering.

"I'm not going to be untruthful. I have a girl in Wilmore . . . at school. Gracie, you're so far away. Ours was an inconvenient relationship, and not even off the ground. And then the distance, and it's going to be that way."

"This is a fine how do you do, isn't? 'Inconvenient'? Don't answer. I'm freezing."

"I didn't want to put that in a letter. I care about you. I do. Tomorrow I plan to show you the kiln."

Chapter 33

I tossed and turned for a good bit of the night, and when daybreak came, I rolled over and, not meaning to do so, fell back asleep, having accepted during the wee hours that I'd come here and not gone to Sister's or to Emma's for that matter. Miss Francine had insisted on her brother's house. Were it not for Marcus having bowed out of the beautiful picture in my mind, we could have posed in a sleigh for a Currier & Ives postcard.

The next thing I knew was the sound of crackling bacon and the realization that I'd slept way too long. I flung off the covers and tiptoed across the cold floorboard to the chamber pot. The restless night had been enough to bring me to my knees beside the Jenny Lind bed, trying to believe God was somewhere in the vicinity of my request for patience and understanding.

Marcus greeted me with a warm smile to match his stepmother's as I hurried into the kitchen. Immediately stood up from the table. "Sit here, and I'll fix you an easy-over egg if that's the way you like it. You're too sleepy eyed to cook, or I'd let you. Lucy and my dad are getting dressed. Can you be ready for church? And afterwards I'll make good on my promise."

"Sure, Marcus. I don't want to be in the way, though. These plans . . . for me to come here should have been changed. You know. When everything else changed, my coming here should have been changed too."

"Don't, Gracie. I love having you here. And Dad said Lucy has been so excited. You coming is all she could talk about. I was beginning to wonder if she'd rather have you all to herself." He laughed and cracked an egg into hot grease in the skillet. "I hope you'll forgive me. If I'd ever dreamed this would turn out like it has with Rebecca, I would have tried to make you understand in a letter." He slid the egg onto a plate and put two slices of bacon on top. "But I didn't. I don't see how I could have. There. Eat."

"And you're going to sit there and watch? Go on. I'll be ready in a few minutes."

He carried his empty plate to the sink and gave me a sideways look.

"I forgive you, Marcus. I don't want to, but I'm not in control, am I?"

<hr />

Marcus and I went after church to the small concrete building down the hill at the back of the Willoughbys' bungalow. The day had turned out sunny but cold and blustery. Marcus trotted ahead of me, got the door unlocked, then lit two gas lamps.

"It's stinky in here," I said, tugging at the fingertips of my gloves with my teeth, and he let out a chuckle. "That odor's due to minerals in the clay. When clay is *stinky*, though, it's usually good. The smell only comes when the clay's spent some time in a wet condition."

"Is this where you work all summer? Doesn't it get awfully hot in here?"

"It does. Over here is the kiln used to attain high temperatures—over a thousand degrees. But Dad and I try to bake the kilns at night when we can . . . in summertime. In winter it feels pretty good to have one going." He ran his fingers over the arch of bricks that surrounded the oven. "It keeps heat loss to a minimum and efficiently allows the potter to control temperature rise and fall inside the kiln. This is the spy hole. Peek through it, if you like. It lets you view what is going on inside the kiln during the firing. And here, the potter's wheel. It's used in shaping round ceramic wares. Circular pieces: pots, plates, and the like." He paused. "When I met you a year ago it was Christmastime. Definitely a hard time with the loss of your mother. And things've been rough, for sure. Going off, and so far away—"

His summary made it sound so wasted. I didn't hear beyond the truth that my world was far away. All I could think of was the clay pot that had fallen from the window and when it had broken into a half dozen useless pieces.

"Sent off, Marcus. I've been taken from my own home. I might as well have been taken by a thief. It's as if Miss Francine devised a plan to keep me away from everything and everybody. And Crescent Springs isn't a bad place, but it's certainly not home."

I wasn't about to let myself cry. It took me a second to breathe the air that I needed to rethink my thoughts. "I'm sorry . . . it's truly not a horrible place. I've made friends, but I do get lonely. I miss Henry. I miss my sisters. I miss the children. I miss seeing them even if I can't be teaching them. I miss Moe Lee."

"Your letters said lots to me about your attitude, though. You've matured, Gracie. I loved what you said about letting God remold you. Faith develops over time." He took his hand off the potter's wheel where he'd been resting it and looked straight into my eyes. "You made a commitment to trust God, but trusting is like deciding every day to renew that commitment. Sometimes it's an hour-by-hour thing."

"Father is someone I no longer know. And this place . . . Your kind stepmother, you, and this whole circumstance all feel a little make-believe."

He had an appropriate look, one of understanding, but he picked up a lump of wet clay and turned it in his hands. "We're a lot like this. Raw material to be shaped."

He'd not heard a word I'd said. Unable to speak, I looked at him in disbelief, then out through the window. Last year's dead, frozen grass and a few leafless trees stared back at me, but nothing moved.

"The potter has the right to do with the clay whatever he chooses. The end result is a vessel to be used for the purpose he intended. That's you, Gracie. You need to know that you are being formed for an incredible purpose."

I wanted to change the subject, say "Jesus wept," or something to take off the heat.

"Love will find you, Gracie. That day will come. And I hope the day will come, too, when you cooperate with the fact that God is the Master Potter. He is shaping you for a beautiful future that you cannot even imagine."

There it was again, I thought. *Marcus leading me to consider that someone else besides me held my future while I stewed in self-pity.*

He watched, gentle eyes on me as I spun Mama's ring on my finger, slowly twirling the delicate gold flower with its ruby center and eight tiny pearls, drawing comfort as I often had during the last year from knowing it belonged to her. Try as I might, not once had I felt the pain of her loss subside.

"You'll look back one day upon this time of struggling, and you'll be able to see how God was shaping you." He picked up the glove I dropped on the floor and handed it over. "We need to spot a tree before tonight's service. Think about what I've said. Let's go find us a Christmas pine."

—◦⟪⟫◦—

The afternoon chill and the ones that followed in the days to come at the Willoughbys' home lacked the iced-over sensation that could have ruined Christmas. As it was, the four of us spent five warm and memorable days playing Monopoly by the fireside, swapping stories of happy times and childhood. The snow drifted down in flurries that covered the little town of Waco in a powdery white blanket. Only the telephone call on Christmas Eve to Henry that went unanswered left a trace of sadness.

Mid-morning on Friday, with my bag beside my feet and our goodbyes said and hugs shared all around, I waited with the Willoughbys as the train whooshed into Waco's station. Lucy pressed my cheeks between her two gloved hands, squashing my smile into a comical one, and in the background Marcus was grinning.

"Want you to know this, Gracie Maxwell, and never forget," Lucy said with one last hug that took my breath away. "We want you to come again! You're always be welcome to come down to the potter's house, anytime."

I stepped up to the running board with emotion aplenty to swell my heart, anticipating the remaining five months of the upcoming new year at Crescent Springs.

Chapter 34

—◦⟨⟩◦—

January 1924 in Northern Kentucky began as frigid as any winter I could have created in my imagination for the North Pole and as ghostly as any picture of peacefulness. Traipsing through ankle-deep snow from the girls' dormitory to the two-story building that housed classrooms and the infirmary was enough to change my mind about returning to Crescent Springs Girls School for my senior year. With not even my junior year ended, I was all too aware that I had no choice in the matter. I laughed at myself for thinking runaway thoughts.

Freida Ledbetter had her baby in February. Ramona Jenkins had hers in March. Both Ramona and Freida were among my favorites, and when their time came to deliver, both relied on the bond of friendship the three of us had formed. Whether it was the coincidence of our off-putting situations that had landed us at Crescent Springs or that kindred spirits simply sought out each other, we made it through the bleak months from January to March.

The ground began to thaw and crocuses popped up in the woodlands, and before we knew it, May had us looking to the day we could finish the semester and return to our homes. When it arrived, I was so ready I cried.

The Crescent Springs schoolmarm plopped herself behind the wheel of the Model T, seized it with purposeful intent, and faced forward, awaiting the crank-up that the elderly man applied at the front end of the automobile. She shooed him from her path once it was obvious his chore was done. I'd become quite accustomed to both their faces during my junior year at school, and many days my observation of them had provided my only amusement.

Residents in the small town of Crescent Springs were few and were a mere part of the country south and west of Cincinnati, Ohio, the community appropriately named for the nearby springs. That and the train tracks that formed a crescent as they passed through the vast treeless area. The scheduled train stop was minutes away with no station to speak of, just an overhanging frame designed to shield in the event of rain or snow. On this Friday in late May, the sun shone brightly across the rooftop of the place I'd called home with eleven other girls whose hugs and goodbyes had brought tears and promises of letters to come.

Miss Woody motored us meditatively down the bumpy dirt lane called Buttermilk Pike and across the train tracks to within a hundred feet or so of the old firehouse north of town. She brought us to an abrupt stop near the frame structure. I could hear the chug of the train coming south from Ludlow.

Her unexpected reach for my hand gave me a start, and she patted it as if I were a beloved old dog, then managed a kind word of dismissal before I got out of the automobile. I grappled my two small trunks from behind the seat and dragged them to a spot beside the tracks. I was going home. Not much else mattered—not the nine long months of buttoned-up environment, not the starched and stern days of a girls' learning institution.

The train trip south to the Guthrie station would be over before late afternoon. All the way, I anticipated the ride with Father in his Model T—perhaps an all-new version of the one he'd had before—from there to Hillbound. Home again, and once more I'd be my daddy's daughter, the past healed, my thoughts reshaped.

But it proved to be Henry at the station, and I didn't stop to ask myself why that surprised me except that he was on time. His smile was reserved with the one of the biggest of his that I'd seen.

"You sure do look like Mother," he said, gazing at me in amazement, his words conveying a tender significance. Our long embrace said even more, then he took hold of my shoulders as if he needed to steady me and scrutinize my face. Meditative as he was, I had made his eyelids raise. "You look well, Sis, for all you've been through."

His comment made me smile. The journey hadn't been so bad, and the year was past. Gazing at him, I couldn't have failed to notice the stubble on his face or the bedraggled bent of his shirt and trousers. Although he hadn't said it, I suspected he'd come for me because Father was knee-deep in business concerns. Whether the duties of stabling thoroughbreds or the aftermath of the Derby or the concerns of other races, any one of a number of obligations could have consumed Father enough to prevent his taking time to travel to Guthrie. *Besides*, I thought, *it was easy enough to send Henry, and Father will be waiting at the house.* The reunion would be glorious, although a raincloud had presented itself hours since I'd departed Crescent Springs. Nevertheless, the approaching month of June would have Hillbound flaunting vibrant colors of flowers in bloom. Tobacco crops would soon peek their shoots through the abundance of rich Todd County soil.

"And you, Henry," I sighed, "you have not changed a bit."

The *plink-plunk* of the raindrops as they bounced on the windscreen sugar-coated my confidence with the rhythm of a metronome.

Henry was subdued, as if he were driving a stranger to a haunted house. His strong, graceful fingers gripped the steering wheel. "Sis," he said once he got settled on the drive, "things are different nowadays. I hope you'll stay close to home. Town talk's not always polite. You've been away quite a spell."

I looked at him, pushing my gloves farther between my fingers. "How so?"

His hilarious eyebrows had furrowed together like a hedgerow, but nothing hilarious registered on his face

"What on earth? I can't wait to be back where I belong," I said, bubbling with enthusiasm. "School was like—"

"Small towns . . . they're known for their nosiness in everyone's business."

Lines creased his forehead, and his cartoon face grew even more serious. It was obvious he'd been stung.

Whatever was on his mind was a festering ailment. It needed airing. In the sweltering silence I dared to ask: "What, Henry. What?"

The muscles in his face had tightened, and his expression was lifeless.

He clung to the wheel. "I just don't want you t' get in the middle. So, be careful. Miss Francine is poison, Gracie. Pure poison."

"What a thing to say, Henr—"

"Moe Lee's gone, Sis. He's not here, none of his folks. Nothing's the same as it was. There was trouble, and I mean big trouble. Miss Francine said he was belligerent. Said he tried to assault her. Then it got *real* bad . . . talk of lynchings. She stirred up a whole lotta grief for him, his whole family . . . his young'uns."

Henry didn't take his eyes off the road in front of us. "Clarice. Amos . . . They stepped in and, well . . . It got so bad they had no choice. Moe Lee, Odelia, the children, all of 'em up and left in the dead of night on a train. Not much more than the clothes on their backs. Went north, accordin' to Luke."

I could feel my heart pounding, but I was unable to move, and not a speck of relief came in the hideaway of my thoughts. If Henry was across from me, I was unaware. In my head I could hear the mockery, experience firsthand the thievery that Miss Francine had doused Moe Lee and the other folks—his children, *my children*—with and then set them aflame.

The *rat-tat-tat* of the Model T paralyzed me, refusing to shut out of my head the hum of machinery coming across the nearby field. Sounds—numbing ones—pounded my ears. Familiar, once pleasant smells like moss and the rich scent of dirt—the kind where huge, slimy earthworms crawl—now gagged me.

"Stop. Pull over—" I said, vomit filling my mouth.

Henry tried to speak but choked up instead. And as best as I could remember, I had never seen him cry.

⊷⫘⫘⊶

The drizzling spring rain had ended. The automobile tires splashed in water that puddled like long, narrow mirrors in the ruts along the road, reflecting spidery arms of the trees above us. Henry was trancelike as he drove us past the opening in the picket fence to a place beside the house where he parked the car. Even after he killed the engine, neither of us made an effort to get out.

A late sun was trying to break through the hazy line of clouds that hung above the horizon, and I sat with my eyes fixed straight ahead. Lingering raindrops dripped from the roof and shimmered on the hood of the Model T.

An image surfaced of Moe Lee walking up the hill from the meadow. And another one of his children, listening to me read to them on an occasion soon after my fifteenth birthday. Thoughts of that summer of 1922 flooded my mind, then more thoughts of the year that had followed when my life was forever changed.

And somewhere between my recollections, Henry left me sitting in the automobile, sensing, perhaps, my need to be alone and drenched in a homecoming with the stark truth of Hillbound that I could never have expected.

I stepped from the automobile onto the fresh green layer of grass that stretched between the house and automobile. The sprinkles of rain had stopped. It was as if I could still hear Moe Lee's voice in the silent scene I pictured—him standing, holding onto the fencepost, steadying his "'bout-to-give-out" bad leg. And I ran to where I could reach out to touch the top of the post, to feel where his hand had rested. I listened again, savoring the sound of him fussing, then walked the mile or so to the hollow house where he'd lived, my eyes watering as they took in the desolation of the yard around it.

Through the open door, a feral cat nosed in behind me and strutted across the splintery wood floor—its head in the air, its tail in the air—stepping around strewn apple baskets and a raggedy plaid shirt.

In the pouring rain, I walked home again, hoping not to see Father, wanting only to go up the stairs to my bedroom and ask God if he could possibly reshape my return home.

Across the not so distant landscape came the eerie clatter of iron wheels as a train crossed the tracks, and in the dark of night, I got up from the bed I'd made soggy with tears, tripped over the trunk that Henry had brought to my room, and lit a lamp. With my diary unlatched, I began to write.

May 30, 1924

*Were it not for the daffodils, I might never know Spring
has come. Surely Moe Lee is seeing the same moon this
night, and God will shape his life as He is shaping mine.*

*"I do not consider that I have made it my own. But this
one thing I do: forgetting what lies behind and straining
forward to what lies ahead, I press on toward the goal
for the prize of the upward call of God in Christ Jesus."
Philippians 3:13–14*

*My term at Crescent is past. The winter is gone. Hope
abounds within me.*

*Sister will no doubt allow me to stay the remainder of
tonight with her. I cannot and will not stay here. Miss
Francine is tearing my home to shreds. Surely the woman
Father has married is evil.*

In the wee hours, before morning had come to the fields, my decision
was made. I crossed my bedroom, tiptoed down the hallway to Henry's
room, and lightly rapped with my knuckle on his door. "Henry!" I waited.
Nothing. I tapped again and turned the knob. "Henry!" I whispered through
the small open space. "Get up!"

Chapter 35

Henry was unquestioning, as if he understood our trip into Elkton was essential to my well-being. That I'd escaped from Hillbound under the cover of darkness needed no explanation. He steered the automobile down South Main Street and stopped in front of Millicent's house.

"Sis, I-I'll tell Father whatever I need to," Henry said, walking me to her door, waiting with me till either she or Jim answered my knock. "Are you going to be alright?"

"Sakes alive! Gracie! Come inside! Henry—"

"No, it's just Gracie." He turned. "I'm going back."

"What's happened?" Millicent said, tugging on my sleeve. "Never mind. You look positively stricken. I'll fix you a place in the little room in the back. We can talk in the morning."

Millicent bustled about her kitchen, making coffee, rolling biscuit dough. "It's absolutely wonderful to see you, Gracie. I spent nights just wishing I could send a letter, but Francine insisted you couldn't be contacted—no telephone. *Nothing*. Crescent's policy, you know. Absurd! And people seemed so closed-mouth about everything."

She glanced off toward the hallway and put a finger to her lips. "If Louise hears us, she'll be jumping up and down in her crib, so we'll have to whisper. I am so, *so* delighted to see you, and looking very well. Tired, but it's to be expected. Were they good to you? That's all that matters. I know your education was a good one, and for a teacher especially. The best."

Sister babbled on, her personality never waning even for having had an early-morning intrusion and lost sleep as a result. "Henry was good to bring you into town. Of course, he would. But you must have suffered horribly, not being able to come home at Christmas. Jim and I would have welcomed you. In a minute! No questions! But I guess it's worked out. Do you want to talk, Gracie?"

Sitting at Millicent's kitchen table as if we were simply catching up on the last few weeks, when it had been an entire school year since she and I had been able to have a good talk, felt odd. I wanted her to soothe the pain of my discovering the awful things that had transpired in my absence at Hillbound. I yearned for her to take my hand and reassure me that my relationship having ended with Marcus was for the best. I hungered for her to fill every space in my heart with hope that the future was going to work out alright—the way she always had.

"I plan not to waste a minute getting my application into Logan Female College, so I'll be ready when I graduate next year," I said, letting my lungs inhale air as if it were the source of courage. "But Sister, you have to tell me what Francine did to him. I have to know about Moe Lee."

Millicent looked across the kitchen to me, baking sheet in hand. "She made life miserable for him, I guess. The Delaneys have been like a blight since they moved here. Felix's death and all . . . Moe Lee apparently said some things that Clancy had told him after the accident." She shoved biscuits onto the wire rack and shut the oven door. "You remember the black man that worked for Felix?"

I nodded, and Sister continued. "Some things didn't add up. There was question about the accident, and when people started talking about it, more and more bad things seemed to start happening. And even though Night Riders haven't had any occurrences around these parts in a good while, there was talk of something awful happening to Moe Lee. Not just him but his whole family. Moe Lee left because he had no choice, Gracie. He would have died. A lot of folks would've. I don't blame him. He was terrified. Who wouldn't be? Miss Francine was stirring the pot."

"And Luke and Bertie?"

"They're out there, but as far as I can see, only because of Father's obsession . . . his horses, his races, his betting. All-consuming. It's hard to know, and with little Louise it's been difficult to go out to the farm. You know Miss Francine doesn't like children. Particularly crying ones. So persnickety . . . and then some!"

"She doesn't want me around either. I could not stay the night. I had to talk to you."

"The night? Gracie, I told you that you're welcome here. It may be the answer."

"The answer? Oh, Sister! I have to find my direction somehow. But may I stay for a while? I do believe God will open doors for me to teach once college is behind me. My going to Logan should do that. I could work. And a scholarship to college . . . I won't require Father to take care of me all my—"

"There is more to it, Gracie."

"More?"

"People can be cruel. I just don't want you to be hurt."

"Hurt by what? It's not like I'm still trying to teach Moe Lee's children. I want to teach here, in Todd County. I just want to make a difference in people's lives. Don't you understand what I'm saying? I believe teaching is my purpose. I've had aspirations, but now . . . now I *know* with all my heart that this will be my future."

"Logan College will be good, honey. Russellville's a nice town and will afford you some distance. That will help, and in time . . . Time has a way of taking care of town talk."

"What on earth, Sister? What has that monster done to my family? Crescent is supposed to be preparing me in special ways to go to college after next year. To be all that my dream holds.

"I know you and Marcus made the best decision possible, putting the child up for adoption—"

"*What?*" I burst into tears. "I don't know how I missed it. Is that what you think? So that's what happened while I've been away? I've supposedly had a baby? I'm supposed to have had a child out of wedlock?"

Astonished, my sister nodded that it was true. "Father and Miss Francine have tried to squelch the subject. All they've said at every turn is that you were pursuing your education at a prestigious girls school in—"

"And let me guess: try as she might, Miss Francine and her venom could not seem to keep it from gossipers, could she?" I gave my sister a knowing look. "Small town. Word travels fast. So I've heard. And the rumors in the months after I was carted off simply rippled through Todd County."

I stood, although I thought I could not. I walked my coffee cup to the drainboard. "Sister." I felt the knot at the back of my throat grow to the size of a rock, "I did *not* have a child out of wedlock."

———⌇⌇⌇———

Only during the previous night's homecoming at Hillbound, the dinner where I'd sat, mostly stunned, was my urgency to be rid of Miss Francine's vicious mastery over people set in motion. The unusual feeling that I was watching on the screen in a movie palace the most recent revelation of her loathsome actions as they passed in slow motion before my eyes . . . Moe Lee and his family's exile and everything he meant to me was summed up in the pouring of the tea and the passing of dinner's fare and the closing of the day. No explanation had been offered for their personhood to be drained or their existence to be consumed or the darkness of night to erase them. And yet they were gone, and Bertie alone served in the house as a helper.

Henry had moped about the rooms of the first floor as if my being home after a year away at Crescent Springs had put him in a state of confusion. And only in my bedroom upstairs did life as I'd known it at Hillbound breathe its last breath.

Sister had been the only person to whom I could run to and reach out, and having broken free from one overwhelming evil, I clung now to the post of the Jenny Lind bed in Millicent's home, grasping for answers in the quiet reality of the lie that was told about me. Miss Francine's lie.

I looked around the room at Millicent's house that was mine now. *Whatever is to befall me*, I told myself, *I will have these four walls to shield me in the night when ugly creatures of my own design or those of people in my conscience point fingers and form odd shadows.*

Rumors whispered in dark corners as I walked in my mind past make-believe people snickering in hushed voices as if I wore a scarlet letter like Hester Prynne in Nathaniel Hawthorne's novel. Turned-up noses in the daylight and ducked-down heads on street corners surfaced while decency parked itself far off.

The small bag I'd packed in the wee hours at Hillbound before coming to Millicent's house held the bare necessities. I took out my diary and tried to think, sorting out rational thoughts to put on its pages and then began to write:

May 31, 1924

A lie so big, so accomplished, so cunning, and nothing less than the material of murder mysteries I have read. A lie devised to keep me from my home, to send me to Marcus's for Christmas so that Miss Francine could carry out her scheme. A lie to keep me from going to my sisters or being near Henry or my home or my friends. A lie that I have been away a year for the distinct purpose of hiding my shame—having a baby—Marcus's baby! Whose else?

Last August we were seen together everywhere, at church, in town, everywhere in the week he spent at his aunt's farm.

A lie made so believable that I will not be able look at a person on the face of God's earth that does not believe it.

We were talked about then. We will be talked about now. I will never be able to face Marcus. And not Lucy or Chester.

What kind of person would go to such lengths to destroy my reputation and position me for ridicule and shunning? Miss Francine has cooked up her own Scarlet Letter for me to bear.

The Coca-Cola calendar on the kitchen wall at Millicent's house pinned the thirty days of the month of June in bold black numerals beneath a lively-looking lady enjoying the beverage at a soda-fountain counter. Day after day went by with sparse connections—few and far between with Henry—to Hillbound, and life with Millicent and Jim and little Louise became the routine. Before I knew it, the days had passed, the paper page was torn off, and July's numerals showed, then August's with my birthday circled in pencil. I saw them as a blur in the fleeting time that I had with Millicent before returning as a seventeen-year-old to Crescent Springs.

From within, I found courage to look people straight in the eye and hold my head high.

When it came time to go back to Crescent Springs Girls School in September, I left Elkton with clear understating of how the location in Northern Kentucky on the outskirts of nowhere was chosen in the first place. Miss Francine deserved a medal for her diligence in tracking down the most isolated, regulated, and rule-oriented educational institution she could find. I couldn't be touched by the outside world, and I, along with my girlfriends with similar heartaches, returned to complete our final year of high school. I was, with a little different twist, nevertheless led there to complete the cover up that so often is never covered up.

What had begun as scrambled puzzle pieces in my life as a fifteen-year-old took shape in the way puzzles do, one piece at a time. When my two years were finished at Crescent Springs, two years at Logan College and two years at Athens College in Alabama fell into place as if they were completing the picture of a scene I could never have expected.

Nothing was going to bring back Moe Lee and his family, nothing was going to let me ever see the flower of the seed I'd planted in the lives of his children or Amos's or bring back Odelia or Clarice to reshape the Hillbound I'd known as a young person. And the jagged lie Miss Francine had positioned to destroy me fitted in instead as the pivotal piece in the complex puzzle of my six years away from home. Determination wedged itself in as a Bible-shaped piece, enabling me to glean from it the promises of God's plan for my life. I put the past behind me. The Gracie Maxwell that had been broken was the same one that exchanged lies for a life worth living.

With a scholarship, I graduated Athens College. Having resolved to honor my commitment to God, I was still planning to walk through the open door that had been set before me, to the mission field in the Sudan.

Chapter 36

After all the years

December 31, 1930

B ecause of my telephone call to Father ahead of time, the drawing room at Hillbound was aglow with all the lamps lit. Father ushered us inside, his dark eyes piercing. "My, my, Simon Hagan from outta the past! You were a strappin' youngster last time I saw ya. Look at ya now!" Their handshakes were hearty, the type of old acquaintances. A convivial air permeated the place as if something had been swept under the rug.

Simon at six foot three inches stood way taller than Father, but it gave him no edge. Father had only to assert his authoritativeness with a convincing smash of his cigarette in the ashtray. Dominance was understood.

"I've looked up to you since I was seventeen," Simon said. "That Model T of yours had me chomping at the bit for one of my own. Think you even bought me my first cigarette there at Carver's, if I'm recollecting right."

"Ah! And you bought my daughter a bar of chocolate in return. We're even."

Father could pour on the charm. His welcoming hug for me was the first I could recall in quite some time. All the same, a marvelous show of affection, followed by Henry's warm embrace and sweet kiss on my cheek.

All outer wraps shed and introductions aside, we seated ourselves comfortably in the room. Bertie brought refreshments and talk of the thoroughbreds commenced. Henry's glances told me he'd loved to be excused, but he sat patiently as Father told of his financial winnings at the track, his less than successful runs with his thoroughbreds, his everlasting aspirations for breeding a Kentucky Derby winner. Even as he spoke, there were clouds where his head seemed to reside.

Before the subject could switch to Simon or Henry or me, in walked Miss Francine, and a hush fell on the room. She was lovely by all accounts, I am sure, in her sleek satin dress, simple with only a demure little bow at the neck and flouncy long sleeves. And off to the left, pinned high on her shoulder, the delicately filigreed fan brooch that I'd given to my mother.

I gasped at the sight of it, and a look passed between me and Miss Francine. Hers was a fairly amused one, self-congratulatory, I assumed, with the deliberate blow she'd landed.

Simon was the first to rise. Henry and Father stood as well. "Aren't you stunning, darling!" Father said to Miss Francine. "Come meet Gracie's friend, then I want to walk him out to the stable. Want you to see what a specimen Luke has made of Bona Fide."

Simon nodded graciously to the rest of us, and he and Father picked up their belongings and were gone.

—◦ⅉⅉ∿∿ⅉⅉ◦—

"Henry," Miss Francine said, seating herself on the piano stool, a cigarette deftly perched between two fingers, "Fetch me that tray. Guess you didn't want to be with the men. Well, no matter. Robert might find you to be nuisance at the stable anyhow. I've had Rufus bring the carriage around, so you and Gracie can have yourselves a little visit while I go into town.

"But before I go I want you to know, Gracie, I've been thinking about . . . *things* . . . since your last visit here. Not that long ago, was it? And I need to set the record straight: this is not your house, not your farm, not your things," she said and swept her arm in a grand flourish across the drawing room.

My mouth opened, but there were no words. Henry was by my side in a heartbeat.

"You flaunt your education and your religion like my nephew does. You two deserved each other, but I guess that little fling just didn't work out for you and Marcus, did it? He's got himself that goody-goody skinny wife . . . Oh, dear, did I forget to mention he married? Possibly you knew. Who cares? He couldn't possibly ever have been seen with you anyhow after that *awful* rumor leaked about your misbehavior. Now that he's a preacher, always pushing, poking his agenda, as if there were a God who judges the sins of backsliders like me and Robert who don't go to church. *Ha!*"

She took a deep breath, her countenance iced over with an ugly glare.

"I've heard that garbage from Chester and that son of his for as long as I'm going to put up with it. They are not welcome here, and neither are you. And speaking of brothers," she said, "I don't care if this no-count excuse for yours hears this either: this place is mine for as long as I want it . . . and everything in it. But it was oh so good of Chester and Lucy to welcome you in their little poor excuse for a house on that Christmas—"

"—when you brought about one of your outstanding lies," I interrupted. "Yes, the Willoughbys' graciousness was offered to me out of the goodness of their hearts. But you used them as you use everyone else, as players in your convenient lies to accomplish your devious plans. That one was meant to destroy me. But you didn't get the last word, did you, Francine?"

Francine peered at me with angry eyes. "Life takes many turns . . . Take Felix and his untimely—"

"Yes, indeed. Take Felix. And how about Moe Lee and Clancy and their sudden departure. Is it because they knew somet—"

One look at Henry and his eyes told me I was in dangerous territory, summoning, perhaps the wicked.

"I will not be shaped by your despicable schemes, Francine. You've done everything possible to my father to cause our separation. But let me tell you this: my father's house will not be given over to evil. A day of reckoning will come."

Chapter 37

The walls of the place where I'd grown up would not let me smother any longer the feelings of abandonment. *Perhaps the injustices Francine brought on my family will never heal*, I thought. I wanted to believe I had swallowed that bitter pill long ago and risen above my disapproval of her, but lies were planted, and like land mines in unsuspecting soil, they were exploding.

Henry walked away from the front window as the carriage carrying Francine wheeled out of sight. "*She*, Gracie, is the real lie. In a way, I should have seen it coming."

"I certainly don't know how. Maybe I was too naive, but I thought she was gorgeous . . . and so fashionable. I wanted to be like her and wear beautiful clothes."

Henry put his arm around my shoulder. "You were fifteen. And, yes, naive."

"And?" I could tell he was hedging. "*And*, Henry?"

"You think the best of people, Gracie. It's a fine quality, for sure. Always finding good even if it's not there. Father's our father, of course. He deserves our honor. But you need to know why Francine is so loathsome. She stands between me and Father because of something that happened.

"What? Why is she treating you this way? Us this way? Don't tell me there is more. How could there be?"

Henry slid his arm from my shoulders and took a seat on the divan, head in his hands. "It goes back, Sis. Way back, to before Mother died. That day you came in and there were the flowers . . . Miss Francine had supposedly brought them for Mother. I had come into the house to let Father know Trojan Girl had that horrible rash. Remember? You were so young, so alive, so innocent."

I knew in the pit of my stomach an ugly truth was about to unfold. I could not sit down. I walked to the piano and braced myself on its edge. "What is it, Henry. Tell me."

"Father wasn't in his office, so I went to where Mother was . . . in the morning room. She was so weak she hardly knew I was there. And Father was not there, so I started up the stairs, looking for him. I didn't set out to track down the sound coming from the end of the hall up there." Henry sat back on the divan and looked up at me. He twisted his hands together as if they were a rag to be wrung. "I didn't intend to spy on the goings on behind the door of our parents' bedroom. But I found Father and Miss Francine—quite compromised. They must've started their conversation in the office. The flowers were there. But Gracie," he said and ran his fingers wildly thought his hair, "I'm convinced she came with it in her mind to seduce him. I'm certain of it. I practically fell down the stairs I was running so fast to get out of there. By the time I reached the office, Moe Lee had come in, and Father raced in there right behind him. Then you—"

"And y'all pushed me away, and I went into the morning room where Mama was dying. Father . . . was upstairs in bed with Francine . . . while Mama lay dying?" I tried desperately to reject those hideous words.

Henry came over to me, and we embraced. The image, worse than those of Father's flirtatious interactions with Miss Francine while Mama was alive, would not leave my consciousness. Knowing Henry had carried the burden and suffered in defeat the consequences that stemmed from Father's affair left my heart ripped from its valves.

I walked up the stairs to Mama's bedroom, pondering what had just taken place and the sad commentary that Henry had delivered, and all that filled my head. There was no mistaking the downward spiral that had defined Hillbound. Slowly but surely it was being given over to the wilds of compromise, bad judgment, and corruption. And Henry, clearly, had been run over like a squirrel in the road.

In a wilderness that resonates deep within all of us, I thought. *Thousands upon thousands of banks are gone under, and Father has yet to win the Kentucky Derby. Not one of his three thoroughbreds in the seven years he's raced has placed at the Oaks, and now he's all but given up the illusion of Hillbound Stock Farm—well beyond the grueling process of selling all but one of them.*

Last year's October stock market crash has signaled hard times. Unemployment is at a record high, affecting a fourth of the eligible workforce, but Father still has his air, I thought.

The repercussions of the economic depression are the worst in the history of the country, and he's still putting up a front, gambling, throwing away his life—and for what?

In my brazenness, I opened the door to his bedroom.

No longer Senator Maxwell, no longer Squire Maxwell, I thought. *His resplendence will surely come to an end, and Henry, it appears is the unlikely heir to the vast acreage that should rightfully be his inheritance.*

Just as quickly, I shut the door to Father's bedroom. The thought of Francine in this room irked me. Every fragment of Mama's history had disappeared. Only the bed where she had given birth to my sisters, my brother, and me still remained. Seeing it again made me resolve to make it my last time to come near this bedroom.

Behind me, Father rustled his watch chain. It startled me. "Simon's waiting on the verandah," he said.

"Ah, I shouldn't be here, should I? Because this is yours—your place to do with as you please. You and Francine figured it all out." I looked past him to the hand railing, then across the hallway to my room. "Funny in a way, isn't it? We think we know the people we've loved, the house we've shared, but in the end they're full of little surprises. Ugly ones, sometimes. I hope Francine's been worth the sacrifice, Father." I rested my hand on the railing and started down the steps, then looked back at him standing very still. "She had a big price tag."

I stepped into the drawing room to tell Henry goodbye, then found Simon outside, meandering along the picket fence, taking in the view across the road, and I thought of how I'd long since buried the treasures and tremblings of my youth. My diary had been replaced by my journal, moreover by my Bible as my anchor and my beacon. Words from the first chapter of Titus floated in my memory: *"But to those who are defiled and unbelieving, nothing is pure, but both their mind and their conscience are defiled. They profess to know God, but by their deeds they deny Him, being detestable and disobedient and worthless for any good deed."*

Not a comfort but an understanding.

I took a long look back as Simon drove us away from Hillbound. Henry stood at the window in the drawing room. Father was nowhere in sight.

I had escaped. Henry had not. I had my power source. Henry did not.

"My bringing you here was perhaps a mistake, Simon," I said, staring out the truck window. "There's a bit more to my family than meets the eye, I'm sorry to say. We're a complicated bunch, I guess."

Simon threw his head back in a delightful chuckle. "All families are complicated, Gracie. And on the contrary. Seeing Senator Maxwell . . . Of course I know he's not now, but I'll always think of him that way. He was sort of my idol there for a while. I wanted to strut like Senator Maxwell, own an automobile like his—"

Perhaps sensing my disengagement, Simon glanced at me, then back at the road. He took a firmer grip on the steering wheel, then moved one hand to rest it on mine.

I was not smiling. "I need some time, Simon. Maybe a good bit of time," I said. "I won't let this trip out to the farm bruise my urgency to help people, but there's no mistaking its ability to keep me from ever coming back. It sounds harsh, but I think it's provided me closure. Pretty final, isn't it?" I smiled at him, solidifying that was precisely what the visit had allowed. I took a deep breath and plopped my other hand on top of his. "I'm so glad you got to see my father again and the place I called home. I'm looking forward to a whole new year. We both have big plans for 1931, don't we? I with my teaching, then off to the Sudan. You with your plans for a tire business. That's all very exciting."

Simon swerved the truck a mite, perhaps to avoid something in the road, but I gave him his hand back anyway. The temperature had dropped drastically, and the truck was drafty. I pulled my plaid wool coat closer, pained to forms the words I knew he had to hear.

He maneuvered the automobile. Still he smiled, and his brown eyes twinkled.

"I am going away, far away. To the mission field." I dabbed a stray tear. "It's definitely my calling. I hope you'll—"

"Let's not forget. You promised, Gracie . . . to go with me to Providence Methodist."

Chapter 38

—⟨⟨⟨〰⟩⟩⟩—

Both school rooms where I taught in Russellville were empty, the log embers dying down in the stove. I bundled my lesson plans and stacked them at the corner of my desk, set the black-handled school bell on top, and walked next door to my boarding house.

Dinner was close to wordless. My landlady wielded her inquisitive eyes but asked nothing, and I excused myself with all the grace of a teacher needing to prepare for her students, then made my way up the stairs to my room.

It had been months since I'd considered my old diary. I opened it, not wanting to dwell on the past. Even so, I picked at the torn-out pages, four or five at least of them, torn from the between written and unwritten ones.

Simon is a stronghold, I thought, *a port in the storm, but I cannot expose him to all my known past. And who's to say what is yet unknown?*

I fingered the ruffled edges of the torn pages still clinging to the spine—those that had told about Mama and the agony of her last days when I knew nothing of the depth of treachery that Father was enjoying and the real reason he couldn't face her. Pages from when I was vulnerable and hurt—angry—from when I'd needed him more that I could begin to express, stuck out a reminder.

"But I was smarter than that," I said aloud, "not thrown off course by what other folks said, and I taught the Negro children without one single regret."

As if I were a young girl again, needing to record my feelings, I picked up a pen and began to write in my old diary:

January 5, 1931

And I rose above the lie. I will continue to rise above them.

I never envisioned my life without Mama or what she would say when I met someone like Simon. Not what she might say when Father's true nature would be revealed, compromised to the core by a seductive woman.

I knew the first time I lay eyes on Simon, when there was a flutter in my chest that I had not felt before, a sudden rush and a weakness in my knees, and I knew in less than a glimpse as he walked toward me, stealing my breath, robbing my judgment, that he was extraordinary.

That alone made me smile, but inside, reasoning was telling me I had no business deepening a relationship with someone—anyone—when I was going so far away for so long. It would be unfair to us both if I were to allow it. I thought of a verse from the Bible and began jotting it down, for posterity's sake, I supposed:

> *"I press toward the mark for the prize of the high calling of God in Christ Jesus. No longer will things past have power over me. I will be shaped by the calling God had chosen for me."*

I shut the diary and stuffed it away in the back of the wardrobe.

That said, I thought, *I cannot see Simon. I should not see him. I will not.*

And in the three months to come when I declined his invitations, abbreviated our phone conversations, and buried myself in my teaching, I felt no less guilty that my excuses were justified by my vision to be a light to the world.

Inside, where my heart resided, the flame I was trying to ignore was flickering. It seemed to have Simon's name written all over it.

Chapter 39

April 2, 1931

"Gracie Maxwell?"

"Yes, sir, this is she," I said through the telephone wires.

"Gracie Mae Maxwell?" His voice was strangely familiar, an older gentleman.

I stood, puzzled, holding the receiver in the hallway at my boarding house.

"Yes, sir," I said.

"This is Geoffrey Hagan here. Hope you won't be taken aback, but a dad's gotta do what a dad's gotta do. Never was much on debt collectin'— collectors weren't well-thought of in the Bible, ya know."

I could hear his smile. I had to laugh.

"Mr. Hagan! Have I been fired from teaching?"

"Not on that score, but on another. You are a mite indebted. You see, I've been a-havin' to put up with this *can*-tankerous overgrown son of mine. First he takes off, leaves me with the farm for ten years, then comes back and starts up mully-grubbing 'bout how you— Well, he said you'd told him you'd come to my church, then didn't. Now, he's cert'nly capable of takin' care of himself, but like I said, I'm stickin' up for him. Wanted to invite you— Actually, it's Hannah, my wife too. We both want ya to come for Easter Sunday morning service and on over to the house for dinner. That'd settle the score. Otherwise we got us a problem."

231

"That's a lovely invitation, Mr. Hagan. Thank you very much. And you're right. I didn't honor my promise to attend church service at Providence. I should regret that, but under the circumstances I was unable."

"Don't want to twist your arm, but you've gotta remember how I was instrumental in getting you that teaching job. That has to count for something, don't ya think?"

I listened to his smile pushing through the words and sensed he was amusing himself as much as me. That and his fatherly influence were about all that were needed to soften my defenses. Deep down I wanted to jump at the chance to see Simon again, if only for a church service and lunch. Still, I couldn't. "Please don't misunderstand. Hannah's been so gracious to offer more than once now. And I would love to do just that, but—"

"Then it's all settled. No more about it."

I closed my mouth, not knowing where to place the blame for Mr. Hagan's cleverly carried out scheme to reunite me with Simon. It was plain to see where Simon had acquired his sense of humor. It tickled me, made me laugh out loud, made me giddy. I wanted to dance, I wanted to sing. I told myself to think quickly. "Do the ladies wear Easter bonnets?"

"You'd be totally out of place if you didn't!" He sounded perfectly serious. "Now, then, it's gonna be my boy Raymond that comes for you. Simon is workin' on his manners."

"I doubt that Mr. Hagan, but I'll be ready," I said, restraining my exuberance. "And I do want to hear about the Shawnee Indians that inhabited your property. Will Big John be around to do that for me?"

"Teachers are like that, I guess. Well, alright then." I heard on the other end of the line the deep breath Mr. Hagan took. He cleared his throat. "And Simon's gonna be surprised, by the way. Probably won't be a mite mad, though."

"Thank you for the invitation," I said and hung up the telephone.

Oh, no, I thought. *Now what have I done?*

A chorus of spring peepers delivered a cheerful welcome to Raymond and me as we stepped from the Hagan's automobile onto the lawn at Providence Methodist Church. The quaint chapel sat amid clusters of evergreens with a few sprinkled-in early flowering trees. Sun poured through the round window above the arched door as if it were an anointing.

Raymond, perhaps ten years younger than Simon, was a chatty individual and had told me all I ever wanted to know about vulcanized rubber and the tremendous demand for it due to sale of automobile tires.

He gave me a grin, and I held lightly to his arm as he and I strolled up the church steps. "And that's precisely why Simon and I are considering opening a Goodyear store," he said, his enthusiasm as crisp as the Kentucky air on this glorious Easter Sunday morning.

Mr. Hagan was waiting just inside the door and greeted me with a warm hug. "This is a wonderful day, isn't it? I'm glad you've come." Having tugged my arm away from Raymond, he enfolded it in his and began walking with me down the aisle toward where Simon was seated.

I had recognized Simon from the back of the church. His head towered above the other parishioners. The pews were quickly filling with all age persons: men in overalls, some in waistcoats, children in their Sunday-best with behavior to match, and ladies in flowered dresses. Not a one donned a hat that bespoke an interest in the latest fashion the way that mine did.

"*Easter* bonnets, Mr. Hagan," I whispered, "aren't exactly bonnets."

"Now, now, " he chuckled, sounding much like Simon. "I didn't think you'd mind standing out a bit."

My *standing out* was an understatement. Cropped black curls peeked out beneath my hat at the sides with the perfect display of attitude. "Not at all. Not at all," I said, noticing the ladies who were gandering at my stylish dome-shaped cloche with its low-flying wings.

Mr. Hagan and I arrived at the front row, and he indicated with a pointing finger that I was to sit next to his eldest son. Simon glanced up, astonished to see me. The service was about to begin.

"Gracie!" He quickly stood—radiant—smiling his dazzling smile.

"Good morning, and a Happy Easter to you, Simon."

Noontime dinner around the cherry wood table at the Hagans began with prayer, hands held. Mine felt like warm clay melting in Simon's grip as his father gave thanks for the sacrifice Jesus Christ had made to fix our brokenness.

Amens spoken, the ruckus began, and Hannah with helpers brought in the food, placed it in the center of the cherrywood table, and the lazy Susan started turning with the help of Big John's hands. Bowls full, platters full—ample food in a roomful of friendly faces amid the charm of the butterscotch-colored stone bungalow situated high on an embankment six miles north of Elkton. The Hagan home positioned itself in my heart, in the void that Hillbound had left.

The account of the skeletal remains of the Shawnee Indian had obviously been told many times. Simon's young half-brother, a redhead with freckles as big as black-eyed peas, easily recited the details. From his perspective as a second grader, he presented a most intriguing tale of the intact remains being unearthed. "*And*," Big John said, "they're in a museum in Frankfort."

He pushed back his chair from the table. "Kentucky," he added with a smile and rushed off, only to return within minutes with his arrowhead collection that he shared as we ate country ham and roasted potatoes.

But it was the captivating stories of Simon's years away that had me on the edge of my chair. From his earliest start at the Henry Ford Motor Company to his being captain on the Detroit police department embroiled with prohibition and the Mafia to Albuquerque and his battle with tuberculosis—I wanted to know everything.

"Should we try one of our famous walks," Simon asked after the dishes were cleared and the stories were told.

"What's famous about a walk?" Big John asked, scooping up his arrowheads.

Simon looked at me with a mischievous grin. "Celebrated, I think. Yes, that's it. By the way, did you find those arrowheads all on your own?"

"Yes, why?" Big John was on the defensive.

"Because some of them are familiar, as in belonging in the ones I might have found," Simon said, his brown eyes sparkling.

"*Did not*!" Simon's half-brother came at Simon with a punch toward his belly. It was caught in midair, and they both burst into laughter. "They're mine. Every last one."

"Alright, then," Simon said. "Maybe I need to take Miss Maxwell on a walk. Show her where some have been found."

"Go on, y'all. I'm taking these up to my room."

Big John was up the stairs in a flash. Simon led me to the front door and across the lawn.

A red barn and a silo sat in the not too far off distance, and down the hill two bay horses grazed next to the fence.

Simon was quiet as we walked, occasionally glancing at me as I surveyed the view in all directions. There had been nothing in my thoughts to indicate I should be anywhere but right where I was, close beside Simon. Everything about the moment felt comfortable.

He took a few more steps, then paused beside an enormous oak tree at the side of the house. "Gracie," he said and lit a cigarette. "I know you have your plans and I applaud them. The calling to be a missionary is a splendid one."

He reached up with a hand to hold onto a branch overtop my head, and his gaze went out to the seedbeds of the wheat fields. He took a long puff on his cigarette and pointed toward the back of the house, smoke trailing his every gesture. "My mother died out there a number of years ago. I was seventeen. Was a terrible thing. I tried to save her."

After a few moment he began walking again. "I failed," he said. "I failed to save her." My fear of asking questions that might go too deep kept me from speaking about Nellie Hagan's death after a bear severed her arm. I had not heard any talk of the incident in recent years, and the recollection of it made me shudder to think back to when I was twelve and the news had kept Elkton in an uproar. I waited out the silence while Simon hesitated.

"Our homes, the places where we grew up, our history, Gracie," he finally said, "all of them hold a part of us. Some good, some not so good. Oftentimes, it seems like the not so good ones are the very ones that reshape us. Least ways, that's been my experience. Probably talking out of turn here, but I guess you've got things in your past, same as I do. Wish we could fix 'em."

He waited for me to respond but the afternoon was far too beautiful, the moment too serene to dredge up unpleasantries. I smiled and breathed in the farm air to replenish myself with its goodness.

"I do know this much, though, and that's where the good Lord comes in. Reshaping us. I don't want to try to persuade you to reconsider your future. I just want to be part of it." He parked us next to the rock well at the side of the house and looked at me for a long moment. "If you've felt the need to distance yourself these last several months because I've been too eager, then I want to apologize. If it's something else, Gracie, would you be willing to tell me?"

I traced the rim of the water bucket and said nothing until I was sure I could articulate what was necessary to say. "It's just that I'm leaving, Simon. No ifs, ands, or buts about it. I've let go of the hold that my past had on me. Sometimes I have to remind myself that I have, but for the most part, with God's help, I have. But I believe I would have chosen to go to the Sudan under any circumstance, so it's not because I need to get away. The decision didn't ever feel like a drastic one but a natural one. It's completely about the urge to go where people are destitute. I want to go . . . but I must admit I do enjoy being with you. I'm glad your father called."

I laughed and Simon did as well. The levity was just what we needed.

Cigarette smoke curled between us. "He's a character, that one," Simon said.

"He is at that. Seriously, though," I said, not taking my eyes off Simon, "I am going far away and for a very long time. It's just not right to lead you on by having you court me. That's probably the biggest reason why I've tried to be sensible."

My heart was pounding. I gave the bucket a little shove and continued to look up at him with his tall frame silhouetted against the afternoon sun's glare. In the silence between us, I waited, hoping beyond hope that he would assure me of something, although I knew not what.

He crushed the end of his cigarette with the toe of his shoe and his hand went up in a graceful manner to shush me. "Gracie, left alone to go off to a strange land, then. I guess I should respect that. I've tried to do that. But now, with you standing here and us having this conversation, I don't think it's right not to tell you that I do want to court you, still."

I turned away. "Alright. Completely honest. I know I've already said it before when we had come from Hillbound, but I'll say it again: there's more than meets the eye. I'm afraid my father hasn't been the best model of morality. As his daughter, I don't want to be disrespectful. Public life may be a different thing. But family . . . my mother." I had to stop talking. I gazed up to the blue sky and regained my composure. "I have to heal, Simon. The day we went out to Hillbound was one of the worst days of my life if not the absolute worst."

Immediately I knew I'd not said what I wanted to say in the way I should have.

"Ahem, I'm right here," Simon said.

"Not because of anything you did. Of course! It's just that on that day I learned who my father really is, how compromised, how duplicitous. It's very scary to grow fond of a man after knowing what my father did to my mother. Can you begin to understand, Simon? Because I'm not sure I understand myself. Perhaps it's a part of the puzzle that in truth is a deep wound. I know you have one as well. Need I go on about it anymore than I have?"

"Well, hearing this makes me even more sure," he said in earnest. "I want to protect you. I do care about you."

"And if I'm gone for two years?" I could feel myself melting beneath an incredible yearning to be held and shielded and loved. Hope that he would see through the wall I had built was welling up inside me. Every other thought vanished. I was about to burst.

"Thing is, Gracie, if you leave, even if it's for two years, I will wait for you. That's how sure I am of my feelings for you—"

"But—"

"Ah-ah." He placed his finger gently over my lips. "Don't say anything. Just think about what I've said. And if you want me to stop trying to call on you, then I'll accept that. I won't like it, but I will stop. I'd just like to know."

The spring breeze sent a chill down my spine. I shivered, smiling. "But, I was going to say, perhaps we could write to each other."

Chapter 40

W ith only two weeks remaining before the end of the school term, I found myself delighting daily in the last days of April's sunshine-filled offerings as if they were gifts of exceptional value. My heart brimmed with anticipation, due in part to the beauty of the Kentucky springtime that by itself was a promise of new life, and in part to my deep satisfaction that came from teaching the children and pointing them to hope for the future. Mostly, it was due to my being in love. Simon Hagan had turned my world upside down, made my days and weeks come to life in a rainbow of colors, my nights turn sleepless, my thoughts tingle with happy notes of what might be in store for me with the man who had stolen my heart.

I tidied the arrangement of students' desks and put away the excess of papers on my own desk, then rushed from the school and hurried to my boarding house to make ready for Simon's arrival. Ever since Easter Sunday and the direction we had decided upon for seeing each other, Friday afternoons had become ones to count down to before my departure to the Sudan. This being the next to last, I proceeded up the stairs to my room, folded a few extra garments, took some personal items, and put them in my bag to ensure the final move to Millicent's the weekend after next would be a little less cumbersome. By the time I'd finished the task and gone downstairs to the kitchen to speak with my landlady, there was a knock on the front door.

"I'll answer it, Mrs. Martin. And I'll see you when I'm back here on Sunday night.

She smiled and kindly shooed me on, wiping her hand on her apron as she followed me through the dining room. "Hard to believe your time here is getting so close. Go on, now, hon. Have yourself a lovely weekend."

Simon was all smiles as I opened the door. He stepped inside and picked up my two bags that sat close by. "It's good to see you, Gracie. You as well, Mrs. Martin," he said and tipped his fedora. "We sure have ourselves a beautiful afternoon for the drive back to Elkton. Might even catch the sunset. Gosh. You've doubled up on baggage here, Gracie." He chuckled, looking every bit as handsome as always with a twinkle in his eyes. "Mind if I put these in the truck bed?"

"Of course not. And it's very nice to see you too."

"Wait here," he said, "and I'll load these and be back for you."

I gave Mrs. Martin a hug and was out the door and down the walkway before Simon could return. "Thanks for traveling all this way for me."

Simon grabbed the truck's door handle and tucked in the bottom of my dress at the floorboard as I sat down. Once he was situated in the driver's seat, he turned to me with a smile. "I thought today would never get here." He reached for my hand, squeezed it, then let go and focused on the road ahead. "So generous of Jim to let me use his grocery truck, isn't it? You're welcome, but it's your uncle you have to thank for letting me travel all this way. Good week, Gracie? Will you miss being at Mrs. Martin's?"

"Whoa! I thought I was the one with all the questions. But let's see, yes, I'll miss kind Mrs. Martin. She's been the perfect landlady these last two years. And my week has been the absolute best." I could feel my face flush. "Lots to be thankful for. Lots to look forward to. Springtime does that for me—thrills me to no end. Leaving my students in a week, though, is like seeing little birds fly out of the nest after you've been watching them develop. Bittersweet, but it's exactly what's supposed to happen. I'll have so many children, so many opportunities to assist with their development. Even without my having anything medically to do, I can be an instrument in God's hands. That's certainly my vision, my passion." I couldn't take my eyes off Simon. I could feel what I said was resonating with him.

"You'll write to me about every single thing that's happening, won't you? I want to know it all. If I'd been able to go on to medical school as I'd planned, as keen as I was on going, I'm not sure I would have ever had the depth of self-sacrifice that you have. It's truly amazing, Gracie. I'm proud of you."

"Not really, not anything to be praised. It's just that I've seen injustice that irks me. It's because of the Negro children . . . way back when I was not much more than a child myself . . . I saw the pain of those less fortunate. It put a mark on me. The fact that they were Negros didn't figure. Not just the teaching. The rest of it too. What they did to Moe Lee . . . I didn't know what people were capable of till then. And I've wondered about Francine's husband. His death was awful. And odd. I can hardly explain what happens when you're overwhelmed with empathy . . . saturated . . . emerged. It's almost as if I became a vessel for compassion. Then came the inspiring, compelling conference while I was on the campus at Athens, and that book I've mentioned before—*In His Steps*. I could almost see the children in the Sudan that I needed to reach out to help." I took a deep breath, wrinkled my face into a queer expression, certain I'd gotten too caught up in myself. "Two years is not that long in the big picture. Going to the Sudan now is something that will happen only once in my lifetime."

Simon didn't look overwhelmed. He looked moved. "I love listening to you, how you take on life. It's beautiful, Gracie. Just beautiful." He turned to face me, and his gaze lingered a moment while the afternoon sun fell across his features, accentuating his high cheekbones and putting a warm glow on his lips. "I've been hoping to work something into our conversation, Gracie, something I want you to know about me. I don't think there's going to be a better time than the present. Just don't want you to think I've been withholding a secret past. I haven't."

I adjusted my position on the seat, instantly thinking back to long ago when Marcus Willoughby had told me he'd met someone else. Replacement by someone new could easily sound like an echoing gong. Simon's tone had the same ring to it—-upfront, honest, with a big "but" at the end of it. Fleeting romances had a way of being just that, and I'd seen my share of them in the past couple of years.

"When I found out that I had tuberculosis, the girl I loved ditched me. I've spoken of her family. The Mallorys along with their two daughters were everything to me. I was brand new to Michigan. They took me in— not to live with them but to see to it that I belonged. Charlie was like a big brother. Great guy. Wonderful guy."

The sounds of the truck's engine and the tires on the dirt road and a few passing automobiles were the only interruptions to Simon's narrative. He looked at me once and continued to speak. "The girls were just kids, but kids grow up. Long after the time I had spent in Highland Park at Ford and was on Detroit's police department, Charlie and Virginia's daughter became my first love. We were involved. Not how you might think, but we were in love—"

"Are you sure you need to, want to, tell me, Simon?" Imaginary as it was for me, Simon's story was unfolding with obvious emotion for him. "It's okay. It can wait."

"No, I don't think so. The night I found out about my good buddy being killed in the line of duty—the sergeant that I've told you about—"

"Roman Davis?"

"That's right. Gunned down in cold blood outside the precinct. It helped during that difficult time to have a woman to love and to have her love me in return. She was my support while I tried to deal with Roman's death." Simon pulled from behind a slow-moving automobile, passed it, then rolled the window down completely, lit a cigarette, and kept on driving. "It was a few days after. I'd planned to ask her to marry me, but that one night I was particularly vulnerable. I couldn't stand to think of letting her slip away. It sounds crazy, I know, but losing the best friend I'd ever had did that, and I didn't wait for Christmas to propose. Afterwards . . . we let our emotions go out of control."

I felt uncomfortable, as if I were an uninvited guest at a party. Simon, I think, could tell I was wondering what to think. He took a deep breath and continued. "I'm getting to what you need to know, Gracie. The details are important. It was right after that night when we were together that I was diagnosed with TB. I told her, of course, and because I had TB she wanted no part of my future. I left right away for Albuquerque to live in a sanatorium."

Simon's countenance was peaceful. "When I found out about the baby, I was still in the sanatorium. When it was possible, we were reunited—married."

I tried not to gasp, thinking Simon had a divorced wife and a child.

The sun in an aura of beautiful shades of orange was beginning to drop on the horizon. It helped to focus on its magnificence to keep my spirits up.

"They are both deceased, Gracie. But, yes, for a brief time I did have a wife and child. If you want to know more about—"

"It's not necessary, Simon," I said, trying hard to process his confession. "Unless you want to tell me more."

"No, not now. I think we have a nice weekend ahead. I'm going to get you to Millicent's before long. Jim said she's planning dinner. And tomorrow we'll go to Pilot Rock." Simon was beaming. "Not a drop of rain in the forecast. So let's take a hike, see the spectacular view from the top." He paused and gave me an inquisitive look. "I know this is a lot to take in. Are you still on board with me? Or have I ruined things?"

"I'm glad you told me. It was the right decision. I'm sorry for your loss, Simon. Truly." I was taken aback by his disclosure, but it served to melt my heart, knowing what he had experienced. "Pilot Rock it is. Let me bring a picnic lunch." I smiled to reassure him and we rode on in silence, taking in the beauty of the sky that was clear evidence of God's handiwork.

Noon on Saturday, Simon and I were bound for Pilot Rock a few miles away. He steered the truck with lettering on both sides (ones that indicated its intended use for *CARVERS'S GROCERY & HARDWARE*) down the road, then into the vicinity of Todd County's own landmark, its highest point.

Slowing down, Simon rolled past some scraggly trees and deftly parked alongside a rather new-looking automobile. He turned off the motor and sat for a moment, eyeing every inch of the automobile next to us—its sleek dark body, its shiny chrome front end. "*Zzzz!*" He sounded a whistle. "She's a '30 . . . Series AD Universal . . . Chevrolet. Not from around here, I'd be willing to bet."

He got out with a nonstop smile and lifted the picnic basket from the back end of the truck on his way around to my side.

"You do like automobiles, don't you?" I said, laughing as I got out. "That is a pretty car."

"It is, at that." He looked longingly at it, then closed the truck door behind me. "The closest I'm gonna get to owning one again, anytime soon, will maybe be because of a tire that goes on it." He chuckled and took hold of my elbow, gently leading me up the path toward the pinnacle of stone bursting from the earth. "If Raymond and I can get our ducks in a row with this Goodyear store, I'll be mighty happy."

"Well, we're up against a great depression. Everywhere. But saving every penny does count. I've been at it for two years . . . to have enough to pay for the flight to the Sudan and back. It's terribly expensive, as you know."

"I do. I do. By the time you return, I suspect I'll be knee deep in tires at Hagan's Goodyear Tire Store." He gave me a look from the corner of his eye and grinned.

It was a short hike to the summit of the large, high hill. The walk was invigorating. The view, breathtaking.

"We're at close to a thousand feet up," he said, muffling a couple of shallow coughs as he positioned the picnic basket on the rock formation. "Right in the middle of farming country. What a view! And I'm fortunate as the dickens to be alive to see this again. Been here only once before. Dad brought me and Alan."

Simon's mention of his younger brother was matter of fact although I understood the sentimentality of his remembrance—perhaps too raw to discuss any further.

"This site is so unique, isn't it? And I'm told what we're standing on was actually formed from the Big Clifty sandstone—the cap rock under which Mammoth Cave lies. Maybe I can take you there some day."

The soft breeze made me shiver. "You're just full of wonderful plans. And good information, Simon. I like that about you."

He took notice of the chill and stepped nearer to me as I reached for the sweater that was tucked beneath the handles of Millicent's picnic basket. But Simon beat me to the basket and got the sweater. He smiled down at me— a smile I thought I'd like to look at for the rest of my life—then adjusted my wooly cardigan closely around my shoulders and tied together its long arms beneath my chin. Slowly, deliberately, his hands cradled my cheeks and—there, in the middle of a splendid April afternoon atop the steep slope of Pilot Rock—he kissed my lips with a tenderness that didn't let go for quite some time.

It warmed me all the way down to my toes.

Chapter 41

My trunk was packed. My last day in Elkton, Kentucky (for the next two years) was nearing its end. Henry sat next to me on the maroon mohair divan in the living room of Millicent and Jim's home.

"—and Louise is going to miss you too," Henry said. "Isn't that right, sweetheart?"

"Uncle Henry, you could come play with me more often. While Aunt Gracie is gone, would you? You never come. Would you?"

I raised my eyebrows at Henry. "Well?"

He nodded, pleased. "I'd like that, Louise. I'd like that a lot."

"Where do you live, anyway, Uncle Henry? Can I come see you?"

"*Ahem.* Who knows? Maybe so, one of these days," Henry said, his voice drifting. "But you didn't answer me about your Aunt Gracie."

"You mean, am I gonna miss her?" Louise ran to me and threw her arms around my knees. She sat on the floor, clinging. "My mama says I'll be out of the fourth grade before Aunt Gracie comes back." She looked up at me. A forlorn expression registered on her little face. "Mr. Simon is gonna come see me. He said so."

"Now, y'all are getting way too mushy. I'm glad I'll be missed, but let's be happy. Sister? Would you and Jim come in here?"

It was only seconds before we were gathered together, standing in the living room in front of the empty fireplace, hands held. And Jim offered a prayer for the months ahead.

The following morning, right on time, Simon was on the doorstep at Millicent's and the few miles to the Guthrie train station in Carver's grocery truck seemed to pass in the blink of an eye. We could barely look at each other. Simon was as intent on my not seeing his tears as I was on not letting him see mine.

Over the clamor and commotion, we said our final goodbye. With little more to be said that had not been previously said about our past history and our hopes for the future, Simon's chest heaved. His lip trembled. "Gracie, I love you." His kiss was salty from tears but nevertheless the sweetest imaginable.

"I love you, Simon," I said over the thundering voice on the speaker from the train platform. And with a wave I stepped out of sight. The train began its move down the track with a massive *chug* coupled with the deafening scream of the whistle. *Chug—wooh-ooh . . . chug . . . wooh-ooh . . .*

Before the train connections to New York City were accomplished, I had penned in my journal my beginning thoughts of what was to be a two-year experience in the Sudan. My vision for changing my little corner of the world had mushroomed. I was ready to take on the rest of the world. The culmination of the fast-paced modernization of the 1920s and a year and a half into the 1930s had me riding high on ambition. Unmistakably, I was urged by an inward calling to be the person God wanted me to be. And if the future was going to include Simon, I was taking the necessary time to be certain. Meanwhile, I was clay in God's hand until I knew for sure.

Simon had not asked me to give up my calling. He'd promised to wait for me.

The airplane out of New York City on Thursday, May 14, 1931, had me trusting God in a new way. I refused to admit to myself that I was terrified. I'd never flown in an airplane—only in my dreams—and I didn't know anyone who had.

The plane was an austere beast. Like a gigantic metal eagle with wings stretched wide, it wanted to intimidate me. Even so, the sensation of climbing the steps to the interior was exhilarating.

"We will hit the two-hundred-miles-per-hour mark, then settle into a cruising altitude of about thirteen thousand feet," said the nicely dressed attendant. She followed her comment with a confident smile. "For the temperature fluctuations, you will be provided blankets as well as oxygen-tank-assisted breathing when necessary."

I jotted the information down, knowing Simon would love the details.

She continued to inform the several of us aboard to expect within the cabin climate changes ranging from arctic to temperate to tropical to arid and then back again.

Upon takeoff, I swallowed hard, sure I'd managed to wet my panties. My quick revelation was that flying was not for the faint of heart. My plans for journaling along the way were quietly abandoned.

"Air-sickness bowls may be found under each seat," came the announcement.

I reached for mine.

In the air, with days of flight ahead, there was plenty of time to think. I was most looking forward to touching down in Cairo. It would feel so . . . biblical. I had to laugh at myself.

I grabbed my journal to fan the heat from my face and for the umpteenth time swallowed hard. Suddenly, there was no doubt. We had dropped hundreds of feet with not a word of warning. The attendant smiled with a tilt of her head as if it were as normal as falling off a log.

I tried reflecting on my former pupils at school and the hug I'd given each of them on the last day of class, the encouraging word from the deep wellspring of my fondness for them. Experience with children had a way of reassuring me of my purpose, and their fingerprints were all over my journey.

Once, in an odd silence when I started to think of Father, the question about whether he still basked in the sexual escapades he'd pulled off with Francine before my mother died reared its ugly head. Immediately, I raced to remind myself of Marcus—the Christmas when I'd gone down to the potter's house if only to be imprinted by the strength of his teaching. I had, as a result, relinquished my life to become clay in the potter's hands.

Somewhere in the air, I found myself wondering what might have happened to Moe Lee. Wondering, too, about the others of his family and how I would ever know. Memories rendered a kind way of drowning the noise of the airplane, and I drifted off to sleep, covered in a blanket of uncommon warmth.

Awakening from time to time, I had to remind myself that I, at twenty-three years old, was flying across the Atlantic Ocean, over eight thousand miles away from home, into the middle of Africa to a remote spot in the Sudan in hopes of helping to spread the good news of God's mercy and grace to people who would otherwise never hear of it.

And when I finally did arrive there, the faces of the children—everyone—were just as I had imagined.

Chapter 42

Homecoming 1933

I t had not taken two years of my life or my coming full circle around the world to know I belonged with Simon Hagan. It had taken two years, week by week, month after month, letter by letter. Two years in the Sudan, seeing God's love touch person after person with His love the way that He had touched me, to know that I had been in Africa for a reason. Every hungry mouth, every penetrating eye, every longing soul was embedded in my brain.

And I had not needed to read between the lines in Simon's mile-high stack of letters. He had assured me, countless times. He was waiting for me.

When I at last stepped foot again onto American soil, Simon had been on one knee beside the airstrip, and I'd run to him. I had felt his heart beating. A warm body, finally. A wonderful presence. Not a piece of paper with a postmark, not a dream in the night but Simon himself, real and imposing and regal—imperial in my eyes.

After a one-year courtship, we married in front of the fireplace at Sister's home on South Main Street. Only Millicent, Jim, and nine-year-old Louise stood in their living room with Simon and me during the simple ceremony. It was May 1934.

The Ellington Hotel (along with its owner, clerk, and bellhop all rolled into one) where we stayed the first night as Mr. and Mrs. Simon Newton Hagan—directly across the street from the Todd County Courthouse on the downtown square—was brimming, tacky with excitement. Elkton's most eligible bachelor had finally married. The fanfare was more than I wanted, more than Simon expected. Mr. and Mrs. Ellington scurried to assist Simon with our two small bags to our room on the next floor.

We'd walked across every mile of paths in Todd County in the year since I'd returned. We'd allowed ourselves the freedom to get to know one another. I had accepted that, at thirty-one, Simon had lived a lifetime beyond the farm, that his experiences were far-reaching. I understood how he had learned to forgive himself for the tragic loss of his mother when he was seventeen. It had meant learning to love life even when he couldn't control it.

And now, alone at last, the night was simply, sweetly, passionately the much-anticipated passage of a man and woman becoming one body, one flesh.

Simon and I moved into a three-room attachment at the back of a cinderblock building with large letters: *GOODYEAR TIRE.* The business that Simon and Raymond had opened together was situated on North Main Street, downtown Elkton.

Three months as a bride had agreed with me. Simon was happy as a lark.

We were fortunate on this particular morning in late summer to be enjoying the out-of-doors in the shadow of the icehouse situated adjacent to the tire store. Each of us sat on a small chair.

"Look here," Simon said, reading the August 5 edition of the 1934 *Todd County Standard.* "Looks like the German president died this past Thursday. Lung cancer." He propped his elbows on the black cast-iron table and continued to read. "Lived a long life. Paul von Hindenburg . . . commanded the Imperial German Army during World War I. Later on became president."

I wanted to show genuine interest in Simon's announcement, although it would have been more readily received had it been about new books for the library or the latest in ladies' fashion. Still, I listened as if the news had significance to our existence, isolated as we were, sipping our coffee in Elkton, Kentucky.

"But with him gone, it says here that Adolph Hitler has declared himself supreme leader. *Führer und reichskanzier*—that's a mouthful." Simon looked up to see if I was listening.

I was.

"This Hitler fella's the leader of the Nazi party. Was also the German chancellor, but according to this, he managed to get papers signed just hours before Hindenburg's death, stating that the existing authority of the Reich president will consequently be transferred to the führer and Reich chancellor." He glanced up over his cup. "That being Adolph Hitler." Simon let part of the paper drop and took a sip of coffee, then peered at me over the top of his cup. His brows were furrowed. "Doesn't sound good. One man with all the power. Glad we have a democracy." He set his cup down. "It's times like these I wish I had a cigarette."

"I'm certainly grateful for our democracy as well. I'm also pleased you're not smoking, Simon."

He grimaced playfully and again picked up the other half of the paper. "There's a picture of the motorcade if you want to see. We can spread the papers out on the bed and—"

"Simon Hagan! You can be so serious one minute and the next . . . I'd much rather hear more about the notorious motorcade *you* led. Not some German funeral far away—"

"In on the bed?" His expression had changed. He had a twinkle in his eyes.

"No, now stop it! Tell me about it, right here in the shade of this elegant icehouse."

Simon folded the newspaper and laid it aside, puckering his lips like a disappointed child. "Those were the glory days, alright. Sometimes felt like they were few and far between, but we were well-seasoned officers. Prohibition was fueling the demand for illegal booze . . . firing up the wave of crime that we faced, day in and day out. I was laying my life on the line for what I believed in."

He reached over and took my hand, pulled it to his lips. "In hindsight, of course, if I hadn't gotten TB, I might not've made it out of Detroit alive. Like you've told me time and time again, we're shaped for the purposes God had in mind for us. I believe it, and I'm sure glad that you're mine, Gracie. We have everything to look forward to."

"Will you take me to Detroit someday, and Albuquerque, maybe, to meet the people you knew? To see where you lived and all the places you've talked about?"

"A visit, yes. But sometimes it's best to let bygones be bygones."

Simon stared off into space for a moment, and I kept quiet.

"That scoundrel, though. Lieutenant Dugan . . . Guess he finally got the justice he deserved," Simon said. "Just doesn't pay to be the kind of person he was. At least he's behind bars for setting up my buddy. You'd have liked Roman. Good officer, good friend. We would have been a significant presence as part of the proud motorcade passing through the streets of the Detroit—low, flat cruiser bodies with huge, bulbous eyeballs . . ."

Simon's chest swelled like a bullfrog's; he ran his fingers through the waves that had turned into curls in the humidity.

"They were powerfully lit headlights, alright. Straddled those massive chrome grills—mean-looking, *good-lookin'*—and we paraded those son-of-a-gun vehicles through downtown, showing off Detroit's newest and finest police cars." Simon paused.

I loved the pleasure that reminiscing brought him. "And? Go on, honey."

"Well, as you know, I was living hundreds of miles from home, and I'll tell ya what: the Purple Gang was in control. They were controlling every speck of the city's drug and alcohol trade. Mobsters. Mostly immigrants from the lower east side, and Detroit's underworld was definitely being run by them."

"You were so brave. I don't see how you made it up there, all by yourself. You were only—what? Mid-twenties?"

"Uh, excuse me." Simon gave me a wink and pulled out a pack of chewing gum from the pocket where cigarettes would have been. "Were you not mid-twenties flying across the world?

Besides, nobody said I was brave, sweetheart. Just doing my job." He peeled open a stick of Juicy Fruit and popped it into his mouth. "About the last exciting moment before I had to move on out to the Southwest was getting to ride in the first radio-dispatched cruiser. What a wild experience. And yeah, I sure as heck did leave Elkton at eighteen. But I'd been in Detroit several years when I was doing all that. Alan took right after me . . . bull-headed, red-headed kid brother that just couldn't—"

"He had a broken spirit, honey . . . So sad. That longing look in his eye, glaring at me, and I mistook him for a pervert of some sort. It bothered me for a long time afterward. And for me to realize it was Alan whom I saw on that occasion in Jim's store. I do wish I'd been more aware. He was suffering. It was desperation. Reminds me of what I'm seeing in Henry every time he comes in town. I know he has his own life. Doesn't keep me from concern." Simon looked sympathetic. "I know. What if he were to find a wife as wonderful as you? That would make all the difference. He is approaching thirty. 'Bout time."

"But Henry never leaves the place," I said. "He's working himself to death. He's compelled to stay and should be. Hillbound's his heritage. And rightfully so . . . He can't be robbed of that, can he?" I felt myself looking to Simon for an answer he couldn't give.

"Henry's got a tough row to hoe. That's certain." Simon wagged his head, conceding. "I want to support you, Gracie. Any way I can. Your family situation and going out there . . . It's truly disturbing to see how far your father's fallen. Hate to say it, but the times I've run into him in town have been awkward to say the least. He's lost face." Simon stood and came around to the back of my chair, enfolded me from behind. "I'm sorry, honey. I know it kills you to have your homeplace disgraced. So senseless. And Francine—she's something else again."

He leaned in to kiss my cheek. "You speak the word, Gracie. I'll do whatever you need me to. Whatever I can do to make matters better. Although, honestly . . . I can't figure what. Your father's sure been lured from the highroad."

All the while Simon was speaking, images of Hillbound's golden years when Mama was alive filled my mind. I felt again the graciousness and charm that had been its crown. Resplendent touches of beauty in the cranberry-glass lamps on the lovely mahogany table in the front hall, flashing their thousand eyes through the crinkled bubbles in the shapely globes. The patterned walls in celadon and pink in the drawing room. The hollyhocks that would be rising against the backdrop of the white picket fence if I could be there to see them. But I could not go there to witness again my brother's plight or taste again the bitter pill of Francine's depredation.

"Are you okay, Gracie? I've said too much, haven't I?" Simon tugged my hands until I stood, then he embraced me with a much-needed tenderness. "Forgive me, hon. The final word on Hillbound is yet to be spoken. You'll see. Now," he said, holding me back at arm's length, looking at me with his big brown eyes, "we need to go inside, get ourselves ready for church, or we'll be late. One of these days, we'll go to Detroit, see it all. Canada, too, Gracie, and I'll show you Windsor in Ontario. Never have been there, but it's just across the Detroit River. That's where the liquor trade was rampant . . . and the booze was being brought across . . . Enough of this. I'll take you there, but for now I think we're gonna be here in Elkton, going to church, doing the Charleston as the most excitement . . . unless you want to skip church altogether and just go inside with me."

He acknowledged my absolutely-not-response with a wicked little wink. "Just kidding," he said.

Chapter 43

Five years later

September 1939

I sat by the window, looking out at the gloriously yellow falling leaves in the Tennessee town of Cleveland, folding diapers.

Simon and I had moved from Elkton to pursue the opportunity for him to open a Goodyear store, broadening his and Raymond's investments. The tire business provided for our livelihood, a good job for Simon and nothing to complain about, but it hardly characterized Simon's enterprise or energy. After seven years of it, Simon often seemed unchallenged and restless.

We'd had our first son, turning two years old in another week. We had chosen to name him Geoffrey Lee: Geoffrey for Simon's father, Lee in remembrance of Moe Lee. Something about the name lent dignity and respect where it was due. Not a day passed that I didn't think of the meaning of worthy connections or the significance of life. After all the years, often in my mind came the faces of Moe Lee's children. Often, too, those of the Sudanese children.

I glanced at the stack of diapers and visually multiplied it by two. Our second child was due in two and a half months. Sister was planning to come stay a spell with me after delivery.

Grandma Hannah and Papa Jeff had offered to come once Millicent left, but Emma claimed she was next in line. Sisters were like that, I guessed. I planned to let them work it out, resisting the banter that Simon's dad and stepmother were always coming to visit us.

My father hadn't seemed to care one way or the other if he saw Jeff Lee. If it wasn't a thoroughbred, he didn't have much use for it. So far, he and Francine had not been to Cleveland. And Simon, I, and the baby continued to stay at Millicent and Jim's on our return trips to Elkton. Louise doted on Jeff Lee as if he were an oversized boy version of a Flossie Flirt doll.

Even so, Father had sent word that he wanted us to come to Elkton for a visit. I owed him the honor as my father to offer him the chance to get to know his grandson. My pride and fear swallowed, I made up my mind to draw on unseen resources for strength enough to return to the farm. Seeing Henry so infrequently was a two-edged sword: Inwardly I died each time at the sight of him. Outwardly, I cried with each letter we exchanged.

Simon and I settled on a date.

"This is such a gorgeous time of year, honey. I'm glad we can go before the weather gets too cold for little Jeff Lee to be outside," I said. "He needs to be out of the house for at least part of the afternoon."

"Are you sure you're going to be alright with all this, Gracie? Hill-bound? It's not worth any risks just to appease Robert. He's had lots of other chances to see his grandson, you know."

Simon massaged my shoulders as he spoke. "We don't have to go."

"That feels good. Helps a lot. Would you put the basket away?" I folded the last diaper and put it on the stack." Thanks. And I'm fine. If I can go across the world to help children, I can go to Elkton to be my father's daughter. Sound ridiculous?"

Simon stood, holding the basket of folded diapers, and laughed. "Not coming from you it doesn't. Besides, I learned a long time ago I won't win any argument with you. What does the doctor have to say about your traveling two hundred miles? Hum?"

I offered him a tremulous smile. "I didn't give him a chance to tell me I couldn't travel. I'll be fine. Just fine. Two hours with Father. Maximum. Then we'll go on up north to see your folks. Sound good, honey?"

"If you say so. I'll put these at Jeff Lee's door. He's still asleep."

We were both eager to go back to Todd County, if only for a weekend. We'd planned to make the rounds to see my sisters before heading back on Monday.

Having taken Friday for travel, we were on the road, starting out at the crack of dawn. I'd packed us a lunch. All things in our favor, we'd hoped to arrive around in the early afternoon. Still, the trip proved to be a long two hundred miles with an active child in our '35 Buick, especially when Simon's week had been a grueling one with travel to two nearby Tennessee towns to troubleshoot for Goodyear tire stores.

Our arrival back in rural Kentucky felt like home, however, and the farm place had a lovely offering of bronze leaves about to drop from the massive trees. By good fortune, several trees had been allowed to remain rather than be felled to sacrifice space for Hillbound Stock Farm and the thoroughbreds (or the breeding thereof).

Simon steered the car down Allensville Road, and I looked in every direction with emotion welling up inside me. Wrinkled and worn, we pulled up next to the graying picket fence and he turned off the engine. With his hand laid lovingly on my shoulder, he kissed my cheek.

"You're beautiful," he said. "And you're doing a courageous thing, honey."

The house had a distinct odor: stale and unpleasant. I held Jeff Lee's hand, guiding him as he toddled into the drawing room.

The piano looked dusty and abandoned.

Father still had his air, the same tilt to his head. He immediately launched into a tirade on his favorite subject. "That Cavalcade—no business at all winning the Derby like he did. I've got a whole lot better blood in my geldings than Brookmeade Stable does . . . any day. Mine are gonna show 'em up next year. Watch out!"

He walked to a crude cabinet that now hung over Mama's favorite side table. "How about a J. W. Rutledge—Cream of Kentucky? Straight bourbon whiskey, Simon?" He seemed to enjoy the persuasiveness of his own voice. He followed up with a sly grin. "Eleven and half years old . . . smooth as silk."

"No, thanks, Senator."

Francine had made her appearance. "I certainly will. Just a short one," she said, tossing her head behind Simon's back.

She seated herself on the divan. "Hello, Gracie." Haughtily she lifted her eyes toward me. "So this is Jeffy? And walking too? Isn't he too cute? Bet you could make a horseman of him, Robert, dear. Keep him away from Sam, though!"

"What's happened to Mister Sam, anyway?" It hadn't been on my mind to ask, but Francine having mentioned him, I was curious. "Come, baby," I said to Jeff Lee, coaxing protectively. "Over beside Mother. There, we'll take a walk outside in just a minute, sweetheart."

"You might want to answer that one, Robert," Francine said and sipped her drink as Henry entered the drawing room.

"Sam Delaney's a slippery one," Father said, offering no further explanation.

Simon stepped in. "Gracie's spoken very highly of Sam Delaney . . . Slippery? How so?"

I rolled my enormous body to one side, preparing to push myself up from the chair, all the while grateful for the obvious attempt Simon was making to take up for Mister Sam's reputation. It was only fair on my behalf, I thought, based only upon his understanding of my deep respect for Mister Sam, not having personally known him.

Father shot a petulant glance in Francine's direction. "How 'bout we just leave it at that?" He continued to sip his whiskey. "So, Simon, how's the tire business? Making any money?"

"Henry!" I jumped to my feet the second I could lift myself from the wingback chair. I rushed to him, leaving Jeff Lee for the moment to fend for himself. "You're looking . . . more like Father all the time. Aren't you?" I threw my arms as closely around his neck as I could reach.

"We're comfortable, Gracie and I," Simon said to Father. "Can't complain. Wouldn't make an ounce of difference, anyhow." He chuckled and walked over to engage in a handshake with Henry. "Great to see you, Henry."

Francine took her empty glass, stood, and quietly made her way toward the liquor cabinet. She glowered daintily as she swished past Henry and Simon, bustling about in her painted face. I made myself disregard the adorning jewels that set her ablaze, but my unborn child landed a wallop as if to notify me that my emotions did not go unnoticed. From the day Francine had arrived, she had been more than an innocent undercurrent, having been there longer than anyone wanted to admit. Henry had shielded me, protected me, while Father slipped about, moving in his portentous shadows, believing everyone was otherwise occupied.

I returned to the wingback chair and sat down. Henry sat on the piano stool next to me, apparently content to be near. He took Jeff Lee's hand and shook it as if he were training the child to be a little man. Henry's face lit up at Jeff Lee's grin.

The destroyer destroys, I thought. *The betrayer betrays*. Nothing resembled the spirit that had once lived at Hillbound. Father had plenty to hide. He had hidden it well. And now, I believed, there was even more to the saga. I pulled Jeff Lee onto my lap and kept quiet, waiting for Father to answer Simon's question.

"Yes, sir, Senator," Simon said. (And I guessed that particular aspect of Simon's adulation for my father was always going to remain intact, no matter its expiry.) "We're mighty pleased to be in Tennessee. You need to come for a visit sometime. But now, am I understanding correctly? You've broken ties with Sam Delaney? That seems like a shame, based on my limited judgment, sir. Not questioning yours. Just an observation."

"Mister Sam is such a gentleman. Slippery, Father? What on earth?"

Father's stance was firm. His knees locked. "I'm selling part of this farm. And Sam Delaney sure as heck doesn't have any claim to it . . . Good gosh! There's money to be made from the land. It was Francie and Felix's land. Period. And Henry here, he already has more than he knows what to do with. Isn't that right, son?"

Henry got up from the piano stool. For a brief moment I saw a spark of the strength once present in his robust demeanor. "Doin' the best I can."

"I see." Simon nodded deferentially. "Well, then, what do y'all make of Nazi Germany's invasion of Poland last week? Not looking good at all, is it?"

"Doesn't touch us, does it?" Father loosened up with the change in subjects. He finished off his drink, went to the liquor cabinet, and stood next to Francine. She had not budged one iota. He poured another drink for himself. "Let that Hitler fella do what he wants over there."

He took a hefty swig and a broad smile forced its way across his face. "Did y'all come here to talk about Germany and Sam Delaney or show off my grandson? Come here and see your grandpappy." Father walked to the piano and set his drink on the keys, then reached out to Jeff Lee. "Is that what he's gonna call me?"

Simon turned to me and shrugged. "'Grandpappy.' Try that and let's see."

Jeff Lee squirmed on my lap, resisting my father's approach, vigorously shaking his little headful of blond waves. I helped him scoot to the floor.

"Well, that fizzled, didn't it?" Father said, his words slurred, his breath alcohol laced. "We'll try again. If you're gonna be a horseman . . ."

Simon glanced at me and took my troubled expression as a cue to lead Jeff Lee away from my father.

"Henry, do believe you've lost some weight." Simon said, standing next to my brother, holding Jeff Lee's hand in his. "Gosh, I know what a huge job you have here. I admire your farming skills. Me . . . I never was much of a farmer. Takes a lot of dedication. How are things going for you, anyway?"

"Fair to midd'n', I guess," Henry said. "Gonna get a world war on our hands? Enlisting wouldn't be far from my mind. It'd be my duty, but who knows?"

Pleased that Henry and Simon were engaged, I decided to let them talk. "If y'all don't mind, I'm going to take Jeff Lee and get some fresh air."

With no one taking much notice, I stepped outside. Francine couldn't have cared less. She had moved to the hallway and was thumbing through mail on the table.

I strolled the yard, looking out beyond to where the plants of the fields stood like tender grass on the hilltops. There was no way I could have calculated the cost, nor could I have rolled back the events of years past or gone another direction. Francine was an inferior trade for the honor that Father had squandered, and Henry was living with defeat stemming from the affair. Early on, she'd done her dastardly deed to make certain I would be out of the picture. And after having tried to blight my reputation with her slander, she had redirected her vengeance toward Henry.

With Jeff Lee's little hand in mine, I walked him to the point where I could feel the essence of his namesake. The spot where Moe Lee's image rested in my memory seemed now to be in a world as far away as the Sudan.

—◦◦◦◦—

The ride out to Simon's old homeplace had me quizzing Simon regarding Henry's mention of joining the Navy. Their discussion surrounding world news, especially the German invasion, had piqued my interest. Perhaps loyalty to country would suit Henry, but he was considering eleventh-hour measures to escape the oppression at home.

Simon's evaluation of the situation was of great importance. We agreed the spiraling downturns had not slowed at Hillbound. Henry had a private sadness that only those of us with a special eye could see.

"Francine has a power over him," I said as I took a last look up toward the window in my old bedroom. The car moved past the house. "Doesn't she?"

"Unfortunately, I'm afraid so, hon. But your father gave it to her. Because of how he treats Henry, your father gave her that permission."

I twirled the ruby and pearl ring on my finger and held Jeff Lee close. He'd been quiet as a mouse. "You and I have such different fathers," I said. "Two entirely different legacies, don't we? What's passed down to us from our fathers is such a crucial responsibility. I can only pray Henry will find God's power—greater than what he has thus far—to direct his life."

Simon reached for my hand, took it in his, and kissed it. "Honey," he said, "Francine stands between your brother and your father. No son should have to earn his father's love. Or admiration, for that matter. There were times when I balked at my dad's views on a lot of things, but deep down I always knew he loved me. I was confident he'd be waiting with open arms when I was ready to accept his love and legacy."

Jeff Lee had laid his head against my shoulder. His warm body next to me was a unique reminder of my gratitude for Simon. Knowing my child had a father who would be a mentor for honorable qualities was worth everything to me. "I just have to say, Simon, I'm extremely grateful to be part of the Hagan family. I see men with character and moral fiber—incorruptible men—in your brothers and your dad. It's an interesting comparison that's running its course in my mind."

Simon was giving me his undivided attention. He smiled. "Uh-oh! I'm bracing myself to hear whatever it is on your mind, inside that pretty head of yours, behind those blue, blue eyes."

We rode in silence while I bundled my thoughts.

"It just disturbs me," I said, "when personal control is so important that it's lorded over another human being. It's as if power-hungry people are saturated with venom. I don't know what y'all talked about after I took Jeff Lee outside, but corruption and power are at the center of world news these days. Isn't it what Adolph Hitler seems to have set his sights on? Isn't that what you've been saying?" I didn't let Simon get a word in edgewise. "I don't like what's being played out on the world's stage. Expansion, dominance. I see how Father has allowed similar unprincipled measures to define his legacy. Where Adolph Hitler's concerned it's a German empire—"

"Whoa!" Simon whipped his head in my direction. "Careful putting your father in a context with Adolph Hitler, honey."

I thought for a moment that Simon was going to run off the road as we bump-bumped across the cattle guard and continued down the lane toward the Hagans' butterscotch-colored stone bungalow in the distance. Jeff Lee had awakened but had sat still, up against the burgeoning, kicking bulge in my tummy, for about as long as he could.

"You're right, Simon," I said. "And I'm wrong to judge Father's corrupt state of affairs. I'm just concerned about what's happening in our world . . . plus the slightest negative influence Father and Francine might have on our children." I took a deep, deep breath. "The patriarchal influence, that's all. Such a contrast between our fathers and the legacies they're passing down."

I kissed Jeff Lee's long, tapered little fingers. "Just another couple of minutes, baby, and we'll be at Papa Jeff's. And Daddy will get to see *his* daddy. And Grandma Hannah will have goodies for you. So, be real still now, sugar."

"He's passed down an awful lot to me, Dad has," Simon said. "Foundation, roots, strength for living. Can't put a price tag on those things. It'll be good to see him . . . catch up."

"Da-da," Jeff Lee said, pointing to Simon's waistcoat. "Choc?"

Simon hesitated with a rueful grin, then twisted on the automobile seat enough to enable Jeff Lee to reach inside the outer pocket of his jacket. Simon looked guilty of murder in the first degree.

"Chocolate? Simon! You've been slipping chocolate to him? Bribing him?"

Jeff Lee promptly stuffed the piece he had found into his mouth.

Simon's smile was infectious. I had to laugh.

"Works with you," he said.

—◁◁◁◁◁∫Ω∫▷▷▷▷—

Simon Maxwell Hagan, at two twenty-two on the early Saturday morning of October 28, 1939, surprised us by coming into the world almost six weeks early. The doctor's attentiveness to my newborn and the precarious situation surrounding Maxwell's birth suggested the danger of my having traveled as far as I had, too close to my due date.

"Millicent has come, honey," Simon whispered in my ear as I lay in Cleveland's Memorial Hospital. "Jeff Lee's in good hands at the house, so you rest."

I raised heavy eyelids to acknowledge him. His presence came with the scent of his Old Spice aftershave. His long fingers enfolding mine afforded comfort.

Dr. Murphy must have known better than to lecture me in the days that followed while I was still hospitalized. And if the trip to Elkton had caused the problem, it was not the mileage but the heartbreak at Hillbound, coupled with the unrest in the world.

Britain, France, India, Australia, and New Zealand had declared war on Germany, and by Thanksgiving the German authorities had begun the deportation of Jews from Polish territories that had recently been annexed by Germany.

"I need to know what's happening in the world, Simon. I don't need to have you hide world news from me," I said, feeling like he was unnecessarily shielding me. "I can read the newspaper for myself."

Simon had his most serious look working overtime to influence me. "Sweetheart," he said, "look, you've lost your milk, and Maxwell needs to be gaining weight. You know what Dr. Murphy said. I think let's focus on what's happening right here at home. Let the outside world rest. *You* rest. We'll get through this."

"Do you think Henry made the right decision enlisting?"

Simon was frustrated. He slipped over and sat down beside where I was rocking Maxwell. "Seems like he did the only thing he could under the circumstances, hon. Henry was desperate."

"Well, the U.S. is remaining neutral, aren't we? Still, we are rearming for war, apparently. And I know that British soil was bombed by the Germans for the first time—in the Shetland Islands. And German armies stormed the university dorms in Prague . . . and other towns in Czechoslovakia as well. They attacked and arrested thousands of students, Simon. It's just escalating. The Nazis executed nine Czechs by firing squad, no trial, simply for leading the recent demonstrations. They've closed all the technical schools too."

"Sometimes I think you're too smart for your own good, Gracie." Simon looked positively bewildered.

"What's it coming to?" I tipped the bottle of milk so Maxwell could finish it completely. "Talk to me, Simon. Please. I need to know these things just as much as you. Don't I? And I want to know what you think too."

"Don't fret, hon. Let's just see what the future holds. True, there's a tremendous amount of turmoil. It definitely has me concerned, what with Hitler trying to take over. He's a maniac and—"

Maxwell's wail was loud and long, drowning out any further conversation between Simon and me.

Whatever happened to me after Maxwell's arrival caused my purpose to intensify. The sights I set for my sons and the hopes for their future regenerated my ambitions. I was having no part of mediocrity. It was no more acceptable to me than colorlessness was to an artist. I had lofty ideals. I believed they were the Potter's hand on the shape of my clay.

Simon was content to raise our family in an unassuming manner, but his dissatisfaction with store ownership presented us with his own form of unrest. Constantly aiming for a better way to provide for me and our two boys, he was hopscotching, traveling from town to town, his dreams for a satisfying career fading in and out.

"It's just a matter of time," I said. "Let's trust that other job opportunities will come. You might be better suited for other work—somewhere else, even. And Raymond could buy you out."

"I need to be here, Gracie. Something's got to give. I belong here, in this house, in this town, not traveling to every southern Goodyear tire store around, searching for higher ground, not knowing what's happening with my family at home while I'm gone." Simon walked to the window and peered out on a blustery November afternoon. "Standing around at the store talking tires, no matter how good they are, or sitting behind that dang desk . . . It's just that I'm not a salesman any more than I was a farmer, Gracie," he said, his breath fogging the windowpane. "I wanted out of Todd County when I was eighteen, and I want out of the tire business now."

"I could go back to teaching if that would help." Saying it aloud sounded like music to my ears.

"Heavens, Gracie! Sweetheart! We have a four-week-old baby and a two-year-old. It scared us to pieces that Maxwell might not even make it. No, honey, I won't hear of it. Not now and not anytime soon. I'm just talking . . . Bad timing to bring it up."

"I'm sure it's all going to work out," I said.

Chapter 44

T he reality of higher ground and the fullness of springtime in 1940 came alive in the wrapping and boxing of every piece of china, every stack of diapers, every stick of furniture. Hope for the future, abundant and fresh, new territory, new horizons to reach for, had all rolled into one plentiful vision come true. Simon and I had an open door set before us, literally, figuratively.

Our new home was a house on a hill, beautifully situated like a precious crown jewel. The minute I walked through the front door, I relinquished my Hillbound longings. My home-shaped emptiness filled to the brim.

Simon was determined to provide for me and the boys, giving every drop to make our move work plus allow all I needed to be content. The supervisory job he'd taken with the Tappan Stove Company in Murray, Kentucky, was the answer. He was enterprising, gallant, and in every way his manner enabled him to redouble his efforts to support us. In the process he could still be close to home.

Busily, I furnished it with Pembroke tables and English antiques. My agenda overflowed with decorating my home—that and once again endeavoring to change my small corner of the world. I'd applied for a job at Murray State College, and my involvement in the Missionary Society (as close as I was ever again going to be to the Sudan), garden club, and teaching a children's Sunday school class had me right where I wanted to be.

When I was happy, Simon was happy. He could talk about every man's thing from the price of gasoline to how deep to stick seeds for a crop. When it came right down to it, I was gleaning from Simon a quiet understanding of the values that really mattered. They just didn't keep me from loving beauty or appreciating beautiful things.

Meanwhile, Americans turned to college football for relief from the turbulent world around us. The depression still had its grip on the nation, and across the Atlantic the Battle of Britain raged. As war crept closer every day, the nation's first peacetime draft called men and women to the defense of the country. Henry was already in the thick of it, and one by one his letters came from the Naval Air Station in Pensacola, Florida.

I didn't have to read between the lines. I wondered if he'd have the fortitude for war if it happened. I worried that perhaps I should have discouraged him from joining the military.

"Gracie. Honey," Simon said and laid aside the cigarette he was smoking. He took me in his arms, "Henry had to do what he had to do. We all have to rise, meet the future with internal strength. You have, I have. Henry will too."

I believed Simon. His discernment was perfect (except when it came to taking up smoking again). The only remaining question was whether Henry had the kind of strength he might need to carry him through.

NAS Pensacola, Florida

April 12, 1941

Dear Sis,

Sorry for not writing, but no better time than the present I guess. Sure hope Maxwell is getting along fine. You wrote me once that you thought he was at the point of death, but I knew a pretty boy like Maxwell would pull through, especially with your prayers.

Sis, I guess I'm getting along alright. I've been moved in rank from Seaman Recruit to Petty Officer. This Navy is hard to explain to a civilian not knowing anything about it much. The man over me taught me all I know about being a gunner. He's a real fellow and told me I was the best gunner he ever saw without any more experience than I'd had. Said he was proud to have me.

I dream about being back at home every night, though. I'm really scared I won't get back, by the way things look.

Sis, I'm going to tell you the truth, and I think most of the neighbors will tell you the same thing. I took care of that farm in lots of ways, and I did it mostly through heart and body and brain. When the bank collapsed in 1929, we walked into the bank and Father tried to get some money, and I don't think he had a hundred dollars in the bank. He asked me if I had five dollars and I told him no, which I didn't. So he told Bowling Trummel he's got to have five dollars, and Bowling gave it to him.

To tell you the truth, I think Father gave his money to Miss Francine to pay off the mortgage on her place. I believe she made him do it before she married him. Millicent told me that Father said he wanted to talk to her before he got married and he never got the chance for some reason.

Anyway, Father had money before he married. I know he had thousands in the bank. He started with those horses because of Miss Francine. That might have been alright, but she did something to him. Bad. And then he was betting and spending.

I am not the one to judge but I stayed at the farm and stood it all those years.

You are different from me. When the right man came around you got married and I don't blame you. You made your own home, which was right.

Father told me he was going to give me a good chance on the farm. Well, I'll admit I don't understand this. I asked Father to let me go to State University but he said no, he didn't have the money. I could have made good in athletics, and he wouldn't give me the chance. At that age I was as good an athlete going, but he told me to stay with him and he would give me all I made.

Well, after Mother died I tried as hard as anybody to make good on the farm, but all it was doing was getting Father and Miss Francine by, and I was having to live like a dog.

Sis, after I went home at Christmas after joining the Navy it was cold. I told them I would be back about 10 o'clock. I went upstairs, and there wasn't a sign of a bed made up and no covers on it. Never felt as bad about anything in my life, and I went back and told them so. I decided I wouldn't take that again. I got really mad, but Miss Francine was making a coward out of me and no part of a man. Father even threatened to run me off the place, and they kept throwing that up to me.

Father was a good man, but he let an outcast woman have too much effect on him. You might still say Miss Francine was alright, but if you look deep down in your heart you know you don't believe it. All Miss Francine was after was

*the money, and you know it. You know she had influence
over him.*

*We won't forget about this, but let's look to the future.
About 18 months, it's a long time when you're not living
peaceful like I should be back on the farm.*

*Hoping I'll live through to show that this is not so for my
heart. The real me is right there on the farm, which I hope
I'll own one of the good old days with a good wife and
family with God's help.*

Sincerely,

Henry

*P.S. Sister, really and truly I don't believe I'll live through
what might be ahead if I don't get out some way. I don't
know why, but I guess it's kinda like robbing a man that's
been free in the country as long as I have. Thought maybe
if I could go out to sea it would be a good thing. Oh, what
I'd give just to be free again. Sis, if I don't see you any
more, it was good knowing you anyway.*

I refolded the pages and sat paralyzed at the kitchen table, staring at the green-and-black squares on the linoleum floor. An ant crawled near one of the legs of the Frigidaire. I watched its search for livelihood until my tears blinded me.

Laying Henry's letter aside, slowly I got up and stomped on the ant as if it were a garden snake, then put water on for turnips. It was getting close to dinnertime. The ant, at least, was out of its misery.

Chapter 45

———◆∿∿∿∿◆———

S imon would be coming in the door at any minute. The boys were playing in the sandbox outside the kitchen window. I peeked out, knocked on the glass pane, and waved to them. Maxwell dumped a little shovelful of sand on Jeff Lee's lap.

Jeff Lee looked at me with the stymied look of a three-and-a-half-year-old, and I went back to preparing dinner. The smell of the raw chicken was about to gag me.

I could hear Simon coming up the stairs from the basement leading in from the garage. He'd had just about enough time to remove his hat and hang it on the door hook.

"Gracie?"

No answer. I pictured him loosening his tie, rolling up his long-sleeved white shirt. At any second—

"Gracie. There you are."

"Stay away."

"Why?"

No answer.

"What's going on, hon?"

"I'm pregnant."

We didn't use the smiles that we had at our disposal. Instead, I rushed toward the bathroom, covering my mouth with the dishrag as I went.

Simon was close behind me. Holding my forehead steady while I bent over the commode, he was there for me.

Having tossed my cookies, I turned toward him and took a deep breath, feeling much better.

"Better? Come on . . . to the living room. Sit." Then came his gorgeous grin. "I'm cutting you off chocolate."

The teaching job I'd gotten would go away after the finish of the term. The University Women's Club would find a new president. And I'd have a new baby come December. Fine. Three children under five.

Simon washed the dishes and put away the leftovers. It seemed like kindness was his new project. And I tucked the boys into bed, climbed in on top of the covers beside Jeff Lee, and reflected on the well-spent time being shaped into motherhood.

Even so, the clay was still wet.

Chapter 46

—━⟪⟫━—

An early December morning in 1941 had me resting on the beautiful sofa from Feinberg's Furniture Store, reading a book. Sunlight streamed through the white organdy curtains on the living room window and across my bare feet. I flipped the book over and perched it on my enormous tummy, laid my head on the back of the plump cushion.

Simon glanced up from reading the funnies, scrutinizing me for a hint of a change in my condition. Detecting none, he started reading aloud about Dagwood and Blondie. We were missing Sunday school and church, hoping this third baby wouldn't decide to arrive too early like Maxwell had. The radio was low, breaking the monotony of having to stay at home. It provided us with timely market and weather reports.

Abruptly, Simon dropped the newspaper onto his lap. He whipped his head toward the rounded-top radio on the table between us, then shot his hand in the air to ensure I'd not say a word. The voice coming through the mesh-covered speaker was not talking weather.

Simon reached over and turned up the volume:

> . . . *have bombed Hawaii. This is no joke: this is war. I am speaking from the roof of the Advertiser Publishing Company Building. We have witnessed this morning the distant view of a brief full battle of Pearl Harbor and the severe bombing of Pearl Harbor by enemy planes, undoubtedly Japanese. The city of Honolulu has also been*

attacked and considerable damage done. This battle has been going on for nearly three hours. One of the bombs dropped within fifty feet of KTU tower. It is no joke. It is a real war. The public of Honolulu has been advised to keep in their homes and away from the Army and Navy. There has been serious fighting going on in the air and in the sea. The heavy shooting seems to be . . .

There was an interruption, then the announcer's voice came back.

. . . cannot estimate just how much damage has been done, but it has been a very severe attack. The Navy and Army appear now to have the air and the sea under control.

I looked at Simon, tears dripping from my eyes. The baby inside me gave me a boot kick, and the blood in my arms turned to ice.

With the boys playing tinker toys beneath the dining room table, Simon and I knelt next to the Pembroke table, pressed our knees humbly on the needlepoint rug. Simon gently draped his arm over my shoulder, and together we turned to the one and only potter who was capable of shaping the uncertain future.

Inconsequential things had never seemed so irrelevant.

Four days after the Japanese attack on Pearl Harbor and the United States' declaration of war against the Japanese Empire, Nazi Germany declared war against America in response to what it claimed was a series of provocations by the United States government.

Two days later, our new baby son, Hickman Winston Hagan, arrived to a world at war.

Chapter 47

June 1942

"The Japanese occupation force was spotted on June 3 steaming toward Midway Island, and B-17 Flying Fortresses were sent out from its coast to bomb the strike force. It failed to inflict damage.'" Simon held wide the pages of the *Calloway County Gazette*, reading aloud from the wicker rocker. He let the corner of the *Gazette* flop down, looking over the top of it. "Want me to stop?"

I couldn't look at him. Simon seemed to know to stop.

The swing moved me in slow backward-forward trips as I nursed six-month-old Hickman, and the calmness in the flight of the butterflies outside the screened porch absorbed me. "Henry . . . He's in God's hands."

It was all I could say, and I believed it. Love for my three boys made me believe, even when the shape of the world around us wanted to make me believe otherwise.

According to a newspaper account on a day that soon followed, a battle was now raging in the far-off Pacific. Unless something had changed, Henry was in the thick of it.

If I wasn't listening to Simon read about it, then it was I, insisting that he hear me.

"Listen to this, Simon. 'Early in the morning on June 4, a PBY Catalina flying boat torpedoed a Japanese tanker transport, striking the first blow of the Battle of Midway. Only six months after Japan's attack on Pearl Harbor and one month after the Battle of the Coral Sea . . .'" It says ' . . . the United States Navy under Admirals Chester W. Nimitz, Frank Jack Fletcher, and Raymond A. Spruance defeated an attacking fleet of the Imperial Japanese Navy Admirals Isoroku Yamamoto, Chuichi Nagumo, and Nobutake Kondo near Midway Atoll . . .' I didn't pronounce those correctly, I'm sure. ' . . . inflicting devastating damage on the Japanese fleet.'"

"I believe that's enough," Simon said.

If he was shielding me, I was having none of it. "He's my brother. I knew I should have tried to prevent him from enlisting. We're like that. You would have stopped Alan from running off to California if you could have."

"You probably need to take it easy. News can be too much at times, honey. It's *you* that I want to protect now. I just don't want you to get so upset, lose your milk, Gracie, like happened with Maxwell."

The carnage that Henry surely faced—if he was still alive—had to exceed what his unfortified spirit could bear. He lacked a power source. His letter had more than divulged it. With his courage depleted in personal skirmishes on the home front in the backwoods of rural Todd County, Kentucky, he'd left behind the isolated world he'd known and gone into battle. Nothing in his past had prepared him—I was certain of it.

My having gone down to the potter's house had turned my brokenness into wholeness and imprinted on me the signature of my maker. I had returned pliable, ready to be shaped to meet life—head on. Henry, unfortunately, as far as I could tell, had been shaped by a duplicitous plunderer, and the compromised foundation on which our father stood had provided little if anything to pass down to his son.

—◦⫘⫘◦—

The Battle of Midway ended just four days after it began. Four days after that, on Thursday, June 11, 1942, I, my sisters, and all of Todd County, Kentucky, got the news that Father—former Senator Robert Rutherford Maxwell—had passed in his sleep.

A telegram was sent to Henry in Midway.

Saturday, about one in the afternoon, Hillbound was quiet. Hollyhocks stood like colorful soldiers against the dilapidated fence. One lone thoroughbred roamed in the pasture as if looking for a reason to exist.

From the kitchen I saw Henry walk in through the front door—unannounced, unexpected. Barely inside, he stepped onto the rug and set a single bag at his feet. Slowly he removed his Navy hat, tucked it ceremoniously under his arm. He could have been a ghost. Jeff Lee stood next to me, unmoving as if he suspected something frightful. Hickman, resting in my arms, burst into tears.

Stunned as I was to see Henry, I managed to pass the baby off to Bertie, then ran to meet my brother as Francine briskly walked from the drawing room into the hallway. Her mouth twisted into a grimace.

"I got furloughed," Henry said and embraced me. For a long moment he held me, his tears dropping on my neck. "I want to see Father. Where is he?"

"Buried this morning," Francine informed him, haughtily, lacking any sense of remorse. "I was told that you would not be coming home, Henry. I simply passed that information along."

Her arrogance stunned me.

She waved the many bangles on her wrist in my direction, then lit up a cigarette with a shaking hand. "There was agreement that Robert should be buried when he was. He was buried this morning. You're too late—again. Robert's gone. And he had nothing to say to you anyway. How long do you plan to be here?"

Henry was trembling. "You knew better! The telegram I sent—"

"Telegram? I don't recall any telegram, Henry," Francine said, turning to go.

I gasped, then burst into tears. "She told us that you couldn't come home," I said, glaring at her. "There was no agreement! Father was buried—" Jeff Lee came running to my side.

Bertie led Maxwell by the hand into the kitchen just as Simon walked in the back door.

"She will stop at nothing," I shrieked. "Nothing! Simon, help me."

Henry put his arm around me. "It's done, Sis. There isn't a thing we can do. I'll pull through." He glanced around, gazing as it were the last time he might see his home. "But I can't stay here."

"Chester and Lucy went with Marcus and Rebecca into town. They're staying at the Ellington Hotel," I said, having regained my composure. "Simon and I and the boys are out at the Hagans'. I'm quite sure Millicent would be very thrilled to have you."

"Absolutely. Henry, we'll be glad to take you in my car. Not a problem at all," Simon said. "The boys can sit close for two miles. Can't you, Jeff Lee?"

"Mister Sam's here too. Staying at the Ellington as well. Said he came because of me. And he had some other business in the vicinity. Just delightful of him to come, though."

"If y'all are finished with your plans, I have things to do myself." Francine turned and left us looking at each other.

"I want to go out to the cemetery, Sis. Tomorrow, maybe? Or later today. I don't care. Either. " Henry picked up his bag and walked out to the verandah.

I followed. "Mister Sam asked if the family could meet him at the hotel early Monday morning, so Simon and I will plan on being back in town close to nine. Would you want to be there?"

"Nah. Thanks," Henry said and stood there, looking out to the tobacco fields. "I'm ready to go anytime y'all are, Sis."

We went on Sunday morning to Millicent's church off Main Street in downtown Elkton for convenience sake. Henry wouldn't go—not out to Providence Methodist, and not out to Mt. Zion Baptist where Mama's service had been held. He'd not set foot in a church in years, as far as I knew. *Lord knows I tried.*

We returned to Millicent's with plans to get Henry and go by the cemetery.

Simon drove us out to Glen Haven Cemetery, but neither he nor I pretended to comprehend Henry's overwhelming heartbreak. I sat in the back seat of our Buick, hoping, praying as we motored past the Goodyear store and the familiar buildings that characterized the peaceful little town of Elkton. Simon's winning ways failed to engage Henry in conversation, so we passed silently through the entrance gates of the cemetery grounds and came to stop at the freshly covered grave of Robert Rutherford Maxwell.

Henry, from every outward sign on his beleaguered face and in his lifeless eyes, had come to an insurmountable stone. Our father's provision, so vast and so bountiful, so easily robbed, so readily destroyed, was gone as far as Henry was concerned. The costly ransom loomed impossible. Henry had to know that. We all did.

The farm was Francine's. Hillbound was lost.

If Henry had any fight in him, I didn't see it. If he was struggling, I didn't see that either. He'd given up.

Laughter had revived him in times past when I thought he'd grown faint, but there was no laughter now. He'd come home from war to be met with a web of transparent wire—more of the same that had previously wrapped him—bound to break him and take him captive once again.

None of us said a word, not in the automobile, not at the cemetery where the earth formed a rectangle next to Mama's tombstone.

Mister Sam herded us all into the small space at the Ellington Hotel's front desk on Monday morning: Chester, Lucy, Marcus, and Rebecca.

Marcus's wife was skinny but likable, and Marcus doted on Rebecca like Simon doted on me. I took the opportunity to express to her what a fine man she had married and told her the way his faith in God had been a powerful influence on my life. The reunion with the Willoughbys was every bit as meaningful as I could have expected.

"You know my aunt Francine is not going to show up here," Marcus said. "I sure wish she could have changed for the better over the years, Gracie. We just don't always see hearts changed."

Meeting the folks at the hotel seemed indulgent at best, but Mister Sam was insistent, tall burley horseman from Lexington that he was.

"Gracie. Henry. I do 'preciate you coming over here—all of y'all," Mister Sam said. "Didn't really think that my sister-in-law would show up. Doesn't matter anyhow."

He'd tamed his straw-colored hair, and his eyes danced, but the non-stop smile I had remembered barely pushed his sunburned cheeks.

"Want y'all ta know . . . I found this among Felix's things on a visit to Madison County, right after his tragic accident. I went back to the old homeplace." Mister Sam was poised, a mite ceremonious, perhaps, as he recounted the time that surrounded his brother's death. "And I have to apologize: I've kept it from ya all this time. Not to protect Francine, mind ya, because she didn't deserve to be protected. Not then, not now."

Sister took a step forward, then clearly thought better of it and smiled politely at everyone. Emma looked at me and the ceiling fixture. I didn't have any idea of what to do. Simon took my hand.

"You see, half of Francine's assets belong to me . . . because Felix's father—and mine—his will says so." He spindled the document in his hand.

"My father, Monroe Delaney, made it clear that if a marriage took place within a year of either of his sons' deaths—in this case Felix's—be it untimely or otherwise, the estate he'd willed to his boys would go to the surviving sibling. That would be me."

I felt myself getting lightheaded, needing to lie down. I pushed hard to keep fainting from my mind.

"I'm a wealthy man, and not bragging in any regard, but forty acres of farmland in rural Kentucky was not something I bothered to keep my eye on. And Francine— 'Scuse me if I sound crass right here in front of ya, Chester, about your sister. You, too, Marcus. But Francine can go to the devil as far as I'm concerned."

"Not following you entirely," Simon said. "Understood about the devil, but are you saying Hillbound somehow belongs to you?"

"No, sir," Mister Sam said, "I'm saying Robert and Francine never married."

Simon steadied me. I couldn't look at a person in the room. I looked instead at the ruby and pearl ring on my finger as if it were a new Bible verse.

"I've gone and had the courthouse confirm it once and for all. No records here or anywhere else. Not in Kentucky, not in Tennessee. It was Francine's way around the whole matter. Now then," Mister Sam said, "I've had Chester and Marcus come here as witnesses that Hillbound belongs solely to the Maxwells. And Francine is not a Maxwell."

Mister Sam put his hand on my shoulder. A smile spread on his face. "I owed this to you, Gracie. If I could have seen a way to rid you of her long ago, I would have. But you know as well as I do, she would have found a way to drown ya."

He reached out a hand to his brother-in-law. "Chester, I'm truly sorry to have to smear your sister in this fashion, but she needs to be removed from the Maxwell home."

Chapter 48

H enry was sitting in the living room, slumped on the maroon mohair divan at Millicent's house, smoking a cigarette on this most glorious of days in the middle of June 1942.

The helper in the Carvers' kitchen waved a welcoming hello to us, assuring me the children were in good hands.

I tugged at Henry's arm until he stood, and I looked straight into his war-worn eyes. "There are fruits to be picked at Hillbound, Henry," I said. "And count on the rotten ones being thrown away. Hold on a little bit longer. We're going out to our home. The day of reckoning is here."

He looked at me as perhaps he should have—completely confused—but we Maxwells rode the two miles down Allensville Road and arrived once again to the pastures and picket fences in need of Moe Lee's care and Moe Lee's songs. Hillbound might have never been personally Moe Lee's. Nonetheless, it's where my childhood friend had left an enduring essence in the beautiful bond that was ours. That much was his to take.

Henry was sitting on the passenger's seat of Simon's old Buick as we motored up next to the two-story clapboard house, far removed from the scandal he had for years held down, the tears he'd held back, his longing to break free and canter like a thoroughbred on the loose.

Emma and Millicent rolled up behind us, pushed open the doors, and got out of their car.

Simon gave me a kiss and a wink and remained in his seat beneath the steering wheel. But Henry climbed out of the Buick, purposefully opened my door, and waited while I peeled out of the back seat. He reached for my hand. I took it and Emma's, and Emma took Millicent's as the two of them caught up to me and Henry.

And on that day, the four siblings of the Maxwell clan marched across the lawn, every bit as rightfully present on the property as strutting peacocks in the yard. We went up the steps to the verandah, and together we marched across the threshold at the front door of our Hillbound home.

Henry shoved the door shut with a bang behind us. "Oh, Francine? Love?" he said.

Not much more than a moment passed before she hauled herself out of Father's office, hands on her hips, an indignant twist on her lips. She took one look at us and her face changed.

Her hands dropped at her side. "Bertie!" she hollered.

"Never mind, Bertie," I said to her when she appeared, coming from the kitchen. "Francine was just about to leave."

I turned to Francine, refusing to let my eyes move one iota off hers. "Did you think we would not find out what you'd done? Did you honestly think you could destroy Henry and have Hillbound for yourself?" I maintained my calm. "This house will not be given over to evil, Francine *Delaney*."

Her shoulder twitched, her eyes remained on mine a few seconds, then she peered at Henry, next at Emma, and next at Millicent.

"That's right. We know your final little secret," Millicent said, "and we want you out of our house."

"This minute," Emma said as she took Francine by the arm. Henry took a hold on the other arm. "Now, please," Emma said, quite sternly.

"I do believe your day of reckoning has come, Francine. There might possibly be a room at the Ellington Hotel," I said. "But you'll not be staying at Hillbound another day."

Francine attempted to appear ladylike when we all knew she was not even close.

Henry and Emma ushered her toward the door, down the steps, and into Emma's waiting automobile.

"I'll go with them, Sis," Henry said, returning a magnificent smile for all to see.

But for the man who did not count the cost of his treachery, whose remaining legacy stretched thinly over the sparse dirt track of horse racing and counterfeit living, his children were not left in a wasteland. They were free, instead, to be reshaped by the Potter.

The wicked little seed that had embedded itself in rich Todd County, Kentucky soil—that one had received its last raindrop.

THE END

About the Author

Author photo by Erin McCaffrey

Annette Valentine is the author of a trilogy entitled *My Father*. *Eastbound from Flagstaff* was her debut novel and *Down to the Potter's House* is the second in the series. Her writing began with a knack for believing in spine-tingling ghost stories and Nancy Drew mysteries. At the heart of this creative and intensely energetic writer is her purposeful compassion that launched an advocacy of the anti-human trafficking movement, for which she is heavily involved. She is a retired professional interior designer and lives in the Brentwood suburb of Nashville, Tennessee, with her husband, Walt, and their beloved Boxer who prefers to be on par with mortals. Annette and her husband have two grown children and six grandchildren. To learn more about the author and her work, visit www. annettehvalentine.com